VIRGI

ROCKY MOUNTAIN DOGS

DRAGONBOOKS
PUBLISHING HOUSE

DRAGONBOOKS
PUBLISHING HOUSE

Names: Fox, Virginia, author.

Title: Rocky Mountain Star (Rocky Mountain Romances, Book 3)/ by Virginia Fox.

Description: First Edition. | Boulder, Colorado: Dragonbooks, 2022.

Summary: When a dog groomer moves to Independence Junction, Colorado, she must muzzle the Rocky Mountain–sized ego of a good-looking hockey player and work with quirky townsfolk to uncage a mystery involving injured dogs.

Subjects: BISAC: FICTION / Romance / General. | FICTION / Romance / Contemporary. | FICTION / Women.

ISBN 979-8-9862800-5-9 (Paperback) |
ISBN 979-8-9862800-4-2 (eBook)
LCCN: 2022922279

Editor: Elaine Ash
Cover Design: Juliane Schneeweiss
Interior Design: Jennifer Thomas

ROCKY MOUNTAIN DOGS

JOIN ME!

Sign up for my newsletter to get insider information, and receive a FREE digital download of my Rocky Mountain Romances prequel, *Rocky Mountain Diner.*

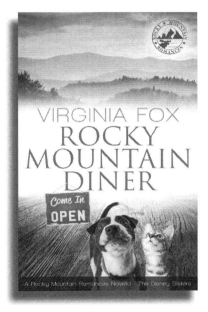

Dive into a little romance, a dab of suspense, and a whole lot of fun!

HTTPS://BOOKS.VIRGINIAFOX.COM/RMDINER_NOVELLA

CHAPTER ONE

It was a bright, blue-sky day and Kat chugged down the highway in her elderly but gently used recreational vehicle. The outside was painted white and polka-dotted with black paw prints. Electric-pink letters read:

Kat's for Dogs
Mobile Grooming

Kat and her traveling companions had just crossed the border from Utah into Colorado and were bound for Independence. *In more ways than one,* Kat thought, trying not to recall the turmoil she'd left behind. Independence Junction was a small town nestled not far from Breckenridge where friends and a pot of hot tea would be waiting to welcome her. Kat shifted her hands on the RV's steering wheel and stretched her neck from side to side. A chance to move her legs and chat over steaming cups of tea would be soooo welcome at this point after driving over a thousand miles from Seattle. Thankfully, the long road was behind her. Good times were just ahead in sixty miles.

She fumbled for her cell phone and called a number that went straight to voicemail. *Hi! This is Jasmine McArthy. If you are calling about classes at the yoga studio, please—*

Kat tapped her screen so the message cut off and started recording. "Hi, Jaz! I'm just an hour away. I'll call again when I'm entering town. Love you! Say hi to Pat for me." She tapped *End Call* and brought up GPS again.

A quick glance into the back of the RV showed her traveling companions, two large dogs, napping contentedly in their crates. With a satisfied smile, Kat turned back to the road.

BOOM!

Distant thunder sounded in the distance.

Both dogs lifted their heads.

BOOM BOOM!

"Woof," went the dogs.

In a few minutes Kat was driving through snowflakes that got increasingly heavy the closer they came to the little mountain town. Wind gusted down from the Rockies and buffeted the old RV. "Whoa, Nelly," Kat said out loud. Nelly was the vehicle's nickname. As if it understood, Nelly stopped rocking for a moment and drove steadily onward. But half an hour later the snow drove harder and the wind rose to a howl.

By the time a sign flashed past in a white bluster, *Independence 3 Miles*, Nelly was groaning against the wind as the dogs whimpered. Kat strained to see out the window in a near blizzard. Beside her on the passenger seat, the cell-phone GPS stalled. *No cell reception* popped up on-screen. The turnoff was just up ahead. Kat slowed to a near crawl and carefully steered into the turn. Blindly, she followed the road into town as the storm lifted a bit. Nelly no longer rocked in the wind. Kat breathed a sigh of relief. "We just might make it," she said out loud.

CRAAK!

The little RV lurched left as Kat hit something invisible on the road under the snow. Nelly started to slide. The dogs yelped, and Kat took her hands off the wheel, hoping Nelly could snap out of it. But with a sickening *crunch* the RV slid off the road, half on the pavement and half in a ditch. The engine rattled and died. The dogs whined, then cocked their ears and made no sound. Only the wind wailed outside.

Kat sat in stunned silence. Beside her, the cell phone still had no bars of signal. She was too scared to cry.

And then out of the cold and dark, a light shone. Was someone coming to the rescue? Kat's heart leaped with hope. "I'm here!" she cried, hoping her voice would carry through the windshield. "Please help me, I'm here!"

TWO WEEKS EARLIER

"Won't you at least reconsider, Mom? I can order your ticket now." Kat turned up the volume on her cell phone and pushed a strand of curly hair behind her ear. Her light blue eyes were full of concern. "You just have to pack your suitcase and go to the airport with your passport. It would be so nice to see you again."

Her mother's voice was mournful. "It's not the right time for a visit, *luby*." Luby meant "dear" in the Polish language.

"Tell him I need to see you," Kat urged.

"Be patient. I'll plan a visit soon."

Kat bit her lower lip. Her mother had been saying that for a long time. "Soon" never seemed to happen.

"I have to go, Kathrina," her mother whispered into the phone. "I can already hear his footsteps on the stairs."

"But—"

It was too late. Only the dial tone sounded on the line. Frustrated, Kat dropped the phone and leaned against the headboard of her bed. A strand of hair fell into her face. Annoyed, she brushed the long brown curls behind her ear. Why didn't her mother see that she was out of date, a throwback? She preferred to stay home and tend a rocky marriage in Poland. As if two weeks in America would hurt it! Kat hated being thrown into competition with her father.

She sighed and drew her knees up to her chest. Her mother spoke excellent English and even had American citizenship. Kat had been born in America. But then, after more than twenty years, her father demanded they go back to Russia. Kat was eighteen at the time and refused to go. Good thing, because the return to Russia backfired and they ended up in her mother's hometown of Warsaw, Poland. That had been more than ten years ago. Since then, Kat had seen her mother only once, when she visited at Christmas a few years ago.

Kat's big male mastiff Rocky brought her back to the present by trotting over with a leash in his mouth. He rested his massive skull in her lap with a sweet clownish look on his wrinkled face. Kat stroked the short reddish-brown fur.

"Are you sure you want to go out?" She glanced out the window. Thanks to the dark clouds that had been hanging over Seattle all day, January was showing its bleakest side.

In response, Rocky nudged her with his nose.

"You're serious," she noted, unable to stifle a grin. Rocky was a huge charmer. His repertoire of facial expressions was expansive. Somehow his facial wrinkles took on a new landscape with each emotion he felt. Depending on what any situation demanded, he could be happy, sad, quizzical, wistful, pleading, or disappointed. He used all of them purposefully and as successfully as any professional actor. At least that's how it seemed to Kat.

"Let's get the rain gear," she said out loud, and pushed herself up from the bed. As soon as Rocky realized that his tactic was successful, he scurried out of the bedroom and down the hallway, surprisingly light on his feet for his sixty-odd pounds of body weight. He skidded to a halt at the front door. Kat caught up with the collar in her hand and attached the leash to it. She slipped into a rain jacket and they were both ready to go. But she didn't move to open the door. Tension formed a lump in her throat. The landlord wasn't exactly Kat's best friend due to some bad timing. No sooner had she moved into this apartment than the building had been sold. The new owner hated dogs and banned all pet ownership. Kat and Rocky were "grandfathered" in, but only tolerated. It made for strained relationships all around.

Rocky refused to understand this and always tried to convince the landlord of his good looks and charm. Unfortunately, his enthusiasm and intimidating size were in the way. Kat prepared herself for a quick dash down the stairs and darted out. This time they were lucky and didn't encounter anyone in the stairwell. In this section of Ballard, in Seattle, many older apartment buildings were "walk-ups" with no elevators.

Outside, the heavy rain had stopped. Only the drizzle so typical of Seattle still hung in the air. She directed her steps to Golden Gardens Park. There she could let Rocky run freely among the tall trees until they reached the beach. Dogs weren't really allowed on the beach but Kat took him there only when it was deserted. She was careful to always pick up after him and leave no trace they'd been there. Her apartment building's close location to this park was one of the reasons she hadn't looked for a new place yet. It was perfect for a large dog needing daily exercise.

While she let Rocky sniff his favorite spots, her mind wandered. She really did need a new place to live. Her landlord asked them to leave at every opportunity. She was sure an eviction notice would have already been delivered except for the fact that Rocky was permitted by their original lease which had been signed by the previous owner of the building. But where could they go? Not far from here was her thriving dog salon. In addition to grooming, she cared for pets there during the day when owners needed doggos minded with love and attention. But after her two best friends, Jaz and Pat, moved to a small town called Independence in the middle of the Rocky Mountains last year, she often felt lonely. Without friends to confide in—and her mother's marital problems that never seemed to resolve—life wasn't getting any easier.

Rocky interrupted her thoughts by pulling on the leash. "Wait," she said, undoing it. After a few seconds she gave him a hand signal that he was free to go. She was always strict about not setting him free until he didn't pull on the leash. Otherwise, she'd find herself flying through the air behind him. *Kind of like kite flying*, she thought, amused. *Or dog flying.* She jogged after Rocky, who trotted on springy paws through the sparse woods toward the water.

Arriving at the beach, he placed a thick branch at her feet and looked up expectantly. "Of course," she said and bent down for it. With a practiced toss, she let it whiz across the water. Rocky dove enthusiastically into the beach water. Soon he had to start paddling. *Good. At least he'd be tired later.* Swimming was great for this breed, as was training and discipline. The mastiff was a working breed and too much downtime led to bad habits.

Kat put her cold fingers in her coat pockets and gazed out at Puget Sound. Only a narrow strip of light still illuminated the evening horizon. She had no idea if Rocky would even find the branch. But at least he was busy. *Busy.* She was grateful that her business was doing so well. She'd even hired an old friend of Jaz's who moonlighted at the dog salon when she needed extra money. Caitlin was reliable and trustworthy, and quietly admitted that she liked the dog salon better than the yoga studio where she usually worked. But something was missing. Kat just couldn't put her finger on where her own dissatisfaction was coming from.

Her eyes were drawn to movement at the shore. The big mastiff galloped out of the waves like one of Neptune's horses and spit the branch at her feet.

"I'm impressed," she said joyfully.

Rocky barked.

"Again?" she asked. A full-body wag was his response. She let the dripping branch fly back into the sea. That fleeting feeling she couldn't quite pin down suddenly came clear. She missed her friends. Jaz's attempts to persuade her to move to her small mountain town were tempting. So far, Kat had only explored the idea as a silly fantasy. Way too impractical. She was settled in Seattle! But missing her friends was a bigger deal than she'd let on.

One thing that was always keeping her tied to Seattle was the hope of convincing her mother to come out. But today's phone conversation made it abundantly clear that her mother was still not ready to leave her husband and might never be. Kat shuddered and pulled her coat collar higher. Maybe it was time to make decisions independent of Mom.

Rocky emerged from the surf without the branch a second time, busying himself by digging in the sand for crabs. Or anything else that wiggled. In reality he was mostly shoveling sand from one side to the other, much of it onto his nose and paws. His fun was going to be her mess to clean. She decided to stop by the dog salon on her way home. Luckily, everything was within walking distance.

Kat whistled to Rocky and started walking back through the park to the street. A block later she walked him through the alley where the salon's back entrance was located. As soon as she approached the door, Rocky stiffened and straightened up to his full size. A deep growl came from his throat. Uncertain, she stopped. What was wrong? Normally Rocky was so relaxed. Her eyes wandered from one corner of the alley to the other. But she could detect nothing that explained his strange behavior. She bent down and unsnapped the leash from his collar. If someone was hiding in there and Rocky needed to defend her, he needed to have room to do it. Rocky whined once, turned his head toward her as if to urge her to hurry, and trotted to the back entrance of the salon. Shaking her head, she followed. He'd probably scented a squirrel. She truly hoped it wasn't a rat.

Abruptly, he stopped and sniffed loudly. At his feet she could make out a shapeless shadow. What was it? Her dog didn't seem to be sure either. Again and again, he nudged the bundle with his muzzle. Kat pushed past Rocky and waved her arms in the direction of the outside light sensor. It came on but the low-watt bulb did a poor job of illuminating the darkness. It was enough to show what lay on the ground, though. A dog. It was tethered to one of the large dumpsters. And not just any dog. But a half-starved French mastiff, of all things, with mangy fur and bloody paws, because it had obviously tried to free itself. A wire was tied from the collar to the dumpster and the poor dog's paw had gotten wrapped up in it. *Who ties a dog up with wire?*

French mastiffs were uncommon dogs. Rocky was a French mastiff. How did one happen to end up tied to the dumpster outside her salon? She approached the animal carefully. Even the friendliest dog could bite if driven to it. She kneeled down and the mastiff weakly raised its large head. It seemed the struggle to get free had exhausted all his reserves. Rocky stood on guard with a worried look. It occurred to Kat that the first thing she had to do was get the dog inside. There she had enough light and an emergency first-aid kit to help.

Kat unlocked the door and entered her salon. She snapped off the overhead UV lights that sterilized all surfaces and furniture while the place was closed—the UV was friend Pat's idea—and turned on the regular lights. Going to the sink she filled a bowl with lukewarm water and gathered soap, towels, and a pair of pliers because she had an uneasy feeling about that wire. When everything was ready she took a deep breath, straightened her shoulders, and went out again.

Neither the strange dog nor Rocky had moved from the spot. When she stepped closer, Rocky turned his head with a sorrowful expression. Reassuringly, she stroked his broad forehead.

"Let's take care of your new friend," she said in a hushed voice so as not to startle the dog lying on the ground.

She crouched down again. Unsure if she should dare touch him, she just let her eyes roam over his body. The paw looked bad. She would probably have to call the vet. On her own, she didn't dare remove the wire. It was too dark out here, she couldn't see enough. If she lifted the dog to carry it inside, there was a risk of being bitten. Even if it was involuntary on the part of the animal. This wasn't something she was going to be able to handle herself. She pulled her phone from her pocket and dialed the number for a 24-hour vet ambulance. The dispatch operator recognized her number from a few previous occasions when there had been emergencies at the salon. She said help would be on the way within a half hour and the ambulance would meet them around back.

Gently, Kat put a hand on the injured dog's shoulder. He was already chilled to the bone. "Help is on the way," she whispered. A slight shiver ran over his soaked fur in response.

Soon, the blue-and-white striped vet ambulance rumbled up and an attendant got out. "Kat Orlow! I was here six months ago. Bulldog with a breathing issue," he said with a smile.

"Cameron! I'm happy to say everything turned out alright for Bully. Am I glad to see you tonight." It wasn't a question, it was a statement.

Cameron glanced at the wet mess of fur Kat knelt beside. "What you got there?"

"I'm sorry the light isn't brighter. It's kind of hard to see," Kat answered.

The man opened the driver's side door and flicked on the headlights. The whole back area lit up, brilliantly illuminated. He walked back to them and zeroed in on the wire around the dog's paw.

"What do you think?"

"I want to cut that wire where it attaches to the dumpster and take it, dog and all, back to the emergency clinic."

Kat looked at the cruel wire cutting into the paw and had to agree. "He'll stay overnight?"

"At least. This isn't your dog, is it?"

"No, I just discovered him."

Rocky's head swung back and forth as they each spoke, listening intently.

"Sure you want to be on the hook for the expenses?"

Kat shrugged. "I want to do the right thing. What else are credit cards for?"

Cameron smiled wryly. "Looks like you've got a soft spot for mastiffs. Am I right?" Without waiting for an answer he gave Rocky a quick pat and went back to the van, emerging with a pair of wire cutters.

Snip! In two seconds, the dog was freed from the dumpster. The mastiff summoned enough energy to give its head a mighty shake. Something fell out from under its collar and onto the ground.

"What's that?" Cameron asked.

Kat squinted. "Looks like a piece of paper." She snatched it up and smoothed it out.

Please take care of my dog. I can't anymore.

The note was heartbreaking. Kat couldn't imagine the circumstances that were so bad a person had to give up their dog. Someone obviously knew she owned a mastiff and brought the dog here for her to find.

She held the paper out so Cameron could read it. "Looks like he's my dog now. At least temporarily," she said. "What does the clinic do with homeless animals?"

"No home to return to, huh fella?" Cameron said to the dog. "Shame," he sighed. "The clinic will wait until he's stable and then have him transferred to a no-kill shelter. He's a big dog, so finding a home won't be as easy as for a small one. But he looks like a purebred, so he's got that going."

Kat stayed silent. Her head was spinning. She didn't understand why the more she and others like her voted to make Seattle a kinder and gentler place, things just got tougher for a lot of people. It made no sense.

Cameron interrupted her thoughts. "I'm going to administer a sedative and give it a minute to work. Then we'll be on our way."

The quick injection worked in seconds. The injured dog's eyes closed and its head lolled. Cameron got a thick pad out of the ambulance and spread it on the ground. "This old ambulance doesn't have a stretcher. Guess that's why we're replacing it soon. This pad will do the trick, though." He slipped his left arm under the dog's shoulder and chest, steadying the head with his right hand. "Can you get the legs?"

Kat knew exactly what he was doing. She went to the dog's hind legs and slipped one arm under the dog's hips.

"One, two, three," Cameron said. They rolled the dog onto the pad in one easy move.

Each grasping an edge of the blanket, they lifted him to the ambulance and into a crate.

"We'll be off, then," Cameron said.

"Just call me at the salon tomorrow with the charges," Kat said. "I'm sure you have my card on file." She peeked into the crate where the dog slumbered. "Bye, Nikki." The name just slipped out. It was the name of her first dog as a child.

"That name'll work," Cameron said, and wrote it on a tag that he attached to the crate.

Soon, the old ambulance rumbled back down the alley. Kat and Rocky watched it go.

CHAPTER TWO

THE NEXT DAY AT THE SALON Kat had her usual day care regulars, all well-behaved and social animals. Many so-called behavior problems were younger dogs full of energy who were not exercised or stimulated enough. The solution to that was a large dog run along the side of the building that could be extended into the back with chain-link gates that opened out and then an accordion gate that blocked off the end. The young and boisterous were taken out every two hours for ball chasing, frisbee, and an obstacle-course run that kept them happy and calm during the time they spent inside. The run was another innovation thanks to Pat, with a rubber floor, easy on doggie joints and paws. Yet it was easily pressure washed with a spray hose. Human clients loved these details, too.

Mrs. O'Halloran had just arrived with her red setter, bringing the number of visiting dogs in the "social room" up to seven. There were three appointments already for grooming, so Caitlin had been called in to preside over the "social" while Kat took the grooming. The salon was surprisingly chic for a place that catered to dogs. The walls were the color of new grass. set off by clean white woodwork. There were comfy couches to sprawl on and even a pair of wing chairs unholstered in leopard print, with matching throw rugs on the floor. The rugs made wonderful napping areas, too, for clients who decided to doze.

Kat was waving goodbye to Mrs. O'Halloran and getting the red setter situated when the phone rang.

"Hello. Kat's for Dogs. This is Kat."

"It's Dr. Chu at the 24-hour clinic. Nikki has stabilized nicely."

"I'm so glad. How is that paw?"

"The wire was removed and the paw will heal just fine. We have your credit card on file. Is it okay to put the charges through?" Dr. Chu itemized his services and gave the total amount to Kat.

"Sure, go for it. What happens now?"

"Another forty-eight hours of observation and feeding. Then Nikki's stay with us is over."

"What then?"

"One of our no-kill shelters will find space." The vet hesitated. "Because there's no home to go to. Or that's what Nikki's chart says."

Kat thought painfully of the crowded shelters, and as if on cue, her own French mastiff looked up from a nap. Rocky's wrinkled face telegraphed a message that seemed to say, *Please do the right thing.* Even though she had no room at home, and was already on thin ice with the management of her apartment building, Kat knew she didn't have the heart to let Nikki go.

"I'll take him," she said quietly into the phone.

"That's good news," the vet replied. "I guess I have another surprise."

Kat swallowed involuntarily but stayed silent. *What now?*

"This dog is female."

"Oh!" Kat said in surprise. "Good thing my Rocky is fixed."

"You want to get spaying taken care of sooner than later," the vet said. "After she's recovered a little more."

"You bet! The last thing I need is a litter of puppies." Kat chuckled with relief and hung up after saying goodbye. *What have I done?* echoed in her brain. The landlord already hated Rocky. How was she going to sneak two dogs in and out? But burning questions were going to have to wait. Caitlin was arriving and that meant it was frisbee time outside. The whole roomful of dogs crowded to the door in anticipation. And Kat's first grooming appointment was pulling up outside. Personal problems were just going to have to wait.

In Independence, Colorado, Jaz stretched lazily in bed as she heard her fiancé, Jake, let himself in the back door of their farmhouse. The jingle of a collar told her their big standard poodle, Rambo, was with him too. The farmhouse wasn't exactly theirs but they lived here and took care of it as Jaz's grandmother, the true owner, lived across town. She now resided in a smaller, more easily maintained home with a companion.

Jaz had moved into the farmhouse initially under strained circumstances because of a boyfriend whose name she tried not to recall often—*Gavin*—and life had turned out better than she could have ever expected.

Leaving the big-city problems of Seattle to open her own yoga studio in Independence was the best move she could ever have made. She'd even gained a life partner out of it. Jake wanted to get married and welcome her into his big, feisty family. Although a big family came with its own set of challenges, she'd never felt so comfortable and secure in her life. *Who wouldn't?* she thought, *With a dozen other people who all cared about your welfare watching your back?*

Downstairs, she could hear Jake stamping snow off his boots, and the flap of Rambo's long black ears as he shook himself. Jake had taken him out for a run on their property, which her forward-thinking grandpa had sorted into parcels and built eight-acre homesteads on. Now that more and more people were seeking a simpler life and growing food, not to mention raising animals, the homesteads surrounding the big old house were filled with young owners and their livestock.

Her mind roamed back about a year ago to the first time she'd really noticed Jake...

Just as the main-street stores were about to open, Jasmine drove toward the center of Independence. She had just arrived. The trip had been sudden and she only had the clothes on her back. Her plan was to duck into Johnson's Sporting Goods, get a few pairs of yoga pants and T-shirts, and then hightail it to her grandmother's place.

Rambo sat in the passenger seat and held his head out the window. His long ears fluttered in the wind. She slowed the car before stopping at the town's only traffic light. Things had changed in recent years. Instead of three warped, weathered buildings, there were now six or seven storefronts lined up on each side. Someone on the street she didn't recognize gave a cheery wave. Jasmine absently waved back. The light jumped to green and she continued on her way.

She swung her Prius into the large gravel lot that served as town parking, and Jasmine got out. Unlike Seattle, parking here was still free. Steps from the door of Johnson's, a car slowed on the street.

"I'd recognize those yoga pants anywhere," a male voice hollered.

Jasmine froze and then turned around. Walking beside her on the leash, Rambo jumped up and wagged his tail like crazy.

It was the sheriff. With a delighted smile lighting up his face.

O-o, she thought. Last night she'd gotten the impression that he might be cute. But now, with his attention on her and that dazzling smile, she realized that was an underestimation—if there was such a word. He was downright handsome. Even in that gas-guzzling V8 SUV he was driving.

Rambo was beside himself with joy, and Jasmine realized she was expected to walk out to his vehicle and say hello. In the middle of the street! No problem, there was no traffic anyway.

She plastered on a smile and stepped out. "Hi, Jason!"

The smile fell from his face. "Jake," he said flatly. "It's Jake."

Her smile wavered. "My mistake. So much going on last night, you know."

"True that," he said good-naturedly. "What are you doing out so early?"

"*Just looking around. You know,*" she said, realizing she'd just used "*you know*" twice in a row, like she was trying a little too hard to be nonchalant.

His eyes twinkled. "*Because if I didn't know better,*" he said, "*I might think you were on a shopping run for some yoga pants.*"

The blood rushed to her face. "*Well, so what?*" she sputtered. "*I mean—*"

"*RUFF!*" Rambo to the rescue. He jumped both paws on the SUV door, begging for a head scratch. Jake obliged, watching as she struggled for composure.

"*Thought you might be headed to your grandmother's,*" he said easily, giving Rambo a good ear massage. "*Where she's been staying, I mean.*"

"*Yes, I was, I am,*" she managed.

"*Got the address?*"

The note Nana left in the kitchen mentioned no address. Jasmine realized with a sinking heart that she had no street, just a P.O. address for mail. Finally, her brain kicked in. "*All I have to do is call. I was reaching for my phone just as you drove up.*" The sheriff looked like he was weighing another crack about shopping and yoga pants but thought better of it. "*I'll take you there,*" he said kindly. "*Follow me*"

She was about to say "*No, no, don't take the trouble,*" but she knew arguing might trigger more tortured conversation. Jasmine closed her lips firmly, nodded, and went back to her car. It figured he knew where Nana was. In a small town everybody knew where everybody else lived.

Finally, the sheriff slowed down and put his turn signal on coming up to a private driveway. Jasmine flashed her lights to let him know she understood this must be her *grandmother's place. He tapped the rim of his western-style hat in farewell. She waved back. Nice of him to take the time to show her the way. One of the advantages of living in a small town.*

Jaz was pulled away from her memories as Jake appeared in the bedroom doorway. "Wake up, sleepyhead."

She gave him a relaxed grin, eyes shining. Her petite yoga-teacher figure made a slim silhouette under the blanket.

He raised an eyebrow questioningly. "What's going on with the late start?"

"I've got to get moving. Thought I'd visit Grandma before I have to open the yoga studio."

"Wagons ho. I've got to get to the station, myself."

"Another day keeping this town safe, Sheriff?"

"You know it."

Jake reached for his hat, put it on, and touched his fingers to the curved rim. "Give my love to Grandma Rose." He flashed his white teeth in a smile and Jaz felt the same thrill of attraction she'd had the first day they'd met. It seemed a lifetime ago but it was just about a year.

Time to get up. She had a good reason for visiting her grandmother. She needed a piece of important advice. And Rose McArthy, the matriarch of the clan known as a wise woman in Independence, would probably have it.

In order to get to the house where Rose lived, Jaz had to drive through "downtown" Independence which was short on size but long on charm. The wooden buildings mostly had peaked roofs, and some were painted different colors with contrasting trim. The feedstore had green paint with red trim. Lily's Flowers had yellow paint with blue trim. Big wooden porches fronted most of the stores, and the owners had prettied them up with potted shrubs and bushes. The hub was Miss Minnie's, a traditional diner where the town's social life was centered. Much as she wanted to stop for a treat, Jaz kept driving.

Rose McArthy met her at the door of her new home with a big hug. Just as willowy as she was in her twenties, Rose kept her long silver hair tied in a French braid that fell down her back. "Come in, darlin' it's soup day," she said, leading the way through the house.

Jaz's nose told her it was vegetable stock made with plenty of onions, celery, and carrots. It smelled divine, and her vegetarian tastebuds set to making her mouth water.

"Nana, you always say you gave up cooking."

"Now that Grampa has passed and you're in the farmhouse, yes, I've given up cooking. For the most part. Now I cook three days a month doing up big batches of Nadine's favorite foods to freeze in portions. All we have to do is heat 'n serve for the rest of the month." Rose twirled a ladle over a bowl and served Jaz up a steaming bowl of soup. "You look hungry, grandchild. Want a biscuit with that?"

"No thanks, what I really need is some advice."

"A bowl of veggie soup with a side of advice. Comin' up."

Jaz giggled like a little girl. "Remember my friend Kat who was here last summer? She's one of my best friends from Seattle?"

"I seem to recall a tall girl with lovely curly hair and a big dog."

"That's her. First, I moved away. Then I was the one who told Pat there was work here so he decided to stay. I feel guilty about leaving Kat all alone. I'm trying to get her to move here." Jaz stuck a big spoon in the soup and sipped at it. The broth was divine.

"Seems to me she needs a good reason to move house all the way across country to Colorado."

"She has a reason. She misses us as much as we miss her. We were like family. But she's tied to her business, seems like."

"Hmmmm." Rose stirred her soup in its big two-gallon pot. The silence was broken only by the ladle tapping occasionally against the inside of the stainless-steel pot. "Somebody needs to tell her that a business is not a family."

Jaz's expression turned sad.

Rose sighed and put the ladle down in a China spoon holder on the counter. Jaz quietly assessed that the holder was likely a hundred years old—an antique from a time long ago and far away.

"You can't force someone to follow you somewhere," Rose said gently. "No matter how much you love them. It won't come to any good."

"You mean there's nothing I can do?"

"You can stay in touch and show how much you love her. And that's my last word."

"Why your last word?" Jaz asked with her soup spoon suspended in midair.

"If it's meant to be, something will happen to make it so."

That sounded a little hopeful, at least. Jaz could live with that.

Forty-eight hours went by quickly. Time to bring Nikki home. Kat left Rocky in the apartment and made a quick trip to pick up an extra bag of premium dog food. She retrieved the twenty-five-pound bag of dry food from her trunk and staggered into the apartment building with it.

Just as she was dragging the bag through the foyer of the building, her phone rang. She set the bag down and glanced at the screen. A smile creased her face when she saw Jaz's name.

"Hello, stranger. Long time no hear!"

"I'm going to remedy that. I'm going to call more often."

"Really?"

"Just because I miss you."

"That would be nice. It's just I'm so busy—"

"Constant dripping wears away the stone," Jaz said mysteriously. "How's the dog?"

"Dogs are fine!"

"Did I just hear you right? Dogs with an 's'? Did you buy a new dog?"

At that moment, someone grabbed Kat roughly by the arm. Her phone hit the floor and went skidding away.

Mr. Kleeves, the landlord, planted himself in front of Kat, breathing heavily.

"Did I hear you say dogs PLURAL?! As in MORE THAN ONE?!"

Kat's mouth worked but no sound came out.

"No more dogs allowed! You're not even allowed to have one!" Kleeves ranted.

"But my original lease says—"

He pointed an accusing finger at her as his jowls shook with outrage. "If I see you bringing another dog in here it's the end of your tenancy. Do you hear?"

"Mr. Kleeves, please. It's not my fault. I found an injured dog. Can't you find it in your heart to—"

"To what?!" His angry eyes bulged at her.

"To stuff this apartment up your, up your—" she could feel a rising tide of words in her mouth, ready to leap off her tongue. "Up your wazoo!" she yelled.

Mr. Kleeves recoiled in shock. Then his eyes narrowed craftily. "Let me make a deal with you," he said. "I'll let you bring that new mutt home with you for two weeks. Two weeks do you hear? But after that, you're OUT!"

"IT'S A DEAL!" Kat roared back at him. She picked up her phone from the floor and continued dragging the food bag to the stairs. "I'm leaving this here and I'll be back down in two minutes to get it," she yelled, taking the stairs two at a time to get away from him.

Inside her apartment, with a trembling hand, she raised the cell phone back to her ear.

"Are you still there?" she asked Jaz.

"What happened? Are you okay?" On the line, Jaz's voice sounded concerned.

"I'm fine. That was my landlord. Oh Jaz, what have I done? I told him I'd be out in two weeks because of the new dog. I must be insane!"

Rocky lifted his head from the mat he was dozing on and woofed softly.

"It was meant to be," Jaz continued. "Now you can come out and join your friends in Independence."

"Don't be as unhinged as I am right now. I have a business here. It can't happen."

"Just calm down and start from the beginning. What about this new dog? Tell me everything."

Under Rocky's watchful gaze, Kat did just that.

Two weeks flashed by. Every day Kat scoured real estate rentals in her neighborhood and dashed out between groomings to see apartments. *Too small, too far away*, or no pets cycled as constant reasons why she couldn't find anything. Now it was the day before she had to move. A decision had to be made.

It was early Sunday morning, the salon was closed. She *should* have been sleeping in. If Pat and Jaz were still here, undoubtedly they'd have been out on the town last night, not saying goodbye until the wee hours. Or, if her mother were here, they'd be preparing for a big brunch to have Jaz, Pat, and friends over. Maybe a big pitcher of mimosas to start off a lazy Sunday of friends and family. "Instead, it's just me and you, Rocky," she said out loud.

In response, Rocky woofed and bowed down on his front paws. He was excited like crazy for a good walk to the beach. He raced back and forth to the door of the apartment, begging to get out. Nikki watched uncertainly. She was still a little afraid to join in. Rocky had been very patient with Nikki and acted like a gentleman for the most part. It was almost as if he realized she wasn't quite fit enough for his exuberant outbursts of enthusiasm. But that restraint was gone with the wind right now. Excitement had swept him up.

"I get the idea, Rocky," Kat exclaimed. Was now the right time to take Nikki with them? Every day she'd gotten a little stronger. The wounded paw was healing well, no tendon had been injured. Kat coaxed the timid dog over, bent down, and unwound the bandage on her paw. Except for a thick scab, it had healed. A walk in salt water would loosen the crust. Afterwards, Kat could clean the wound again and apply a fresh bandage.

Kat started walking for the door. "Come on Nikki, you too," she said. The smaller female wasn't quite sure what was going on, but she seemed to trust Rocky. If he signaled that what was about to happen was fun, fun, fun, she would go along in her own shy way.

At the beach, no one was around. Puget Sound rippled with small waves and the sand stretched as far as the eye could see. Rocky went off the leash and every few feet he collected a new piece of flotsam. Nikki took it more slowly. Every now and then she stopped and lifted her nose into the wind to sniff. Kat stepped up to her and, with long movements, gently stroked her coat, which looked in better condition each day. Nikki's ribs no longer stood out so sharply. Slowly but surely, the good food and clean environment were working magic.

Rocky ran up so he got an ear ruffle too, before he changed his mind and ran back to the water. Kat stretched her face to the rare rays of sun above them. The wind ran through her long curly hair gathered into a ponytail. There was something about the sound of waves and wind—it brought her back to what was important. Whenever she was plagued by insecurities, she would come here and let the earth elements take hold of her. After a while she felt grounded. Worries were put into perspective. Should she give in to Jaz's pleading and join her friends in Colorado? Resettle her business, give up the dream of relocating her mother to Seattle? It would be so very nice to live in the same town with her friends, again.

She watched as Nikki ventured down to the water's edge. Every time the waves reached the sand at her feet, she took a few bumpy steps back, only to limp after them with a curious look on her face when they receded again.

"Looks like you've never seen the ocean in your life," Kat said aloud to the dog. On impulse, she took off her shoes and stockings and rolled up the pant legs of her old jeans. She walked over to Nikki and nudged her closer to the water. When the waves returned, Kat stayed put and let the cold water wash over her feet. Nikki retreated back to dry land. She wasn't quite ready to trust this new experience yet. Rocky, on the other hand, knew no restraint. The fact that his mistress was standing in the water was an invitation to play in his eyes. He jumped towards her in great leaps, a misshapen stick in his mouth. Kat laughed as he looked at her expectantly. She reached for the slippery piece of wood. "Off!" she said. Obediently, the dog released his prey. She lunged and threw the branch out to sea. With a mighty leap, Rocky plunged into the waters and swam after it. Nikki seemed worried as she watched the goings-on. She pranced awkwardly in place and let out a low bark several times.

"You're a real scaredy cat, aren't you?" exclaimed Kat. "Or do you want to join in?"

Nikki seemed indecisive. Kat decided she'd better return to the apartment before she threw all reason overboard and joined them in the water. The salt water would have been good for the wound, but it was probably enough for one day.

At that moment a decision came to Kat. She would stay in Seattle. Sure, she missed Jaz and Pat, but her business was here. She would have a storage company pack her up tomorrow, put everything in dry dock, so to speak, and simply move into the salon with the two dogs for a few weeks until a suitable home materialized. The couches made comfy beds, and she could sleep on one of them. There was a microwave in the back, a washer-dryer combo, and there were plenty of takeout places around to have food delivered. How could it be that bad? She had to trust that she was supposed to be here and things would fall into place, all in good time.

It was Kat's third night sleeping at the salon. The couch wasn't quite as comfy to humans as she'd expected, and going to the gym for a shower wasn't quite as convenient as strolling to her own bathroom. A couple of aspirin helped her forget her stiff back. A cold taco from last night's food delivery served for breakfast. At eight a.m. Caitlin breezed in with steaming takeout coffees.

"Keith is at it again," she grumbled, handing over a huge cup with a lid.

"You mean your boss at the yoga studio?"

"Yeah, him. I wish I could work here full time, Kat. That would be a dream."

"I'd love that too." Kat's mind flipped through hours and projected clients, but the math just didn't work for a full-time employee. *Unless...* she turned to Caitlin with a smile. "Let's put on a cup of tea and talk about grooming."

"Sure. But you're the groomer here. There aren't enough clients for me too, are there?"

"I'm thinking about mobile clients. As in we advertise to more neighborhoods and go to them."

Caitlin lit up with a big grin. "Sure, I'd be up for that." Just as quickly, she frowned. "Don't we need a truck with equipment?"

"Yes, we do." Kat pulled out her phone and looked up a number. She dialed while Caitlin looked on with a *What are you up to?* look on her face.

"Hi, it's the owner at Kat's for Dogs. I was wondering if Cameron was there."

"He's just leaving from the night shift. Let me see if he's still here."

A minute later there was a fumbling sound over the phone and Cameron came on. "Kat! What's up?"

"The last time you were here, you mentioned the old ambulance was being replaced. Did you happen to know what you were going to get on a trade-in?"

"Oh that. Yeah, they were willing to give us a grand."

"Why so little?"

"It's a converted RV in the first place, an old Vanagon with 150,000 miles. The dealership wasn't very excited about it because we had gutted it to make an ambulance."

"Plus, it has blue and white stripes painted on."

"Yep, that, too."

"Would you be interested in a private sale? Something that would get more money than a trade-in but still a good deal?

"Well, possibly. But you have to know we're taking all our equipment with us. The only thing left will be the largest dog crates bolted to the floor. Oh, and there's a built-in sink. That stays, too."

"Perfect. I want to convert it into a mobile grooming truck. I can run a hose from the sink and wash dogs in a portable tub."

"Sounds like you've got it all figured out."

"I'll give you twelve-fifty for the RV. Cash. Interested?"

"Sold!"

"You wouldn't know anybody who does automotive paint jobs, do you?"

"Let me call the dealer and get a referral. When do you want to come by?"

A few more details and the deal was set. Kat hung up and grinned at Caitlin. "Looks like we're in business."

She looked at the clock. "Clients will be here soon. As soon as we get everybody in and the owners on their way, I'm going to look at some Internet advertising."

"You mean I can give notice at the yoga studio?"

"Why not? I'm not in business to stay small. Let's go big!"

The RV needed an oil change and a tune-up but it was basically sound. Cameron was still standing in the driveway with a handful of cash as she got behind the wheel, shifted into drive, and rolled forward.

"STOP!"

Kat hit the brakes hard.

"Wait up!" It was Cameron, jogging behind her. She rolled down the window, alarmed. "What is it?"

Cameron jogged along the side of the vehicle to her window. He was puffing a little. "Did you get Nikki fixed?"

Kat slapped her forehead. "Yikes! No. I forgot all about it."

"We can take care of it for you."

"Give me the first appointment. I'll bring her in."

"Let me check Dr. Chu's schedule."

"I'll wait."

TWO DAYS LATER

Kat spent her miniscule spare time planning the exterior color scheme for the RV. A good logo painted on the side was like a rolling billboard to attract clients. And she was willing to put some money into it, since a good design and decent paint job would pay for itself in new clients and business. Cameron had recommended a good body shop and she was just waiting for the call that it was ready. What a day it would be when she parked in front of the salon!

Sleeping on the largest dog couch took effort, but she felt she was getting somewhere. Expanding the business, waiting until just the right apartment came free, would pay off. She had Caitlin combing daily through online rental postings while she was grooming so if anything promising came up, she could pounce right away. Unfortunately, she had forgotten that at this time of year, in the dead of winter, people didn't move as much. Spring and summer saw tenants on the move.

The phone rang.

It was the 24-hour Pet Ambulance place. Nikki had only gone in a few hours ago. Perhaps the operation was over already?

It was Dr. Chu. "Hello, Miss Orlow?"

"Yes, it's me. Hi Dr. Chu."

"I have a surprise for you." He sounded quite happy.

"You do? Everything went well?"

"You could say everything is going well, yes."

"That's good isn't it?" Kat felt a little alarm rising inside.

"Not quite. We can't fix your dog."

"Why not?"

"Because in another four weeks or so you're going to have four more little dogs. Puppies!"

"WHAT?!"

"Nikki is about thirty days along. Conception must have happened only a day or two before you found her and brought her here."

The rest of what Dr. Chu said went in one ear and out the other. All Kat could think about was living at the salon with six full-time dogs to care for at the same time she ran the business while sleeping on the couch. How could she possibly find and move into a new apartment with six dogs? No landlord would ever go for that. Her thoughts whirled. It would be at least ten weeks after the puppies were born before homes could be found for them. Ten weeks of sleeping on the couch, eating takeout food. She'd be worn to a frazzle by that time.

Her fate was sealed. She knew when she was beat. Now, her mind started working in earnest. *What about an extended vacation to Independence?* Nikki could give birth in the RV so as not to inconvenience Jaz. Puppies destined to grow into big dogs would be easier to place with people who lived on homesteads with plenty of land. Here at the salon, Caitlin could take over grooming and she could get someone else to take over the dog-sitting side of the salon under Caitlin's supervision. Most of the clients paid by credit card these days, so deposits went to the salon bank account electronically. Kat could handle bills the same way she did now, on her cell phone.

A day later, Kat was set. There was little to pack, she only had her bag that she'd brought to the salon. It was already inside Nelly, as she'd named the RV. It was stocked with dog food, toys, blankets, and dog beds. Jaz was ecstatic with the news she was coming, if only for a visit. Kat hadn't bothered to share that the real reason was Nikki's pregnancy, that detail could wait. Right now, the business day was ended, Caitlin had said goodbye, and as the new manager she would open up in the morning. It was seven-thirty p.m. and a good time for Kat to leave Seattle, avoiding traffic.

She took one last look around at the salon, her pride and joy. "Be back soon," she whispered. "I'll miss you." Her lips pursed to whistle up Rocky and Nikki when a knock came at the door. "We're closed," she shouted.

"I know," came a male voice. "Miss Orlow, I need to talk to you."

She recognized that voice. It was Kleeves, the landlord! A thrill of fear ran through her. Maybe he was coming for revenge over telling him off. What was it she'd said? *Stick it up your wazoo!* "I'm leaving town," she shouted back. "Send me a letter and I'll have the new manager forward it to me."

"Please, no, Miss Orlow. This is important."

The polite and pleading tone sure didn't sound like Kleeves. Maybe this had something to do with a dog. Kat went to the door of the salon and unlocked it. When she opened the door Kleeves looked agitated. His bulgy eyes were red-rimmed and his clothes were rumpled. He looked like he hadn't slept in a week.

"What's this about?" she said.

"Well, you see," he stammered, "the new owner and me want to know if you'd like your old apartment back."

Kat's mouth fell open. No words came out.

"We got another tenant who also snuck a dog in although it's way worse than yours. Poop in the stairwell, non-stop barking. Everybody with a dog seems to want to live in our Ballard neighborhood now because of the park. It's like the whole world just discovered it."

"What do you want me to do about it?"

"The owner wants me to offer your old place back. Both dogs can stay with you so long as they behave like that one always did." He pointed to Rocky who had protectively inserted himself between Kat and the open door. "At your old rent," he added.

Kat looked at his apologetic face, but knew she could never up his offer to include the puppies, too. The minute they were discovered Kleeves would feel he'd been taken unfairly and the eviction threats would likely start again. She thought about going back to life as it was three weeks ago. It was tempting. Maybe Nikki could go to the shelter to have her puppies and everything could go back the way it was. Kleeves would probably be thrilled that the number of dogs had reduced to half without Nikki. A cold nose pressed against the back of her hand. She looked down. It was Nikki. Her doggo eyes looked up, sweet and trusting.

If I sent her and the puppies to a shelter, who would I be? Especially when I have another option? An internal voice started up an oh-so-reasonable argument. *Maybe the original owner is doing better now. You could put up neighborhood posters asking to give Nikki back.* The cold nose pressed into her hand again and Kat looked down into worshipful eyes. She knew at that moment, if she took Kleeves' offer, she would never enjoy the apartment, never stop worrying about what had become of Nikki. Kat pushed the voice out of her head.

"Mr. Kleeves, thanks for your offer. But the answer is no."

"You're living here, aren't you?" he went on. "You must need a place."

"I'm going to a place where dogs are welcome. Yesterday, today, and tomorrow. In fact, I'm leaving right now."

In front of his astonished face she whistled up the dogs and stepped outside, letting the door latch and lock behind her. She marched the dogs to their new travel home painted white with black paw prints and *Kat's for Dogs Mobile Grooming* splashed in hot pink letters across the side.

"But, but," she could hear Kleeves saying as she urged the dogs into their crates. Kat hopped in and got behind the wheel.

"But, but—" Kleeves blubbered.

She started the engine.

The last thing visible in the rearview mirror was her former landlord scratching his head, watching them go.

CHAPTER THREE

ROLLING OUT OF SEATTLE got Kat feeling adventurous and free. It wasn't until she was out of range for local radio stations that she heard a weather report mentioning the next few days were snow-free. That was good because, snow? It hadn't even occurred to her to ask about special tires, or taking a shovel, or anything like that. It didn't snow in Seattle except for a few days, maybe, and the white stuff was gone overnight. Sure, she knew it was going to be cold, and that's why Nelly had a propane heater for inside use at night, plus she and the dogs had insulated coats. But the prospect of driving through snow hadn't dawned until now.

A rest stop was coming up. "Ready for a potty break?" she asked the occupants in their crates.

"Woof," came Rocky's reply.

Nikki cocked her head and whined softly.

The rest stop had bathrooms, gas, plenty of periphery to walk the dogs, and groceries. As Kat lugged a carton of water and a bag of food back to the van, a biker on a big Harley cruiser watched her hoist a pack with twelve water bottles inside.

He pointed his chin at the supplies. "Good weather we're having," he murmured appreciatively from under his beard.

She gave him a smile. "I'm counting on reaching my destination before the snow."

He cast a critical glance at the brilliant blue sky. "Me too. That's why I'm out on my cruiser. Snow isn't the right driving weather for me, either." He hung the fill nozzle back on the pump. "Got a set of chains just in case?"

The confused look on her face betrayed she didn't know what he was talking about.

He stroked his graying beard with one hand. "Good thing you're at a truck stop. This is the right place to ask about getting some chains. Where you headed?"

"Colorado."

He shrugged. "Let's both hope the weather gods are merciful. Take care of yourself and the dogs."

"I will," Kat replied, slightly irritated that someone felt they had to tell her to be careful. *Wasn't she always?* she thought, just barely able to stop herself from rolling her eyes. After all, the man was just trying to be nice.

The left corner of his mouth smiled as if he knew exactly what she was thinking. He probably did. Jaz had told her many times that her poker face needed improvement. Kat waved in gratitude and stumped back to the cashier at the rest stop to ask about tire chains.

At sunset Kat headed off the highway into a small town. She wasn't looking for a hotel. Who needed the expressions of dismay when hotel managers saw Rocky and Nikki? Kat had collected enough rejection of herself and her animals to last a lifetime. Driving around a bit she found a nice little street with nice little houses. She pulled over, checked for one with no car in the driveway, and parked outside. She let the dogs out of their crates and took them on a long walk until it was almost dark. Back at the van they had a supper of dry food and plenty of water. She dove into a bag of trail mix for herself. When it grew chilly, Kat pulled out her Little Buddy heater with propane fuel, safe for inside use, and soon they were toasty warm. The dogs sprawled all over the floor and she rolled out a sleeping bag and got into it right beside them. It was quiet and peaceful, and much darker than Seattle.

She felt for the flashlight in her jacket pocket. Outside, the snow reflected the light of countless stars through the windshield. She craned her neck and marveled at the dark canopy of sky that seemed to be covered with diamonds. In Seattle, one never saw so many stars at once. The millions of lights of the big city prevented that. This view of the real night sky put her own life, with all its rough edges, into perspective. Perhaps the ocean was missing here but this view more than made up for it. There was also a feeling of relaxation, as if some stress had lifted off. It was the last thing she knew until morning.

Dawn came bright and clear. After letting the dogs out, walking them and then feeding, Kat got on the road for Salt Lake City and stopped for coffee and an egg sandwich on the way to a branch of her gym. BodyFit Planet had reasonably priced gyms linked all over the country along with hot showers and changerooms. Every bone in her body ached from three days on the road but they'd soon be at their destination. The idea of sitting in

Jaz's homey kitchen in five hours—well probably more like six if she factored in the stops and elderly limitations of her vehicle—and eating something other than gas station grub was just too tempting.

Six hours later, stomach grumbling, Kat wasn't so sure. They had wasted hours at the last truck stop but she was glad that at least the snow chains were mounted. She'd paid to have them put on rather than have someone take pity and mount them for her. She hated being dependent on help, *male help*, especially. It was her mother's dependency on her volatile husband that was at the bottom of all her problems, in Kat's opinion. But Kat had been sensible enough to realize that she didn't have a clue about snow chains. So she paid, and grateful for the help.

According to her calculations, and it was also the opinion of her GPS, that she should already be outside of Independence. She fumbled for her cell phone and called a number that went straight to voicemail. *Hi! This is Jasmine McArthy. If you are calling about classes at the yoga studio, please—*

Kat tapped her screen so the message cut off and started recording. "Hi Jaz! I'm just an hour away. I'll call again when I'm entering town. Love you! Say hi to Pat for me." She tapped *End Call* and brought up GPS again.

A quick glance into the back of the RV showed the dogs napping contentedly in their crates. With a satisfied smile Kat turned back to the road.

BOOM!

Distant thunder sounded in the distance.

Both dogs lifted their heads.

BOOM BOOM!

"Woof," went the dogs.

In a few minutes Kat was driving through snowflakes that got increasingly heavy the closer Nelly came to the little mountain town. Kat turned her headlights on but saw only a translucent white wall. Daylight was fading. Visibility was just plain bad and she didn't dare drive faster than a snail's pace. Wind gusted down from the Rockies and buffeted the old RV. "Whoa, Nelly," Kat said out loud.

In response, both dogs whined through their noses.

As if the RV understood, she stopped rocking for a moment and drove steadily onward. But half an hour later the snow drove harder and the wind rose to a howl.

By the time a sign flashed past in a white bluster, *Independence 3 Miles*, Nelly was groaning against the wind as the dogs whimpered. Kat strained to see out the window in a near blizzard. Beside her on the passenger seat, the cell-phone GPS stalled. *No cell reception* popped up on-screen. The turnoff was just up ahead. Kat slowed to a near crawl and carefully steered into the turn. Blindly, she followed the road into town as the storm lifted a bit. Nelly no longer rocked in the wind. Kat breathed a sigh of relief. Even though the daylight was fading, she whispered out loud, "We just might make it."

CRAAK!

The vehicle lurched left as Kat hit something invisible on the road under the snow. Nelly started to slide. The dogs yelped and Kat took her hands off the wheel, hoping Nelly could snap out of it. But with a sickening *crunch* the RV slid off the road, half on the pavement and half in a ditch. The engine rattled and died. The dogs whined, then cocked their ears and made no sound. Only the wind wailed outside.

Kat sat in stunned silence. Beside her, the cell phone still had no bars of signal. She was too scared to cry. With trembling fingers she tried to undo her seatbelt. But the thing was stuck. She suppressed the rising panic and forced herself to take a deep breath. Behind her, the dogs whined in their crates. The dogs! Hopefully nothing had happened to them. Kat would never forgive herself if they had hurt themselves. Determined, she tackled her harness again. Finally, it worked and she was free. She breathed a sigh of relief and climbed to the back to check on the dogs. Both seemed to be fine. The whining was probably due to her own tension.

She knelt down next to Rocky and propped herself against his crate. *Now what?* She let her gaze roam the RV. It was time to take stock. No one was hurt, she had enough to eat and drink, blankets were also plentiful. They wouldn't starve or freeze to death. She ran her hand through her hair. Lost in thought, she reached into her pants pocket and pulled out her flashlight.

On the negative side was the fact that the dogs had to go out. Her own bladder was squeezing, too. At least she had a bucket for emergencies and didn't have to squat in the snow. She hoped Nelly's rear end wasn't sticking out too far into the road. Maybe she'd better check the situation first before letting the dogs out. She pushed herself up and stretched her tired limbs.

Wrapped thickly in her hat, scarf, gloves and parka, she grabbed the flashlight and opened the door. The wind was howling. It almost ripped the door out of her hand. She pulled her head in to keep the icy air from creeping under her winter jacket. She blinked the snowflakes out of her eyes. Even with the flashlight, she couldn't see much. It wasn't clear where the road began and where it ended. Only the slight slope suggested that she had ended up in a ditch. Great. Now she'd need help from a towing service, too. If there was such a thing in Independence. A longing for the Seattle she knew without surprise snowstorms grew by the minute.

After circling Nelly once, she returned inside the vehicle and let the dogs out of their crates. Happy for the change, Rocky jumped around while Nikki was content to let her big tongue hang out and wag her tail enthusiastically. Snapping leashes on both, she let the dogs out.

In the beam of the flashlight, Kat worked her way against the wind and snow to the rear fender of the vehicle where the dogs began to sniff and do their business.

Kat stood shivering in the snow, waiting for Rocky and Nikki. She didn't dare go too far from the RV, her fear of getting lost was too great. Finally, they were ready to get back inside. Nelly had cooled off already and the inside would soon grow chilly. Rather than turn on the engine and waste gas, Kat got the Little Buddy going and then got back into the driver's seat. Only the comfort of heat kept her from falling into a deep despair.

And then out of the cold and dark, a light shone. Was someone coming to the rescue? Kat's heart leaped with hope. "I'm here!" she cried, hoping her voice would carry through the windshield. "Please help me, I'm here!"

FIVE MINUTES EARLIER

Sam Carter inched along the road to Independence in the snowstorm. He was bound for his parents' homestead and truly hoped the driver ahead knew where he was going and was familiar with the road, because it was getting harder and harder to see where the road ended and the ditch began. The only thing holding Sam to the road was the pair of red taillights ahead, and he kept his eyes glued to them. The taillights suddenly slid to the left and tilted. Uh oh, his guiding lights had just gone off the road and into the ditch.

Sam cautiously pulled to the side and watched the red taillights wink off. In his headlights he saw the outline of an old Vanagon. That vehicle wasn't going anywhere today. The ditch was hard enough to get out of in good weather. With the snow, it was going to take a tractor to pull the RV out.

Sam grabbed a flashlight from his jeep's glove compartment, jammed a beanie on his head, and got out. When he was only a few steps away from the driver's side of the vehicle, he shone his light inside. He gulped. The driver was a woman. She was zipping up her thick jacket over a tight black long-sleeved shirt. He caught a quick flash of curves before the jacket enveloped her. His lips parted in an involuntary reaction and he took a step back, even though he realized she couldn't possibly see him as long as he was standing behind the light.

He lifted the light higher and pulled it back so he was partially lit. With his other hand he waved and tapped on the window. Inside, warning barks sounded. Sam flinched. The barks sounded like they came from big animals, at least two of them. He liked dogs. His family had always had dogs. But he also knew what dogs were capable of when they perceived someone as a threat. Growls accompanied the barking.

"Miss?" he called out in his best hockey captain's voice, the one he used during games to shout something to his players. There was no other way to drown out the howling of the wind.

The woman seemed to pause inside the car. She didn't know who he was, and even if she followed hockey, she'd likely know his name better than his face because a hockey helmet was over it all the time on TV. But what else could she do? There was no telling how long the storm might continue, it could be for days. The dogs stopped barking and Sam could imagine they were looking at her questioningly. He was becoming uncomfortable in the thick snow flurry outside. Would she finally open the door? He knocked once more. Immediately the dogs started barking again. But since death-by-freezing was becoming more and more likely if she didn't let him in, he ignored it.

"My name is Sam. My family lives here. I want to help you."

A startled look came over the woman's face. She seemed to make a snap decision. "Go away," she called. "I'm fine by myself."

"What?" repeated Sam incredulously. "You can't be serious! It's snowing like there's no tomorrow and it's colder out here than, than..." He was actually at a loss for words. "Are you waiting for roadside assistance? Because I don't think they're coming." He was astonished and even a little hurt.

The woman seemed to study his face, probably looking for the fake innocence that he assumed murderers and rapists liked to project. To his surprise she cracked the door open. "I do need your help," she said gently as Rocky stuck his head out the door.

He had been right, the dog was big. He peered past her and spotted the second one with a bandage on its paw. "How far away are you from where you want to go?" he asked.

"A few miles."

"I don't think either of us are going to make a few miles."

Her face fell. "I agree," she said glumly.

He looked around, trying to pinpoint where they were. "Look, we're almost at the foot of Wilkinson Butte. I have a friend staying up there in a big house. They'll take us in until you can get towed out of here." He waited for her reaction. She looked like she was thinking, trying to make sure that would be safe. "Come on, the dogs can come too. You'll be okay with them along, right?"

"Do you think Nelly will be okay if I leave her here?"

"You mean the RV? I have some reflector tape we can tie to the bumper and side window. That should help."

She seemed to make up her mind there and then. "What are you driving back there?"

"A four-wheel drive with snow chains on. We can make it up the hill."

Grinding and roaring, the jeep crested the hill to the house. Kathrina was holding on with both hands and the dogs had long since jumped to the floor and braced themselves there. The big tires with chains bit into the snow as Sam wrestled with the wheel. Finally, they arrived at the house. Even covered with snow Kat could see how gracious the place was. It had a long front lawn, now white, and the house itself was Prairie style— low-slung and rambling with a deep roof and lots of windows.

Sam parked in the driveway, jumped out, and jogged around to her door, opening it before she had gathered everything. She was impressed. The old saying *manners make the man* jumped into her mind. She shook it away and snapped leashes on the dogs before they jumped out.

Wading through the snow to the front door, Kat was getting a funny feeling. This place seemed so familiar. *What name had Sam called this hilltop? A butte? Wilkinson Butte?*

Sam jogged the last few paces and raised the giant door knocker.

"This seems like the house my friend—" Kat started.

The door swung open.

"PAT!" she screamed.

"Kathrina!" The two friends glued themselves together in a giant bear-hug. The dogs gave short barks and snuffed, trotting in circles.

"We thought you were on your way to Jaz's place," a voice said behind them. Pat and Kathrina broke free of one another to greet a slim blonde woman who moved with the grace of a dancer.

"Tyler!" Kathrina exclaimed, hugging her.

They all stamped inside. "I hope the dogs are okay."

At that moment a long canine nose poked from around Tyler's leg. "Meet Ranger. Former police dog and now my constant companion."

The dogs all rubbed noses and sniffed in a friendly way.

"We love dogs," Tyler said. "Hi bro." She gave Sam a quick peck. "Let me get some towels so you can dry your guys off." She bustled away with Ranger at her heels.

"I'm going to get you some thick socks for your feet," Pat said, "You both must be frozen." He disappeared too.

Sam ripped the beanie from his head as Kat peeled off her jacket. Now that his coat was off she could see the muscles defined under his sweater. "I remember you," he said. "I'm Sam, a bro of Paula. We met about six months ago. During the Indie Rock Festival."

At his words, the memory of the Carter encounter rushed back. *Oh no! Not that arrogant hockey player!* Her traitorous body responded with a yearning tug in her belly. Her cheeks grew hot. Of all people, it had to be Sam who rescued her? Sometimes she really didn't understand life's little jokes. The Carter family was well established in Independence. Sam was the oldest of the children. He played hockey professionally with the Colorado Blizzard team. If she remembered correctly, the game schedule, regular practices, and promotional activities kept him busy on the road. She knew all this from a chance encounter at the diner on her summer visit, and she'd had enough of him then. What bad luck it was that he was in town now!

"I remember you," she said softly. and then reluctantly added, "Thanks for bringing me here." Arrogant or not he'd saved her butt. And the memory of their first meeting came rushing back...

Last Summer

The diner was hopping. Miss Minnie directed traffic while her sister Miss Daisy kept the food coming out of the kitchen. A man dining at the table next to Kat smirked and folded up his newspaper. "Around here Mr. Wilkinson is considered the unofficial mayor," he said to no one in particular.

"Oh? Why unofficial? Is there an official mayor?" she asked with interest, keeping her eyes fastened on the revolving door Miss Minnie had disappeared through.

"Sure. A female mayor. There's a community council that consists of seven people. The Disney Sisters and Mr. Wilkinson are the power players of Independence."

"Miss Minnie is a force of nature," Kathrina mused, turning to face the stranger. She almost fell off her stool. She held on at the last moment and squirmed inwardly when she saw his amused look. The man looked like a true Viking; reddish-blond hair, an angular face, and moss-green eyes. Broad shoulders, and if she interpreted the contours under the long-sleeved T-shirt correctly, sinewy muscles. Finally, she found her voice again and croaked, "You wouldn't happen to be related to Paula Carter, would you?"

His mouth twisted into a broad smile. "You know my sister? And survived the encounter?"

"Hey, don't say that about your sister!"

At least he shrugged guiltily. "You're right. But the term 'social skills' wasn't exactly invented for her."

"So far, she's made a better first impression than you," Kathrina replied flippantly. She had no idea which little devil was sitting on her shoulder right now. But it was getting on her nerves that this guy was sitting here, talking about his sister to strangers and acting as if he had the whole world at his feet. Which was probably true if you looked like him.

He seemed more amused by her outburst, which only annoyed her more. "And yes, I met her recently. We have a mutual friend," Kathrina added.

Immediately his expression became serious. "Jaz. The new yoga studio owner." It was a statement, not a question.

Kathrina squirmed uncomfortably in her seat. She didn't quite know what to do with this suddenly very human side of the Viking. Did it have to be like this? she thought, still annoyed, but also fascinated against her will. When a sympathetic side was added to masculine good looks, a man was practically unstoppable. She consoled herself with the thought that this would not be a problem for her. After all, she wasn't interested in him and he certainly wasn't interested in her. Her hormones, which were doing a dance of joy in her belly and cheering her on to throw herself at him on the spot, were not interested in her rational considerations. Distance was the order of the day.

She felt uncomfortable. Her face felt hot. She desperately needed distance from this hunk of testosterone that was suddenly showing emotion, too. Time to back off. "Well then, it was nice to meet you, brother of Paula."

"Sam."

"What?" He was completely throwing her for a loop. Now, to make matters worse, he was smiling.

"My name is Sam," he repeated patiently. "And you are?"

"Kathrina. Friend of Jaz's, and passing through." She got up from her chair. In doing so, she nearly tripped over the chair leg. In a flash, his hand shot forward and steadied her at the hip. All the nerve endings in her body seemed to short-circuit. She took a big step back to break the contact. This time without almost falling down. Wow. The effect this guy had on her...

Kat came back to the present. She and Sam were standing in the entryway, kicking off their boots. Sam hung their coats to dry as she restrained the dogs.

Tyler returned with towels.

Mutely, Kat accepted them.

"I'm getting some hot food ready," Tyler said. "Be back in a jif."

Kat busied herself with toweling the dogs. A wave of uncertainty swept over her. "About earlier... I'm sorry I was so rude at first." She glanced at him out of the corner of her eye.

He just nodded. "No problem. You can never be too careful." He hesitated for a moment, as if having an internal debate. Then he winked at her.

Was he flirting? Kat wondered. No matter. She would just stay away from him. *Starting tomorrow,* she vowed to herself. Tomorrow she would meet Jaz and no longer depend on his hospitality. Avoiding this Norse god shouldn't be a problem. At least she hoped. Independence wasn't exactly big. But as far as she knew, he spent most of his time in Denver with a hockey team. Oddly enough, this thought did not please her as much as she wanted it to. She suppressed the unwelcome feelings and removed the soaked bandage from Nikki's paw. The wound looked fine. She decided to let it air dry for a while.

Pat returned. "Here," he said, handing them mugs of hot chocolate.

Gratefully, she accepted the drink. On top, little marshmallows floated. After three days in Nelly, eating takeout and trail mix, this was heaven.

Pat led them into the house while the dogs trotted behind. To Kat, he looked good—fit, relaxed, and happy. Happy was something he hadn't been in Seattle. An architect, he'd had an unhappy split with a business partner and came to Independence to clear his head. Never left.

They reached a spacious living room. Pat stepped to one side so they could see. Everything seemed to be made of wood, brick, or stone. The dark, newly refinished floors gleamed in the light of a fire leaping in a huge stone fireplace. A full bar was built-in beside it. It looked original and had been nicely restored. Dark leather couches contrasted nicely with light gray-colored walls and pristine white woodwork. The windows were large with deep casements so the views of the storm outside were spectacular. Pat gestured to the couch and disappeared again.

They were left standing a bit awkwardly, looking around the magnificent room. Kat plopped herself on the couch.

"Everything okay?" Sam asked, sitting down next to her. Pat and Tyler still seemed to be busy in another room. She hoped they'd come and take the tension off soon.

Sam was being attentive. And too close, she realized. She would have loved for Rocky to join her on the sofa, as a sort of living buffer between them. But she was pretty sure Pat and Tyler didn't let dogs on this beautiful sofa. It looked new. She looked around the room. So did the whole place, really. She was under the impression that Pat and Tyler just had a room here while renovations were finished. But they seemed to have the run of the place.

"Everything okay?" Sam asked again with a smile.

"Yes, everything is fine. Except for the fact that I should have listened to my friend," Kat replied contritely.

He frowned. "Jaz? Why?"

She plucked invisible lint from the sofa. "Even before I left Seattle she warned me about being prepared for snow." Ruefully, she stuck out her lower lip. "After getting lucky with the weather for the first two days, I guessed I could make it here before the weather turned. Are we even in Independence?"

Sam looked at her. "Don't you know?"

"Not sure," she admitted. "My sense of direction and my navigation system think so. But I'm not sure how much my sense of direction can be relied on when I can't see farther than the nearest snowflake. And I don't know if the GPS can be trusted in this storm either."

"It works via satellite," he replied dryly.

She rolled her eyes. "I know, smartass. But maybe it's snowing in space, all that stuff has to come from somewhere." She gestured with her big mug of hot chocolate toward the window.

Sam erupted in a laugh. She could see her feisty retort surprised him in a positive way. Well, knowing a few of his sisters, he was used to feisty. His mom and sisters made sure of that. She was under the impression that he enjoyed their company very much. Maybe it was liberating for him to spend time with a woman who wasn't figuring out how to get him into bed on the first date. *Ha! Who am I kidding*, she thought.

Sam brought her back to reality. "Don't worry. You're in Independence, just outside the downtown. Don't blink or you'll miss it. We're in the Wilkinson house."

"Pat restored this place!"

"Somebody talking about me behind my back?" Pat entered with a platter in each hand piled with mini tacos and sliders. Tyler was right behind with a steaming carafe on a tray with glass mugs. In each mug was a branch of real cinnamon. She set everything down on the coffee table before them.

"What you got there, sis?" Sam said.

"Hot rum toddies to warm you up." Tyler set the tray down and poured the hot rum mixture into the glass cups. It smelled delicious.

Kat jumped to her feet. "There's just one thing. I should call Jaz. She'll be frantic."

"There's no cell reception, remember?" Sam interrupted.

"No worries," Pat said, putting the hot food down. "Mr. Wilkinson is old school. He has a landline. And so do Jaz and Jake at the farmhouse."

"Speaking of which, where is he?" Tyler asked. Mr. Wilkinson was the official owner of this house.

"He got caught in the storm at the diner and was afraid the old Cadillac might not make the hill. He got a room at the bed-and-breakfast."

"Where did you say the phone was?" Kat asked.

"Over there behind the bar. Help yourself. Jaz's number is right beside the phone."

While Kat dialed and explained the predicament, Tyler handed her a hot toddy. Nikki followed Kat to the phone and waited anxiously as the call progressed. Jaz was relieved and promised to meet them all for breakfast next morning at the diner if the roads were clear. By the time Kat got back to the couch, Rocky was laying at Sam's feet enjoying an ear rub.

"Tyler, how's that knee of yours," Sam asked, popping a mini taco in his mouth.

"It's healing nicely. But I'm not going back to Las Vegas anytime soon." She looked at Pat affectionately. "I'm having too good a time here."

"Any plans?"

"I still own the building Jaz holds her yoga classes in. There's a whole floor empty. I'm thinking about what to do with it."

Pat slid an arm around Tyler. "I keep a workout bag on the first floor and we go over there. Tyler works at the ballet barre while I work out the bag." They smiled at one another.

Kat tried not to show her surprise. It seemed really serious between those two. Tyler had been a driven professional dancer in a Cirque du Soleil–type show in Las Vegas. Now she had given it all up to hang out with Pat in a small town. Kat almost shook her head in disapproval. Not that it was any of her business, she supposed. But still, giving up her career for a man wasn't the way she wanted her life to go.

"So what's the deal with the house?" Sam asked. "Is it finished? Almost finished?"

Pat put his sock feet up on the table. "The Colorado State Registry for Notable and Historic Architecture will refund a large portion of the cost to restore the house if we do it authentically. It has to look exactly the way it was back in the day from the street. But we were able to build Mr. Wilkinson an apartment on the back with two bedrooms—one for him and one for when his great granddaughter Avery comes to visit. He's planning to rent this main part of the house out."

"Really?" Sam looked intrigued.

Pat picked up the toddy carafe and refreshed everybody's glass. "He's letting Tyler and I stay in a bedroom here in the main house until the last of the restoration on the back."

"It's safer that way," Tyler chimed in.

Kat figured everyone was thinking of the intruder who had stalked Pat and actually broke into this old house when the outer walls were under restoration. It was all over now, but that was something no one would soon forget. There was a brief silence but no one brought it up. Tyler, in particular, didn't need to relive that experience.

"Anybody tired?" Tyler asked. I have six bedrooms and four bathrooms waiting. Take your pick."

"I'd love a hot bath," Kat admitted.

In minutes she was soaking in a hot bath while the dogs got fed and watered in the kitchen. Thankfully, Ranger didn't mind sharing some of his dog chow. Submerged in bubbles, Kat wondered how she was going to break the news to Jaz that she'd brought six dogs to stay with her instead of two. She knew how that news would go over while visiting anyone in Seattle. She hoped the news would go over a little better in Independence.

CHAPTER FOUR

THE NEXT MORNING before anyone else was up, Kat left a message for Caitlin and emailed her mother a cheery note. From this vantage point, she could see the surrounding valley. Everything glistened under white splendor. If it weren't for all the snow on the ground, one could almost forget that a blizzard raged just yesterday, so blue and cloudless was the sky today. All around, mountains towered majestically. The February sun was warmer than expected. Hopefully she wouldn't get a sunburn on her nose. Her fair skin wasn't very fond of the sun. Maybe she'd need sunscreen in this place. She had clearly underestimated the high altitude.

Whistling up the dogs, she went down the hill to check on Nelly. The RV was right where they left it, halfway in a ditch and enough off to the side that it wasn't in too much danger of being hit. Sam's reflector tapes were still where he'd tied them, fluttering like cheerful banners. Kat had only been walking for a few minutes and already felt an urgent need to sit down. She was pretty much out of breath. She unlocked Nelly's side door and got in. The two dogs sat down next to her with their tongues hanging out.

"I hope I haven't overworked you now," she said to Nikki. She crouched down next to her and stroked her fur.

Rocky sat up and pricked his ears. Then he let out a joyful bark. When Kat poked her head out she saw a big SUV pulled over and someone walking toward them. A woman with chin-length blond hair waved. She had a poodle on a leash also barking joyfully. Kat began to beam. It was Jaz.

Kat jumped from the RV and ran pell-mell to meet her. The dogs were right behind. The two women hugged each other tightly. Both wiped a few tears from the corners of their eyes as they broke away.

Kat snorted, "We are two crazy chickens, aren't we?" She pulled Jaz and Rambo a little to the side. "I know there's no traffic, but let's get a little farther off the road."

"That's just the way it is," Jaz said, unconcerned. "Didn't I tell you to watch the weather?"

"I thought Nelly and I could drive away from the storm."

"Next time, at least try to make sure the storm is behind you and not in front of you," her friend said dryly. Then she brightened up. "But I love the paint job! Black paw prints and pink letters. Adorable!" Jaz burst out laughing with delight.

Their banter was interrupted by Nikki, who pressed shyly against Kat's legs and looked uncertainly back and forth between them before venturing a cautious step in Jaz's direction.

Jaz crouched down and slowly extended her hand to Nikki, giving her a chance to decide if she wanted to make contact. "So you're the new addition." She looked up at Kat. "The wound looks pretty good already, though."

Kat nodded. "She's healing nicely. I just hope I didn't put her through too much with my walk through the snow."

"She's had a little rest now. Let's go up to the house." Jaz rose with a smooth movement.

"What should I do about Nelly?"

"I'll call Joe. He does snow removal, some towing, and taxi service too, when needed. He'll get you out."

An hour later Jaz pulled open the big door to the diner with *Miss Minnie's* etched in the glass. Her friends piled in right behind her, shaking themselves and stamping off the snow. Red padded booths lined the walls of the diner and four-top tables with wooden chairs filled the center. A big counter had silver stools that swiveled. Platters of hot breakfasts piled with pancakes and eggs, toast and hash browns, sausages and bacon, whizzed back and forth on plates almost the size of Thanksgiving platters.

Jaz was intercepted by Miss Minnie herself, standing ready with a pot of tea in her hand. She gratefully accepted a cup.

"All alone today?" Minnie chirped.

"No, I'm expecting quite a crowd."

"Hmph. At least make sure you eat enough. How else am I supposed to get meat on your bones. Especially since you don't even eat meat," Minnie muttered.

"I promise," Jaz, a vegetarian, replied.

At that moment Sam, Pat and Kat all bundled through the door. Jaz hurried over and threw her arms around everyone. She glowed with the happiness of having friends surround her.

"I'm so thankful Joe was able to pull Nelly out of the ditch," Kat said breathlessly.

Jaz was about to go in for another hug when they were all intercepted by a little man in a great big hat. A little shrunken but still dapper, he wore a wide-brimmed western hat, a string tie, and a pair of handmade boots with big heels that made him five-foot-six if he didn't slouch. The hat added another four inches on top.

"That's Mr. Wilkinson," Jaz whispered in Kat's ear.

"Howdy!" he boomed at them. Picking out Sam, he said, "Why if it isn't the handsomest man in town besides me. What are you doing here?"

"Hey Mr. W, lookin' good," Sam said, patting his shoulder.

"Shouldn't you be chasing a basketball around somewhere?" the feisty little man shot back.

Sam just laughed at the teasing.

"Mr. Wilkinson," Jaz said in a more serious tone, "Meet my good friend Kat from Seattle."

Mr. Wilkinson adjusted his string tie. "I'm on very good terms with people from Seattle. My old woodpile is getting a facelift by another friend of Jaz's from that city. I see you already know him." He pointed to Pat. "An architect all the way from See-attle."

Rather than let Mr. Wilkinson drive the rest of the conversation, Sam took charge. "Let's find a table. I'd like to talk to you, Mr. Wilkinson, about your plans to rent out the house."

"I'm always ready to talk horse tradin'."

Kat looked at Jaz, confused.

"Business, he's ready to talk business," she whispered. "It's the way the old-timers talk around here."

As they made their way to a table Jaz asked, "Where's Tyler by the way?"

"She offered to stay at home with the dogs. It's too many to bring into a cafe and it's too cold to leave them in the car. Besides, she likes to sleep in. I think it's a habit from living in Las Vegas."

Jaz saw a funny look come over Kat's face as if she had some news that was troubling her. But Minnie was urging them toward the biggest table in the place and she soon forgot about it. As they got seated Mr. Wilkinson said, "Pat why don't you give us a report on the restoration?"

Pat rubbed a hand over his face. "Sure. We're reasonably on schedule, which is excellent considering the weather has been so bad."

"At first, I was thinking of selling the house," Wilkinson said. "But then I heard about renting houses to seasonal guests. It's getting so popular these days. Pat suggested I could have an apartment to myself and rent the rest of the place out."

Pat nodded. "Since the house is so huge I suggested the apartment with a separate entrance."

"The extra bedroom is for when my great granddaughter visits," Mr. Wilkinson said proudly.

"We'll be finished with the extra work in the next two to three weeks," Pat said. "Meanwhile, Tyler and I will still stay in our room in the main house."

"What happens after that?" said Jaz.

"We find our own place."

"Well, I have an idea I'd like to put in front of you, Mr. Wilkinson," said Sam.

"I guess I have to listen to the second best-looking guy in the town," the older man teased.

Sam gave an easy grin. "About that seasonal rental. I'd like to be your first customer. I want to take the place until the end of hockey season and maybe longer."

Mr. Wilkinson's eyes grew bright while Pat's mouth fell open.

"I want a place to bring my hockey buddies when we have a few days off from the game schedule." He turned to Pat. "And don't worry about having to leave in a hurry," Sam continued. "What is there, six bedrooms in the place? Stay as long as you need until you're done with the restoration and can find a place for you and Tyler."

"Seems like we can get this sewn up in a jiffy," Mr. Wilkinson said. "How long did you say you want the place?"

"Let's say until the end of hockey season."

"Done." Mr. Wilkinson held out his gnarled hand to shake.

"Do you want me to sign something?" Sam asked.

Mr. Wilkinson snatched a paper napkin up off the table and conjured a pen out of his suit pocket. He wrote a number on the napkin with a flourish. "How does that suit your pocketbook?" he said, showing it to Sam. "Due the first of every month."

"Suits me just fine," Sam said.

"Just initial it," Mr. Wilkinson said, handing him the pen. "We don't need any more paperwork than this. A Carter's word is his bond."

It was hard to tell who was more pleased, Sam or Mr. Wilkinson.

And at that moment, Minnie arrived with both hands full of breakfast platters. Everyone dove in.

A few hours later Nelly chugged up to the McArthy farmhouse where Jaz lived. Years ago, Jaz's forward-thinking grandfather had sold the largest parcel of farmland so it could be divided into eight-acre homesteads. Jake's sister, Paula lived right next door on her own homestead, with her dogs and horses.

Right now, Jake was just leaving the house, getting into his sheriff's SUV. He tipped his big, western-style hat at Kat as she shifted Nelly into "Park." Jaz came out and waved. Rambo slipped out the door behind her and loped across the expanse of front yard.

"Come in come in," Jaz called.

Kat jumped out with her dogs and bags. Jaz escorted them through the house while the dogs sniffed one another and then trotted dutifully behind. "The furniture is old," Jaz said, waving a hand at things as they passed. "Some are nice antiques I'd like to refinish with Nana's okay."

"There are so many pieces here," Kat exclaimed.

"I admit, it's a little crowded. But Nana collected the stuff other people couldn't bear to part with but still had to get rid of." Jaz sighed. "She can tell you a story about every object in here."

Kat's eyes wandered over chairs and side tables in the living room, as well as two spinning wheels tucked into a corner. Jaz turned down a hall and they passed doors, some of them open to bedrooms. Kat spotted a full-size weaving loom in one room.

"Jake and I are gradually cleaning out. You know how it is."

"Having just packed everything up and into storage, I certainly do," Kate sympathized.

Jaz stopped outside a solid oak door. She swung it open. Inside was a brass four-poster bed covered with an embroidered quilt. Beside it was a stately mahogany chest of drawers, and a washstand with a ceramic jug and bowl. The mirror over the washstand was so old the reflection in it was rippled. Kat put her bags down.

Jaz looked at her closely. "This may sound a little strange, but would you like to lie down for a nap?"

Kat walked over to the bed and fell backwards onto it. Her curly hair splayed out over the quilt. "Do I look that tired?"

"Just a little. It's been a big trip. Take the time for a little cat nap and when you get up we can take the dogs for a walk."

"Sounds like heaven." As Jaz closed the door, Kat stretched out, confident that Jaz would take the dogs and give them treats and water outside.

ATCHOO!
ATCHOO!
ATCHOO!

Kat woke with a start. She was having a sneezing fit.

ATCHOO! Her nose was running like crazy but there were no tissues in the room. She took the end of her T-shirt and wiped up. So much for this clean shirt. Thanks goodness she had more in her bags.

Getting up, she caught her reflection in the warped mirror. What a job it did! Her nose was swollen and her eyes were puffy slits. Kat laughed at the funhouse effect and dug out her purse to look in a small makeup mirror. She screamed. The small mirror reflected the same thing as the big mirror. She looked like a gargoyle.

A knock came on the door. "Kat, are you okay?" It was Jaz's voice. "Did I hear you cry out?"

The door opened. "OH!" Jaz shouted as she stared in shock. "Kat is that you?"

"Yes it's me. I'm having an allergic reaction."

"What to? What's in here?"

"Oh Jaz, I'm only allergic to one thing."

"What's that?"

"Dust."

"All this old furniture is full of it. I do my best but—"

"Please don't apologize—*ATCHOOOOO.*"

"Come on," Jaz said, taking her by the arm. "Let's get you out of here."

Fortunately, Jake's sister Paula was home next door and answered at the first knock. She took one look at Kat's face as Jaz hissed, "Antihistamines. She's having an allergic reaction!"

"Leslie!" Paula called behind her. "Run upstairs and get my allergy medication."

There was the sound of footsteps running and soon a teenaged girl appeared with a package of pills. Kat and Jaz followed her to the kitchen where Paula got down a glass and ran some filtered water from the fridge. She handed a dose over and Kat gulped them down.

An hour later, Kat's red and swollen nose was nearly its right size and faded pink in color. Her puffy eyelids were receding and she only had the occasional cough as opposed to a dozen sneezes one after another.

Leslie had gone in another room to watch TV while Paula, Jaz, and Kat sipped hot tea in the kitchen. While they waited for the antihistamines to finish their job, Paula told the story of Leslie, and how she came to be staying here.

"Sometimes she still wakes up in the night with her heart pounding," Paula explained. "She ran away at fourteen after a series of foster homes. She was sleeping in my barn with the horses."

"How did the situation ever get that bad?" Kat wondered.

"Poor thing didn't know her parents. At the age of two, she was placed with a foster family. She says they were a nice family but when she was four, her foster parents split up and she was placed somewhere else. Then one foster family followed the next. No one really wanted her. The older she got, the more she rebelled."

"I never knew all that detail," Jaz said. "How exactly did she end up here?"

Paula set down her teacup and ran a hand through her spiky auburn hair. "Last summer she finally ran away. The truck she'd been secretly stowing away in had stopped in Independence. So she walked around on foot. When she had passed by my place she saw the horses. And the house. Said she'd always dreamed of a white ranch house with a wraparound porch. She imagined that was the kind of house a happy family lived in."

"Sweet," Kat said. "It is a homey, friendly looking place. I could see that through my slits when we walked over."

Jaz laughed and so did Paula.

"I realized someone had moved in when I saw small signs around the barn. The straw was flattened as though someone had slept on it. The barn floor was swept and I knew the horses sure didn't do it."

"Were you afraid?"

"Not really. What dangerous intruder sweeps up after themselves? Nothing was ever taken. So, I started leaving food in the stable. I thought it was likely a man, a vagrant. But one day I surprised her and found she was a girl. Pulled the wool over my and Jake's eyes for a bit telling us she was eighteen, but I saw through that early on."

"Did you adopt her?" Kat asked.

"We're crawling through the paperwork. The system grinds slowly," Paula said simply.

"And now let's talk about you," Jaz said, turning to Kat. "You can't stay with me, obviously. I put you in the cleanest room in the house."

"I'd offer you a bedroom but I don't have one," Paula explained. "Leslie took the spare and my office is the other one. This house is a lot more modern and smaller than Jaz's original farmhouse."

"I can stay in the RV until I find a place," Kat said airily. "Just let me run a cord for power and I can dash in and out of the house to use your bathroom. The dogs won't mind."

"And that will work just fine until the next snowstorm," Paula said. "What are you going to do for meals or TV? For a night or two, fine. But it's going to take some time to find your own place."

"It's true," Jaz admitted. "There's very little for rent here in Independence Junction. Searching for something to come up can take months. I suppose there's the bed-and-breakfast."

"It's ski season," Paula pointed out. "The highest rates of the year." She looked pointedly at Kat, "I take it you're not made of money."

"Wait!" Jaz said and snapped her fingers. "Sam just officially rented the Wilkinson house. He's got all kinds of room. At least you can bunk there until Pat and Tyler have to get out."

Kat groaned. For so many reasons, she didn't want this option.

"What are you groaning about?"

"Oh, just—"

"I know, you don't want to be a bother. Well, Sam needs some bothering. He needs to think about somebody besides himself," Paula stated flatly.

"What about the dogs?" Kat protested.

"Mr. Wilkinson loves Rocky. Remember how he minded the dog last summer when we all went to the music festival?"

Oh yes, Kat remembered very well. And Rocky returned spoiled and happy. "Who is going to ask Sam?" she asked. "Not me!"

"Don't worry about a thing," Paula said. "I'll set it all up for you."

Just as Paula said, it was all set up. Sam was totally willing for Kat to return to the Wilkinson house. Kat warmed Nelly's engine before loading the dogs and leaving. A minute went by before Jaz came out with Nikki and Rocky. As Jaz made her way to the RV, Kat realized she was definitely nervous at the thought of facing Sam. Back in Seattle, she'd thought she was immune to male charm. But it was simply that she'd never met anyone like Sam before. He was putting all her convictions to the test.

As Jaz led the dogs nearer, Rocky spun excitedly in a circle around Nikki.

"Looks like your dog can't wait to get back to his new place."

"I can tell," Kat muttered. She fiddled awkwardly with her jacket. "Unlike me."

Jaz came around and jumped in the passenger seat to say goodbye. "Admit it. You're looking forward to Sam, too," Jaz teased her.

Kat turned to face her. "Honestly, I'm scared of everything. I've known the man barely two days and every time I think I know what makes him tick and what convenient drawer I can put him in, he surprises me all over again. It totally throws me off balance. I can't stand that." She gritted her teeth.

Jaz tilted her head and studied her. "I don't know. It's possible there's something good about your life finally having a little variety."

"I like my life boring. Thank you."

"Come on. What's going to happen that's so terrible?"

"What could go wrong? There's nothing at stake except my independence, my self-respect, and my heart." Oops. Spoken aloud, her list sounded more melodramatic than in her head. And who was talking about love and heartbreak? Since when did she immediately think about marriage without even having kissed him properly?

Jaz looked surprised. "I didn't know you were taking this whole thing so seriously. You're usually the one who gets guys into bed in a snap and gets rid of them with another snap."

"Except it won't be so easy this time, since he's practically your brother-in-law, right?"

Jaz shrugged his shoulders. "I think you're making it complicated. Sam doesn't want to settle down anytime soon. But if you're going to pass on the Norse god—hey!" She screeched as Kat pinched her thigh. "I'm giving you the honest-to-God truth here!"

"Doesn't mean I want to hear it."

"What I was really going to say is, maybe you'll gain a new friend, plain and simple. The Carters really are a nice family."

At Jaz's last sentence, Kat breathed a sigh of relief. Right. Friends. She could handle that. She'd forgotten all about that option. Behind her, Rocky whined. "I'm coming." She reached for her bags and hugged Jaz with her right arm. "Thanks for setting my head straight. I swear it must be the high-altitude air that causes me to make a mountain out of every molehill." She got out and walked around Nelly to open the crates for Rocky and Nikki. They scrambled inside. As she passed Jaz's side again, the window rolled down.

"Or it might be your hormones. Take care!"

Before Kat could think of a glib reply, she jumped back into the driver's seat as Jaz jumped out, started Nelly, and backed out onto the road. And within the hour, Kat and Nikki and Rocky were all back at the Wilkinson house, bags on the doorstep.

"I guess Paula told you this is only temporary," Kat blurted out as Sam opened the door.

"Sure. Come on in," Sam said. He swung the door wide and Rocky trotted right in. Nikki hung back with Kat.

"What I mean is, I want to pay you for my stay and all. I don't want to take advantage of you."

Sam paused with one arm up on door. He looked like he might be having second thoughts. "You don't trust me, do you?"

Kat grew flustered. "It's not that, it's—"

"No, that's exactly what it is. Where are you from originally?"

"Poland."

"Well, I'm offering you some old-fashioned Colorado hospitality. It comes rent-free. I'm doing a favor for Jaz and Jake, and my sister Paula, and hospitality comes with it. That's the way we do things here. Take it or leave it."

Kat's cheeks were so hot they burned. "I meant no disrespect. Honestly, I didn't. I'm just trying to do the right thing—"

"You can start by coming inside. Take off your coat. Relax. I'm not looking for a fight. Are you?"

"No, of course not. I—"

In one fluid motion Sam picked her bags off the front step and whisked them inside. Kat followed. Nikki too.

"Wait, WAIT! One second," Kat protested. "You don't understand. There's something I have to tell you."

He turned to face her and his expression said, *What now?*

"It's Nikki." She hesitated. And then it all spilled out. "She's pregnant. She'll have puppies in another three weeks or so." Tears sprang to her eyes and one slid all the way down her cheek.

Sam's eyes searched her face, amazed. "Girl," he said, "don't you know dogs have puppies all the time? Get in here. You're in Colorado now." And then he turned and waved one hand in the air saying, "I'll let you pick whatever room you want. They're all furnished."

CHAPTER FIVE

WHILE KAT WAS OFF deciding where she'd unpack, Sam's mind wandered back to the first time he'd really noticed her, last summer...

Sam was sitting at the diner and had just finished up reading the news in the local newspaper. Next to him was an attractive young woman with long curly hair and healthy curves. As the star player on the Colorado Blizzard hockey team, Sam had his pick of women. But most of those women were model-thin. Always on the verge of starvation and still on a diet. As interesting as a glass of water in his opinion. He longed for a woman who didn't immediately stab him with a hip bone. Or burst into tears just for raising his voice. He wasn't violent or anything, for heaven's sake. His peaceful father would turn his head around single-handedly if he showed a tendency that way.

How had he even come up with this absurd train of thought? Oh, right. Curves. And what curves, he thought, as his gaze returned to the woman at the next table. He promptly caught her eyeing him.

Embarrassed, she averted her eyes.

Interesting. "Are you aware that around here Mr. Wilkinson is considered the unofficial mayor?" he ventured.

"Oh? Why unofficial? Is there an official mayor?" she asked.

"Sure. A female mayor. But there's also a community council that consists of seven people. The Disney Sisters are

part of that, as well as Mr. Wilkinson. The power players of Independence, if you will."

"Miss Minnie is a force of nature," Kathrina commented, and when she turned to look at him, he knew she liked what she saw. Her voice had a croak when she said, "You wouldn't happen to be related to Paula Carter, would you?"

He felt his mouth twist into a broad smile. "You know my sister? And survived the encounter?"

"Hey, don't say that about your sister!"

"You're right. But the term 'social skills' wasn't exactly invented for her."

"So far, she's made a better first impression than you," the woman replied flippantly.

Sam stayed cool. He knew he was getting to her.

Miss Curly Hair squirmed uncomfortably in her seat. Her face grew hot and she gathered her purse as if needing distance. "It was nice to meet you, brother of Paula."

"Sam."

"What?"

He was completely throwing her for a loop. It made him smile.

"My name is Sam," he repeated patiently. "And you are?"

"Kathrina. Friend of Jaz's, and passing through." She added the last bit almost defiantly as she got up from her chair. In doing so, she nearly tripped. He reflexively shot his hand out and steadied her at the hip. She took a big step back to break away from his touch. But they both knew a spark had been ignited.

Sam smiled to himself at the memory. Oh yes, he remembered Kathrina very well.

Meanwhile, roaming the hall of the Wilkinson house, Kat knew she'd like the farthest bedroom possible away from Sam. That was the idea. But as Nikki grew more pregnant, making it to the second floor might pose problems. So, Kat stayed on the first floor and peered into the rooms. The first one Sam had claimed for himself. The furnishings matched the rest of the house. The walls were painted light gray and contrasted nicely with the dark wooden floor. A blue blanket lay neatly folded on the bed. A yellow pillow added an upbeat splash of color.

There was not much to discover of Sam's personality. There was a photograph on the nightstand, however. She stepped closer and took it in her hand. Five smiling faces gazed back at her. Judging by the identical pairs of eyes, they were the Carter siblings as children. She recognized Sam and Jake, as well as Paula. She didn't recognize the third, who was probably brother Cole. He didn't live in Independence anymore. The little blonde had to be Tyler. Everyone in the snapshot was laughing. It was clear from their body language that they were very attached to one another.

Wistfully, Kat placed the framed photo back on the nightstand. She had always wanted a sister or brother. The idea of having an ally when her father had "another one of his days" was tempting. Perhaps it was better, though, that she had remained an only child. Otherwise, there would now be two people with a therapy-resistant relationship problem.

A Colorado Blizzard jersey hung on a chair by the door. As she walked past it, she let her fingertips slide over it and just barely managed to stop herself from smelling the fabric. *Get out of here fast*, she thought.

Since she already knew the bathroom, she walked past it to the next room. Off-white walls, a big bed with plump pillows, and a green comforter to match the curtains gave the room an inviting atmosphere. Sam obviously intended this room for her, as her bags were on the bed. Well, there was a bathroom between them, at least. She dropped down on the bed next to the bag and stretched out. Pat and Tyler had done a good job. The furnishings were not only stylish, but practical and comfortable. If she wasn't careful, she would fall asleep. A few minutes later she was all moved in. She came out to join Sam, Ranger, and the dogs in the living room. "I guess you're looking at the newest resident of Independence," she said lightly.

Sam walked over to a shelf to look at the DVDs. "Honestly, I have no idea what Tyler dragged in here. She thought they needed movies to spend the quiet evenings."

"Speaking of, where are they?"

"Pat and Tyler went to Breck for a vacay. The storm held them up a day."

"Breck? What's that?"

"Short for Breckenridge. Everybody shortens the name to that." He skipped through the DVDs on the shelf. "I'm sorry we don't have *Turner and Hootch* starring Tom Hanks."

"I saw that! In the movie he owns a mastiff."

"Ever heard of *Ice Age*?" he asked, holding up the package. "It's good for a laugh."

"Um, yeah, sure. Why not?" she replied in surprise. Cartoons were a secret indulgence and it pleased her to know that Sam didn't consider himself too grown-up to watch such things. Then again, that was probably to be expected from a man who made his living chasing a puck around on skates.

Sam put on the movie and they settled in on the leather couch. An hour later Kat was fast asleep. In her sleep, she'd slid against Sam's shoulder. He pulled her a little closer and let her head rest on his shoulder. After another while he turned off the TV and carefully wriggled out from under her. The couch was large and also comfortable, so she would sleep well. He tucked a throw blanket around her and stroked her head with his hand. When she unconsciously nestled against his hand in her sleep, he smiled.

The two dogs blinked as he quietly slipped out to go to his own room. He disappeared, waited a second and then looked back. Rocky had jumped onto the sofa and was curling up at Kat's feet with a deep sigh. Nikki was settled on the floor. They looked as though their world was back in order.

When Kat woke up the next morning, she had to get her bearings. Sleepily, she blinked at the sun's rays streaming in and looked around the strange living room. How embarrassing. Apparently she had fallen asleep during the movie. She was even tucked in with a blanket. Very considerate of the man, she had to admit. With a sigh, she snuggled back into the couch. Hopefully she hadn't been snoring. A small smile crept onto her lips. What would it be like to have a man like Sam for a boyfriend? If she believed the butterflies in her stomach, the answer was "hot." Not that she would find out, she reminded herself sternly.

She was now in a small town. She had to behave accordingly. Uncommitted affairs with the locals were probably not the order of the day. Unfortunately, it had been over a year since her last adventure. And her little battery-powered friend wasn't a cure-all, either. No wonder she wanted to pounce on Sam as soon as he got within five steps of her. She scolded herself silently.

The smell of coffee smell tickled her nose and cleared her sleepy brain. Nikki and Rocky saw she was awake and started nosing her to get up. She cuddled them both and checked Nikki's paw, which still seemed to be healing well.

Finally, the lure of coffee became too strong, and she crawled out from under the blanket. Still wearing yesterday's socks, she plodded over to the kitchen. As she did so, her gaze went out the window to the Rocky Mountains towering in the distance. All around, everything was deep in snow. Except for a lonely truck track leading from the house to the road, it was completely untouched. Very different from Seattle. But beautiful.

A thermos was waiting on the counter along with a cup. Next to it was a note:

Went to town. Should be back in two hours. Fresh towels in hall closet. The dogs already were outside. Sam.

A warm feeling spread through her heart. He had let the dogs out. And left coffee. She wondered if Sam might be worth relaxing her strict rules about men. But then she shook her head resolutely. She couldn't and wouldn't take the risk of ending up like her mother.

She poured herself a cup of coffee and convinced the excited dogs that she could handle things just fine in the bathroom alone. In she went, only to find she had forgotten to bring fresh clothes. So, she wrapped herself in a too-small towel and crept barefoot down the hall to her room where her bags were stowed. Why she was sneaking, she didn't really know. Probably because she suspected Sam would be back any minute. She rummaged in her bag looking for fresh underwear, which seemed to be hiding, as it did every day on the road. She could have sworn that her things moved on tiny legs every night.

Cursing loudly in Polish, she presented a delightful backside to Sam, who had just come down the hall and was looking through the open bedroom door.

"That's a sight I could get used to," he said, and got the pleasure of seeing her blush all over her body.

Kat straightened up and slowly turned to face him, careful to hold the towel tight. There was definitely no need to give him any more of a show than she already had. But in the process, she dropped the underwear that was tucked under her arm along with a T-shirt and jeans.

She moaned. At least she had chosen the set of pink lace and not her ancient cotton underpants. *And why did you do that? Huh?* An annoying little voice in the back of her head wanted to know. Shut up, she told the voice, and concentrated on the situation.

"Um, I was taking a shower—"

"I can see that," Sam replied with amusement.

"You might as well act like a gentleman and pretend I'm fully clothed, you know?"

"Sorry, that's not an option with the way you look. Wrapped in a towel or," he dropped his gaze to the underwear still lying on the floor, "clothed."

Defiantly, she looked him in the eye as he slid his gaze up her body. *Let him see what he's missing*, she thought in a sudden burst of self-consciousness. "Seen enough?" she asked as he bent down and handed her the underwear.

"Not by a long shot," he replied cheekily. "But I suspect you're getting cold."

She narrowed her eyes, knowing that nothing about her indicated that. The terry cloth was too new, too thick, and too fluffy for that, thank God. But she could play this game, too. "I'm in no hurry. I'm not cold either. On the contrary—"

He raised an eyebrow. "I brought waffles, by the way. Just for you."

Just in time, she remembered she was no longer twelve years old and the situation demanded maturity, not competition. So she marched past him and ignored his stifled chuckles which followed her all the way to the bathroom.

"I'll keep those waffles warm for you," he called.

Before venturing back out to the kitchen, Kat made sure her pulse had calmed down and her skin had returned to its normal pale color. Last night she had googled Sam's name on her phone and found dozens of pictures of him at parties and functions with stunning female company. Accordingly, she decided to act immune to his charm at the next encounter. Things were not going exactly as planned. She hoped she could recover.

In the kitchen she dropped into a chair and gratefully accepted a plate of hot waffles from Sam. Apparently, he had put them in the oven just like he promised. They were hot and crispy on the outside. Of course, her traitorous heart smiled briefly when she noticed it. "Thank you."

"Don't mention it. I've already been sufficiently compensated," he replied with a mischievous grin.

She tilted her chair back and closed her eyes as the aroma of the waffles, melted butter, and maple syrup wafted upward. Her sense of smell had come back since the allergy attack. "Mmmm. Yum. If I don't have to do anything for this excellent delivery service other than stand around wrapped in a towel for five minutes, I'd like to sign up for it."

He laughed.

"Thanks for letting the dogs out," she mumbled between bites.

"No problem. I also ran into Jake and let him know you were here."

"Fine. I guess."

"He was definitely glad to hear you spent the night."

Kat raised both eyebrows. "How exactly did you phrase that?"

"Well, like I just said." He winked at her over the rim of his cup.

She moaned in exasperation. "You do realize he's probably planning a wedding right now."

"Jake!? Really now?"

"Paula likely hasn't explained things to him yet."

"What things?"

"That this is temporary and a businesslike arrangement."

"Hey, remember what I said about Colorado hospitality—"

"And Jake is happy and wants to marry Jaz. And Jaz is on cloud nine and believes that everyone deserves the same happiness, whether they like it or not."

"And you don't want that? A relationship I mean."

She shrugged, suddenly unsure whether she should really reject it as categorically as she had always done in the past. "I don't want to get married. Yet." she answered evasively. To avoid him following up she quickly added, "I've got a business to run back in Seattle. Which reminds me I've got to call Caitlin, she's running things while I'm away." Kat shoved the last bite of waffle into her mouth. As she chewed, she gestured with her fork. "I mean, I expect to work while I'm here. My RV is set up for grooming. It would be a shame if it all went to waste."

With an impenetrable expression, he eyed her. "You mean you want to groom dogs in the middle of winter in that thi—I mean, your vehicle?"

"Sure. Even though Paula convinced me that I could forget my original idea of living in the RV." She frowned. "People live comfortably in campers even in winter. I admit that the comfort of your home beats my little Nelly hands down, of course."

He ran a hand over his face. "I thought I could spend a weekend here every now and then with some of the guys on the team. I'd still like to do that."

She blinked. That was all he had to say? "Why sure," she said easily. "Just let me know and I'll make myself scarce for the weekend."

"It won't be often," he assured her.

"Hey, I'm the stranger here," she teased him. "Come as much as you want. You're doing me a huge favor by letting me stay."

She watched him out of the corner of her eye. Her nostrils flared as he stood up and walked close to her to put his cup in the sink. He smelled like snow, coffee, and Sam. Strange that his smell was already so familiar to her. Abruptly, she put her own dishes together. She needed to get out of here, get some fresh air and be around other people. She probably had blizzard poisoning from yesterday. She got up and thought about gathering her winter clothes. Jacket, hat, scarf, gloves.

"I have to go," she muttered.

Sam seemed to be watching her with interest. Maybe he had caught how her pupils had dilated a few times so that her otherwise blue eyes seemed almost black. Other boyfriends had told her that happened during attraction no matter how she tried to play hard to get. The only question that remained was what Sam was going to do about it. She didn't want to feel uncomfortable in Independence just because she'd plunged headlong into an affair with a man. As tempting as the thought was.

Before she could go, he rose from his chair with a predatory movement and walked toward her. If she hadn't known better, she would have said he was stalking her. But when he finally stopped, his toes touched hers. He propped his hands on the countertop to her left and right. She didn't move, just looked at him challengingly. She was tired of pretending not to notice the sparks between them. It was time to stand by and see if they would burst into a flame.

Sam, noticing her change of mood, smiled with satisfaction. He seemed to like her even more that way.

"Did you want something in particular?"

"Yes," he replied, his face so close to hers that she could feel his warm breath brushing her lips. "To make you see the error of your ways."

"Nice. What would those errors be?" she managed to get out as his mouth lowered to hers. For the duration of the kiss her brain stopped. So much for romantic immunity.

He murmured something in her ear.

"What was that?" she whispered.

"I said I'm not nice. I'm helpful, yes. And my mom made sure I had good manners. But nice? Never."

Before she could process this statement, he kissed her again. This time she didn't hold back. Dangerous or not, certain things were just worth the risk. Especially when they tasted sinfully good, like coffee, maple syrup, and Sam, and made her blood boil. Somehow, her hands landed on his stomach. Through the fabric of the shirt, she felt the play of his muscles. Fascinated, she broke the kiss and explored his upper body. He looked down at her.

To prevent things from going any further, she said softly, "I need to get some things in town. I should go."

"Do you want me to go with you?"

Kat narrowed her eyes. "Do you want me to call you 'nice' again?"

He looked at her meaningfully. "Go ahead," he replied. "I thought the effect of that word was pretty spectacular."

She allowed herself a glance at his lips before turning away. "That was a little preview. Go and enjoy your day. I have work to do now."

Sam sighed.

She refrained from telling him he could be very persuasive when he wanted to be. For now, it seemed he'd accepted that a little restraint on both their parts would be quite wise. So, he left her alone to gather her coat and winter things. She felt his eyes watching as she called the dogs and rumbled down the stairs to the basement. Then she led the way out to Nelly and they all hopped in.

She wasn't on the road very long before the driver of a hotel shuttle van did a double take and pulled a U-turn to follow her. Kat watched in her side mirrors, wondering what was wrong with Nelly, and saw the driver waving at her. Figuring she had the two dogs with her and would keep the door locked until she knew what was up, she pulled over. The exhaust from Nelly's tailpipe sent steamy white clouds scudding over the ground.

A woman appeared out of the passenger side of the shuttle and waded through the white clouds to Kat's window. She tipped back the hood of her parka and gave a friendly wave. Kat cracked the window.

"Hello there," the women said. "I'm Jill, the manager at Breckenridge Vacation Resort." She tipped a business card over the top of the window.

Kat took it and rolled the window down a little farther.

"I see you're a dog groomer."

"Among other things, yes," Kat said. "I have a salon back in Seattle. Day care, grooming, all things dog related."

Jill broke into a delighted grin. "Day care? You're singing my song. We are very interested in someone who can provide day care for our guests who want to bring their dogs with them. We're getting a lot of requests. More and more people want to travel with their animals."

"I'm not surprised," Kat said. "My day care service is pretty popular. Dogs are part of the family and they're not always happy when they're boarded in pet hotels."

"That's what we're hearing," said Jill. "We'd like to have you come to our location and talk to us about launching a service with us. It might be a little late in the season for this year, but we could advertise it in advance for next year if you thought it's something the resort could realistically offer."

"I'd love that," Kat said. "Getting business in this area was at the top of my to-do list. Or it was before the storm, that is."

Jill gave a short laugh. "Just digging out now? Please give me a call," she said, indicating her business card. "We can set up a meeting. You could even be my guest for lunch."

"Thank you," I'll do that," Kat said thoughtfully.

Jill gave two light taps on the window to say goodbye and disappeared into the white clouds again. Kat watched the shuttle drive away. While stopped, she picked up a message on her cell from Caitlin advising that all was going well, and the bank deposit should have posted online by now. Then she tried to place a call to her mom in Poland but only got the voicemail. She left a message saying all was well, put Nelly back in gear, and headed down the road.

Back at home with a load of groceries, Kat decided to take Rocky for a walk. Sam's car was gone and she figured he'd probably taken Ranger with him. The groceries would stay cold in the van so she didn't have to go inside and get out of her coat and boots. She let Nikki into the basement where she scrambled up the stairs to return to her puppies. Kat and Rocky turned back to the outdoors.

Outside, it was freezing cold. Sunny, but any bit of warmth had disappeared. The air was so dry that the first few breaths Kat took made her feel as if all the moisture in her mouth and nose would freeze on the spot. Kat pulled her hat lower and her scarf higher on her face. The snow crunched under her shoes. Rocky was trotting around and sniffing at everything. "Curious boy," Kat called at him. "Stay close, now." He shot off into the trees. Blinking, she tried to make out where he was. He had headed into the forested area that went down Mr. Wilkinson's land all the way to the road. When she finally spotted Rocky, she heard him let out a whimper and disappear into more trees. Oh great! She was going to have to go on a search for him before they both froze their paws off.

Kat jogged toward the sound of a bark. Thank goodness he wasn't too far away. If this kept up, she'd be taking him on a tow line. She didn't feel like a repeat of this every time they went outside. She whistled once. But no dark shadow ran toward her. Only a repeated bark from him echoed across the snow. Clenching her teeth, she followed the tracks in the snow, trudging downhill toward the road. In places, she kept sinking into knee-deep powder. A whine came from a clump of trees. Perhaps Rocky had tracked an animal there? She glanced back at the house but it had been swallowed by trees.

She turned her attention back to the trail when Rocky appeared from behind like a ghost.

"Finally! Come on, let's go." She turned around, mentally already thinking about hot chocolate back inside. Rocky bounded over but immediately turned around when she tried to reach for his collar. Strange. He may not have been the best-behaved dog on earth, but once she found him, he usually came along without a problem. He ran off and disappeared again. For some reason, the hairs on the back of her neck stood up. With a gloved hand, she rubbed over the spot and continued in the direction Rocky had disappeared.

A car passed on the road with a whooshing sound. They were really close to the highway here. Another reason her four-legged friend needed to learn to stay close to her. She swept her gaze in a full circle around the trees. There. Now she had spotted Rocky. He was standing nose to the ground, seeming to nudge something. Great. He had probably spotted a dead rat. Or a squirrel. Or whatever was carelessly prowling around in the snow. She just hoped he hadn't rolled in it. Then again, it probably wasn't a problem in these temperatures as anything dead would be frozen stiff. In any case, she smelled nothing but the bitingly cold clear air and spruce needles.

She approached and saw that a shapeless something mostly covered with snow had caught his attention. At first, her brain refused to understand what her eyes were seeing. But then, with an involuntary cry, she dropped to her knees. It was a dead animal. Rocky allowed himself to be pushed aside. On one knee she pulled off her glove. With trembling fingers, she gingerly grasped the fur. It was still warm. At least warmer than her ice-cold fingers. As she pulled her hand away, she noticed it felt wet. Blood. She dropped back on her heels and brushed the snow off the rest of the body. There was a badly mauled dog in front of her.

Rocky nudged the body with his nose. Kat leaned against him a little and swallowed. "It's no use, Rocky. I think he's dead."

To confirm her suspicions, she stretched out her arm and tried to find the dog's carotid artery. But the entire throat was one bloody hole. Who or what would mess up a dog like that?

She wiped her bloody hands on her pants, noticing her bare hand was stiff with cold already. Quickly, she slipped back into her glove and bent to lift the dead dog into her arms. She didn't want to leave him out here. Probably an idiotic move as predators would be delighted with the find. She also understood that this was the nature of things. Eat and be eaten. But dogs were, after all, her weakness. This one deserved to have someone find out what had happened.

She swayed a little as she stood up. Somewhat awkwardly, she adjusted the dead weight in her arms. "Come on, Rocky. Lead us home."

By the time she had staggered up the hill, she was drenched in sweat. Exhausted, she laid her burden down in front of the house. The body was starting to stiffen. She dashed in the back door and grabbed a roll of paper towels, then opened the door that led to the basement. She spread paper towels on the concrete floor. Rocky pushed past her and sniffed all around, inspecting. Then she went out again and brought the fallen dog inside, laying him down carefully. It was cold down here, but not freezing. The perfect temperature for—she searched for the right word—storage.

Taking two steps at a time, she quickly ran up the stairs and down the hall to her bedroom. She was praying there was no one to see her like this. There wasn't. Closing the door, she peeled off the stained clothes and threw everything under the bed.

Again in dry clothes, it was time to feed the living. She measured out portions of dry food for two dogs. Nikki was given a spoonful of special powder Dr. Chu had sent along before they left Seattle—a little extra help for pregnant moms-to-be.

While Rocky and Nikki munched away, she realized she craved a hot drink. Jaz had slipped her some tea during their visit, to take home. Knowing her friend, it probably had a thousand and one mysterious properties. All that mattered to her at the moment was that it was hot. She put a kettle on to boil. When it was ready, with the cup in her hand and a bar of chocolate, she sat down on the sofa. Now that she had a dead dog spread out on paper towels in the basement she wasn't one hundred percent sure of the next move. Maybe she should call Jake?

She imagined her way through the conversation.

"Sheriff, I found a badly mauled dog."

"Where?"

"In the woods."

"Do the wounds look like someone intentionally inflicted them on the animal?"

"The wounds look like another animal jumped the dog."

Long pause. "An animal. If it looks like an animal jumped the dog, it probably was. It's just the way things happen in the woods."

"So you don't want to look at the dog?"

"And do what? Deploy deputies to search the woods for a murderous animal? I can't arrest a coyote."

Still, she ended up calling Jake. The conversation went pretty much as she had imagined. but she gave him credit for not making fun of her. And he did add something helpful, "If you want to talk to anyone else about it, you could call Paula. She's very sympathetic to animals."

"Do you think that will do any good?"

"I don't know. All I know is that she cares about the animals as much as you do. And at least she knows her way around here, and she might be able to tell you if this is a common thing or not."

Kat breathed a sigh of relief. "Then that's what I'm going to do. I don't know why, but something still bothers me about that dog." She brushed a strand of hair behind her ear.

"Good." Jake gave her the number. "And keep me posted, will you?"

Kat broke off another piece of chocolate and typed in the new number. She described the problem. Then she stopped and waited for what Paula might say.

"Hmm. It's possible that the dog was a runaway. It would be weakened if it was attacked by a coyote or even a bobcat."

"There are big cats in Colorado?"

"Sure. Lynx, bobcats, and mountain lions too."

"Up here on the butte?"

"Likely not, but you can't rule it out. They roam around, you know."

"I just figured out what's bothering me. Wild animals are hungry. Why rip out a dog's throat and not eat it? Predators usually eat their prey right away. That wasn't the case here."

"No. But it's possible that Rocky disturbed the culprit. How about tracks. Did you see any?"

"No. Honestly, I was so shocked that I didn't even pay attention. Plus, it was so cold—"

"I see." Paula paused, seeming to sort out her thoughts. "You could take the body to the vet. He'd be the one to determine what happened."

"Right. That's a good idea. Do you know any?"

Paula snorted. "I was afraid you were going to ask me that. Nate Bale is the new guy in town. I've had my differences with him but he is good." She rattled off the number.

"Thanks. Do you want me to say hi to him for you?"

Paula snorted again on the other end of the line. "I'd rather not. We're not exactly friends."

Kat thanked her again and hung up. What she remembered Jaz saying was that Paula had differences with a lot of people. In fact, people she didn't have differences with were the exception rather than the rule. It was just the way she was, and her bark was way worse than her bite.

The veterinarian snapped on an extra-bright examination lamp and motioned for Kat to come in. He'd already uncovered the dog's carcass from the protective garbage bags Kat had used for transport and laid it on the steel table in the center of the room. "That's an animal attack alright," he said simply.

"What's bothering me, Dr. Bale, is that the dog wasn't eaten by its attacker," Kat said.

"You must have surprised the attacker because the body wasn't completely cold."

"True, but now that I'm thinking about it, there wasn't a spray of blood or a bunch of displaced snow from a struggle."

"The animal could have been dragged there."

"But there was no trail of blood in the snow."

The vet threw up his hands. "Then the dog died as a result of an animal attack and a human took the body and disposed of it on the Wilkinson property. It seems a lot of trouble to go to for a dead mutt."

All Kat could do was shake her head. In Seattle, this would be a very big deal. But as she was learning, things were different here.

"In any event," he said, "I can dispose of the remains for you."

"Thanks, how much will that cost?" Kat said, fumbling for her purse.

"No charge. Happy to do it."

"Thank you," she said gratefully. "As a matter of fact, I have a pregnant mastiff that could use a checkup. I'll make an appointment to bring her in."

"You do that. Welcome to Independence. I can see you'll be a welcome addition."

Kat could see Nate Bale was a decent and friendly man. There was no reason for Paula to dislike him so. "By the way, Paula Carter says hello," she added.

"She does?" he said, astonished.

"Yes, in fact she sent me here and recommended you."

A smile spread over Nate's face. "Well, please tell her I return the greeting."

CHAPTER SIX

PAULA WAS AT HOME putting a casserole in the oven when the dogs started barking. Leslie, who was sitting at the kitchen table doing homework, looked at her questioningly. "Mailman?"

"Probably." Paula glanced at the clock on the wall. "He's usually earlier."

"When I got home from school, he wasn't here yet. I'll get it," Leslie offered.

"You do that. Kat's coming over later."

"Kat?"

"Jaz's girlfriend. Who now lives in the house Pat renovated."

"Oh, the woman with the two big dogs. Now I remember."

"Exactly. And one of the dogs, Nikki, is about to have puppies."

"How sweet! Can we visit them when the little ones are here?"

Paula grinned. "Sure. As long as it stays at looking and doesn't turn into taking one home."

"I can promise so long as we always have Barns and Roo."

Paula made an approving noise, glad that Leslie liked her two blue-heeler cattle dogs. Another dog wasn't on Paula's wish list right now. But at least she had made

Leslie smile. She was happy every time she succeeded. The young teen was slowly thawing out.

Followed by Barns and Roo, Leslie made her way to the mailbox a few hundred yards ahead at the very beginning of the driveway. She tilted her face up to the winter sun and took a deep breath. It was so beautiful here. From homeless to her dream homestead. It couldn't get any better than this. Paula even seemed to like having her around. Paula's family and friends were also nice to her.

Arriving at the mailbox, she opened the flap and slid her slender hand inside to take out the mail. In the process of lifting it out a letter fell into the snow. She bent down to pick it up. But before her fingers touched it, she froze. She knew that return address and logo. The envelope bore the official stamp of the Colorado Department of Human Services, Child and Family Division. She turned it over and over in her hands. Good news never came from this place. Maybe they were planning to take her away from here. Maybe she could slow things down by getting rid of the letter.

Leslie's stomach churned at the thought of betraying Paula. When she thought about having to leave here, though, it made her sick. With a quick decision, she slipped the unwanted letter inside the weekly flyer of supermarket specials in Breckenridge. *It could have slipped there by mistake*, she told herself. If she was lucky, Paula would not discover it there. Most of the time, she didn't have time to read the supermarket specials at all.

Somewhat reassured that she had averted immediate danger, Leslie made her way back to the house. She put the mail on the entrance table. She took the precaution of putting the flyer on top of a pile of wastepaper.

"Will you bring in the mail for me?" Paula called from the kitchen.

Crap, Leslie thought, but grabbed the stack and walked through the house. She shoved it into Paula's hand as she walked by. "Here. I need to finish my homework."

"Thank you," Paula replied, looking after her in wonder. What had happened to on the way to the mailbox that had spoiled Leslie's mood? She brushed a strand of auburn hair out of her face and turned back to the mail. *Probably teenage hormones*, she told herself. She frowned. Where had the supermarket specials gone?

"Leslie? Didn't the sale flyer come today?"

In the other room, Leslie felt the tips of her ears begin to burn. She tossed her head to make sure the red parts were hidden under her brown hair. "I got it." She was saved by the excited barking of the dogs. "That must be Kat," she said with relief.

Paula glanced out the window. "She's here for the whelping box I told her about. Come, you can help me get it out of the barn."

Leslie wrinkled her nose. "What's a whelping box?"

"It's like a comfy bed that the mother dog gets in to give birth. The sides of the box keep the puppies from getting out but are low enough so the mother can get in and out."

"That's all it does?"

"There's a railing inside so she won't roll over and crush the babies during sleep, too."

"But why do they call it whelping?"

"It's just what vets call giving birth when dogs do it."
Leslie's nose unwrinkled. "Okay," she said.

"Please get an old rag and a bucket of soapy water.
I'm sure that box is dusty!"

"I will," Leslie replied eagerly, glad for any distraction
from the missing paper and the secret she was hiding.

Paula opened the door a crack and blocked Roo and
Barns from getting out. "Go ahead and let your dogs
out," she called to Kat, who was sitting in Nelly with the
windows rolled down. "They have plenty of room out
here to sniff each other in peace."

"Okay, thanks. That's a good idea." Kat pulled Nelly's
door open. Two large, auburn monstrosities rushed out
and toward Paula's front door. The two cattle dogs pawed
and whined to get out.

Paula let the door go.

Like two cannonballs, Barns and Roo shot past her
toward the newcomers.

"You'd think they'd be more careful when the visitors
are so big and impressive," Paula wondered.

"In their minds, they're at least as big and twice as
mean," Leslie replied dryly, stepping up behind her with
a bucket in hand.

While the dogs went through a complicated greeting
ritual, Kat came to the porch. "Nice place you have here,"
she commented, letting her gaze drift over the house and
the snow-covered paddock. Three horses stood together
in the pasture, searching for grass under a blanket of
snow. "Are they all yours?"

"The horses are Leslie's specialty," Paula replied,
putting an arm around the girl's shoulder.

"Nice to see you again, Leslie."

Leslie smiled shyly. The idea that she should be the "specialist" of not one, but three horses, was so absurd that she fizzed with giggles. "I don't own them, though. The little one is a Shetland pony. Her name is Dolly. She's the boss and she's all no-nonsense. The big brown one that looks like he has a dusty coat is Rufus. He is older. I ride him sometimes. The black and white pinto is here for training. At least as soon as spring arrives. In winter we can't do much with him. It's not like we have an indoor riding arena or anything." She ducked her head and blinked at Paula, as if surprised at how much she had just talked. She shot a quick glance at Paula to see whether it was okay. When Paula gave her an encouraging smile, she visibly relaxed.

"And what's his name?"

"The training horse?"

Kat nodded.

"Happy Go Lucky, but we just call him Lucky. It's easier."

Kat laughed. "Is he as happy as his name promises?"

Kat looked over at the horses. "I don't think I'd dare ride them."

"Why not?" asked Leslie, puzzled. "It's the most beautiful thing in the whole world!"

Paula interjected into the discussion. "If you do want to try riding, just get in touch."

Kat made a sound that sounded somewhat approving. In reality, she wouldn't be taking advantage of that offer anytime soon. "You said you had something for me?"

"Exactly. My old whelping box, and you're going to need it soon. I have it in the barn behind the house. There's a section there reserved for things I might need someday. By the way, how is Sam about the puppies? Now that you guys are roommates?"

"I told him Nikki was pregnant before bringing my bags into the house. He said dogs have puppies all the time in Colorado."

"Very reasonable," was Paula's response.

"To tell you the truth I haven't seen him since yesterday morning. We keep missing each other."

"I was under the impression he might want to see more of you."

Kat waved it off. "I don't think he'll mind. I'm sure he has enough female companionship."

Leslie felt there was a lot more story behind that light comment but before she could ask, Paula said, "Well let's go inside." She pushed open the door and felt for the light switch and clicked it on.

Kat looked around at the junk pile in disbelief. She was too polite to comment.

"Hey. Aren't you glad I have a whelping box for you?"

"Yes, yes, of course," Kat replied, almost choking on a laugh.

Leslie looked uncertainly back and forth between the two. Were they about to fight or were they just fooling around? Friendly teasing had never been a part of her life until recently and she didn't quite trust it.

Paula began to move boxes and objects aside. A bale of wire, clippers, a small wheelbarrow. Kat hoped Paula had at least a rough idea where the box was.

"Did you take the dead dog to Nate?" asked Paula casually.

So casually that Kat looked over at her in surprise.

"Yes, I went to see him. He confirmed that the injuries were from another animal. He couldn't say whether it was a coyote or a dog, or something else that did it, though."

Paula frowned. "That's strange. I don't remember us having a case like this before. The coyotes actually keep to themselves. And a dog isn't exactly at the top of their menu, either."

"Jake was worried that it might have been rabid."

"He has a point there. We've had an increasing number of rabies cases in recent years. Did Nate test the dog for it?"

"He just said he couldn't see any signs of disease."

"But your dogs are vaccinated, I assume?"

"Yes. Rocky definitely. I don't know about Nikki. I can't get her vaccinated for now either, while she's pregnant. No vaccines for pregnant moms. It's not safe for the puppies."

"Right." Paula tugged at a board that was jamming the progress of their search. Leslie came to her rescue and pulled away some of the things that were in front of it. Finally, the wooden board moved.

"Why don't you call Nate if you're worried?" Kat asked, watching Paula closely.

Paula ignored the question and said, "Whew. I think I see it in there." She glanced at Kat. "Call? I'll hear soon enough if Nate has a suspected rabies case. No need to get the bear riled up."

Kat laughed. "Nate's an excitable bear to you?"

Paula just rolled her eyes instead of answering.

Kat decided she probably had to improve her interrogation technique. Otherwise, she wouldn't get very far in this town where information was traded as common currency.

"Here." Leslie pointed to more stuff in the way. A birdcage, a stack of red bricks, an ancient case of tractor tools. She knew Paula was not exactly thrilled about Nate and thought it better to direct their attention elsewhere.

Paula stuck her hand into the pile and tugged and yanked at a few boards. "Got it! It comes apart to store but goes back together easy. Let's take everything outside. We'll have better light there."

Leslie lifted the box and a few pieces of wood that attached to it, and eagerly took everything to the exit of the barn. Praise always had that effect on her, as Paula knew by now. She was pleased every time, even if it made her sad to think about what the girl's life must have been like up to now if it took so little to elicit that reaction.

Touched, Kat watched the two of them. She really hoped that Paula would get the legal side of fostering under control soon. She waited until Leslie was out of sight and hearing until she asked, "How is her status here with you, anyway? Have you made any progress in your research?"

Paula shrugged one shoulder. "It goes like this. We still don't know who she really is. Her name is in no database that Jake has run her through. None of the missing persons reports match her. But she's flesh and blood and she needs a home. So I have temporary caretaking of her."

"You mean she ran away somewhere and no one reported her missing?" she inquired incredulously.

Paula nodded.

"Thank goodness she ended up with you," she groaned. "So where do we go from here?"

"I contacted Child and Family Services to find out what I needed to do to be officially considered a foster family. I figured if I already had the necessary qualifications, if I got serious about looking into her past, there was a better chance that she would be able to stay with me." Paula expelled her breath in frustration. "I don't understand all the delay with granting official status. I mean, it's obvious that the last place she was, whether it was her real family or an adoptive or foster family, sucked. Not just because Leslie ran away, but mostly because no one has even noticed she's gone! I mean, who does that?"

"Unbelievable. It always shocks me when that happens with animals. Just look at Nikki. But a child? That's a whole other category. Not that animals don't have the same value to me, but you know what I mean, right?"

"Sure. I totally agree with you."

"So, was your foster application approved?"

Paula let out an unhappy laugh. "I wish. Currently, I'm waiting for the application materials."

"Let me know if there's anything I can do to help."

"Thank you. Half of Independence has already agreed to vouch for my character."

"This tight-knit community is really good for that," grumbled Kat, who was still struggling a bit with all the features of Independence.

"Say, are you coming?" called Leslie from the doorway. "I'm already done cleaning here."

"Sure," Kat shouted, hurrying to help take everything outside.

Back at the Wilkinson house, which Kat was slowly starting to think of as home—temporarily—she unloaded the whelping box, plus a container holding generous helping of Paula's tuna noodle casserole.

Once inside, Kat got the animals settled.

A tap came at the door. "Yoohoo," a familiar voice called. It was Mr. Wilkinson.

"Door's open," Kat called, as the dogs bayed and ran to meet him.

The older man cracked the door a few inches and popped his bald head in. "Can't stay," he chirped. "Just dropping off a care package." He plopped a paper bag in the front entryway. "Don't want to let the dogs out. Toodleloo!" He withdrew his shiny dome and shut the door.

Kat rescued the bag as the dogs sniffed and scratched at it. Inside was a note saying, *This strudel was baked by the ladies of Rugged Cross Church of Independence.* Kat broke off a piece and popped the pastry in her mouth. It melted in her mouth. Those gals at the church really knew how to bake. Before getting carried away, she set it on the kitchen counter so any human entering would instantly see it was available for the taking. Then she settled on the couch and looked around a little bit. What to do next?

She took out her phone and began idly searching news in Seattle. She pulled up the Search bar and typed in "Sam Carter." A dozen news mentions and pictures popped up. In lots of those pictures Sam had gorgeous women on his arm. A different woman for every occasion, it seemed. And then came the capper. Picture after picture of Sam in advertisements wearing only his underwear! A sidebar in one article said the contract with the underwear company was worth a small fortune. But still. Every woman in the world must know what he looked like stripped down!

After just a few minutes Kat reaffirmed to keep it "friendship only" with Sam. Besides, she could never compete with those hot Denver babes in their tight little dresses and false eyelashes. End of story.

She enjoyed a quick dinner of casserole and strudel, and went to bed.

Morning. Kat was glad to be out in the fresh air again. Even with her two dogs for company, the house seemed huge without Sam and Pat, and Tyler. She took a deep breath and let her eyes glide over the mountain peaks. The snow was great. But she couldn't wait to experience the area in the spring and watch nature awaken from winter slumber. A black cat sat in the comfortable crook of a tree branch and watched them with bright eyes. "Where did you come from, kitty?" Kat said, taking note that the cat looked neither nervous or hungry.

Into the woods Kat went, but only a few yards deep. This time she led the dogs north along the property, away from the house, but still close to the cleared land. Rocky was behind her for once, engrossed in the unseen trail of a rabbit or squirrel. Suddenly he shot past her, barking. She almost tripped and landed in the snow. What had gotten into him? Sometimes she cursed his good nose.

She started running, trying to keep up. Just as suddenly he stopped with his neck fur bristling and ears tilted forward. He usually only acted like that when he couldn't make sense of something. She closed in on him, eyes raking the trees, trying to see what had his attention. Oh no. Blood again in the snow. That's when she heard it. A pitiful whimper. There was a bundle of fur in the snow. This one was still alive.

She approached. It was a dog similar to the last one she had found. A mongrel. Probably with fighting dog blood, as could easily be seen from the broad head. A terrible suspicion rose in her. But now she had no time to deal with it. This poor animal needed emergency help.

She kneeled down sideways next to the hind legs so that the animal could see her but not feel crowded. She took stock of the situation. She was bleeding in several places. Kat saw gouges on the face and neck, and a gash on the flank.

Rocky came close and sniffed the snout of the smaller dog. A tongue flicked out to lick Rocky's lips. A clear gesture of submission. A good sign. She hoped this animal's tolerance extended to humans as well. She had to get her back to the house. What was the best way to transport her? Making a snap decision, Kat took off her jacket and laid it on the ground next to the dog. Carefully she grabbed under her shoulders and hip, trying not to touch any wounds. Easier said than done, as she was covered all over with them.

Finally, Kat managed to pull the dog onto the jacket. She wrapped her up as best she could and lifted. Relieved that she didn't struggle, Kat expelled the breath she had been holding. She swayed briefly until reasonably balanced and started walking with the bundle in her arms. The injured dog was small and stocky. She estimated her at just about twenty pounds.

Fifteen minutes later, sweaty and straining, she staggered in the basement door.

"Kat? Is that you? I just came in the door," Sam called from above.

"Sam, I need your help," she croaked, still panting heavily.

Seconds later he clambered down the stairs. "What happened? Is that blood? What have you got there?"

Kat knew her hair was disheveled and her cheeks were flushed. She was perspiring.

"I found another dog," she gasped. "Badly hurt."

Sam hurried to her side. Kat carefully lifted the jacket a little so that he could see the wounds.

"You're sure she's still alive?" He stared doubtfully at the lifeless body in her arms.

"Yes. Or alive when I found her, at least. Oh Sam. What if I just made it worse?"

Without thinking, he grabbed her arm and gave it a gentle squeeze. "Out there in the cold and without help, she would have died anyway. You did the right thing."

"What do I do next?" Without waiting for an answer, she said, "I don't want Nikki exposed to her. We don't know if this dog is healthy. But we have to keep her warm. Can you get my keys out of my purse and bring in the Little Buddy heater? It'll warm everything up down here."

"Okay."

"And maybe bring the dog bed from my bedroom. And towels. I'll buy new for the house after this."

"Okay, don't worry about that."

She took another quick look at the dog and was relieved to see she was blinking. At least she was still alive.

"Hang in there, little fighter," she whispered as Sam raced back up the basement stars, two at a time. She heard him speaking on the cell phone to Nate Bale about coming on a house call.

Kat sank down on the stairs and leaned her head against the wall. She was pretty sure that this dog, just like the last one, had been dumped on the property. Whomever was doing this probably didn't know there were dogs at the house. They probably thought it was just old Mr. Wilkinson in there and he would never find what was in his woods before other animals ate it. But who would dispose of injured dogs this way?

Nate arrived and gently examined the little dog's injuries. He had lightly sedated her and worked with a sure hand.

"Blood pressure is pretty stable, considering the circumstances. I take that as a good sign. It speaks to the fact that she has no internal injuries." He gave Kat a warning look. "But I'm not sure. Without an ultrasound or MRI, I can't say for sure."

"What are her options?" she asked in a thin voice.

"Honestly, I don't think she has any. We can do our best here and now, stop the bleeding and suture the wounds. I'll take her back with me to the clinic. Then it's wait and see. Time will tell if she makes it."

Kat swallowed and looked down at her latest rescue. Then she looked up, a look of fierce determination in her eyes. "Just help her." Nate picked up a sterile needle and thread as she touched him on the shoulder. "And thank you. For your open and honest opinion. Most vets I know beat around the bush."

He just nodded and started to take care of the dog.

Three quarters of an hour later, Nate put his instruments aside and pulled the latex gloves off his hands. He had placed a drip in the dog, providing her with the fluids and medication she needed. She lay motionless on a clean pad of towels. More towels were stained red and ripe for the garbage disposal.

Probably have to make another trip to the pet store for a dog bed, Kat thought wearily. Or maybe the local feedstore carried something similar. With Nate taking over, she'd had time to think, to figure something out. Who could possibly be causing this carnage on the Wilkinson property? Someone who was holding illegal dogfights in the area, that's who. And then conveniently disposing of dead or badly injured dogs in the woods.

The next day, Kat resolved to do something, especially since Nate had taken the newest canine patient back to his pet hospital. She put through a call to Pat in Breckenridge asking if she could use his laptop and printer for something quick. He was fine with it, and when she didn't offer to explain, he didn't ask either. She printed fifty copies of a single sheet of paper and rushed out of the house, after penning the dogs in the kitchen. Sam was still in bed.

Her first stop was the mini-mart. After stocking up on a few things for the house and some beauty products like tissues and lip balm—the dry cold here was really relentless—she got in line at the checkout. As she handed money over to the cashier she pulled out a sheet of paper and said, "I found an injured dog. Could you possibly tape it to the side of your register so customers can see?" She held up the roll of clear tape she'd just purchased.

An indifferent look passed over the cashier's face. "Sure." But then her gaze returned to the poster. "That's a pit bull mix isn't it? Probably attacked by its own kind. I don't like those dogs."

Kat took a step back. "I don't think you understand. The dog isn't dead. I found her."

"All that expense for a pit? Just put it down," the cashier muttered.

"Will you let me put this up?" Kat had to clench her teeth to keep her voice steady. She had to really pull herself together not to reach out and shake the woman at the register. What kind of attitude was that toward animals?

The woman hesitated for a moment. Then she shook her head. "No. Like I said. Nobody misses dogs like that."

Completely perplexed by the unfriendly refusal and the last words, Kat left the mini-mart with her purchases. What had the saleswoman meant by that? She went down the street, inquiring with all the retailers if she could leave a flyer. In some stores it was no problem. Lilly, who ran the flower store, had almost snatched the note out of her hand and hung it prominently on the door. She wanted to know all about the injured dog and promised to stop by in two or three weeks, when the puppies were bigger and the dog hopefully on the mend. Nate, the vet, had posted the flyer, too. She tried to ask him about the strange reaction of some of the store owners but he had only shrugged his shoulders and mumbled something about maverick mountain people. Then she remembered Nate had only recently moved to Independence.

She was turned down at the hair salon and even at the feedstore. But now one of her flyers was hanging in the yoga studio. She also brought one to the police station. Jake seemed to take her suspicions about the injured dog more seriously.

An hour later she arrived at the diner. Her groceries were staying cold just fine inside Nelly, so long as she kept the heat off. She jumped out with the folder of flyers. She had by no means gotten rid of them all.

Inside, she dropped heavily onto one of the red leatherette-covered stools at the bar.

"You look like you're in desperate need of coffee and something decent to eat, child," Miss Minnie greeted her.

Kat gave a grateful smile. It was true. With all the excitement she kept forgetting about food. Her stomach was grumbling. "Gladly. I haven't eaten much. Can you make me a double portion of whatever breakfast special you have on today and wrap one up? Sam is still at home."

"Now that's what I call fast work. You and Sam? That's beyond all expectations of our betting pool!" Miss Minnie winked at her in amusement.

Kat laughed out loud and immediately felt better. "Thanks. But it's not what you think, We're just housemates."

"Sure. But the opportunity to razz you was just too good." Miss Minnie laughed as she poured coffee. "You just sit here. I'll let my sister know her lumberjack breakfast is called for."

Miss Minnie returned fifteen minutes later with a huge plate. Fried potatoes. Sausages and bacon. Scrambled eggs with peppers and delicious melted cheese. A whole stack of pancakes drenched in maple syrup.

"She left out the steak," Miss Minnie said with a knowing smile. "She said you'd burst otherwise."

"Really," Kat answered weakly. But then she set to work. To her surprise, a quarter of an hour later the plate was spotless.

Even Miss Minnie raised an eyebrow, impressed, as she put it away. "Where do you put it all?"

Kat shrugged her shoulders. "I don't know. Good metabolism. I keep busy. That reminds me..." She reached for her folder and pulled out a flyer. "Can I put this up here? I'm trying to track down the owner."

Miss Minnie reached for the sheet of paper. When she turned it over and looked at the photo, she drew in her breath sharply.

"What is it?" asked Kat, growing suspicious after all the negative reactions.

"It's one of those," she also promptly replied. "One of those dangerous dogs."

"It's still a dog. He was just thrown into the woods to die. Apparently even a bullet was too good for him."

Miss Minnie recoiled a little. But then she leaned over and patted Kat's hand. "You're absolutely right. I'll be happy to post the note."

Miss Minnie looked as if she had more to say. After a furtive sideways glance, she leaned over and whispered in Kat's ear, "We had trouble a few years back. Some lowlifes moved in on the edge of town and they had dogs like that. They let them run wild. The dogs were harassing people here in my restaurant, too, and letting their dogs roam free all over Independence. Local animals got attacked and one girl was injured. Finally, Jake ran them out of town."

Kat leaned back on her stool. "That explains a lot. Although you still can't lump all these dogs together. Dogs that are out in a pack are unpredictable, no matter what breed they belong to."

"True. Still. People here associate these dogs with nothing good."

Kat had to lean forward to understand Miss Minnie's last words. "Why are you speaking so softly?" she whispered.

"Because there's no need to broadcast all that old stuff up again. If you want to know more you should talk to Scrooge before you go."

Kat followed Miss Minnie's outstretched index finger with her gaze. She saw an old man at the end of the bar pouring something from a flask into his coffee. Despite the fact that it was only eleven in the morning.

"Scrooge likes his firewater. Lives in the woods in a trailer right on the edge of the Wilkinson property, which means he's about half a mile from the house. Brews his own hooch. Probably sitting on a pile of gold, too. No matter. It may be just a rumor. On the other hand, he's not on welfare either. Always pays cash. Maybe he's got the old-age security going already."

Kat's head was buzzing from all the new information. "And what would I talk to him about?"

Miss Minnie moved her head from left to right. "He knows things other people don't. Especially about things that happen in the woods."

She was probably right, Kat thought, and stood up. At the front, she taped a flyer in the large window to the left of the door. She turned back to where Scrooge was sitting. Or rather, slumping over his spiked coffee. A shiver ran over her. It was not a rational reaction, she knew. But drunks, especially older male drunks, always brought back memories of her father and his outbursts when he came home after a bender. Her mother's screams, the sound of him slapping her, the smell of stale beer and sweat, and the memory of her hiding under the bed in fear were burned into her cells. She shook herself to get rid of the ghosts of the past and walked resolutely toward the man. When he didn't move, she gently tapped him on the shoulder. Scrooge grunted but didn't look up.

"I'll buy you some fresh coffee," she said.

A bloodshot eye opened.

"I heard you knew the woods around here very well?"

A second eye blinked. With a quickness she wouldn't have credited him with, he reached for the spiked coffee. After downing it in one gulp, he exhaled noisily. "Nice of you to offer. You could pour me some straight coffee, I suppose."

Minnie had disappeared into the kitchen, so Kat got the coffee pot, poured him a hot refill, and then put it back.

He pointed to the flyers in her hand. "What have you got there?"

She stared at the papers in her hand. "Oh, that. I found a dog." She tried not to narrow her eyes suspiciously. "Have you lost a dog?" she asked. It didn't seem likely, but you never knew.

"What would I do with a dog? I have a cat. Right now she seems to be away on vacation, though." He wiggled his head as if the idea were completely absurd. "Can I see that?"

She handed him one of the flyers. When he saw the photo of the injured dog, he whistled softly through his teeth. "Those bastards."

Surprised by the unexpected emotional stirring, Kat paid him a little more attention. Eagerly, she leaned closer to him despite the penetrating smell of hard alcohol. "Do you know whose dog that is? Or who beat her up like that?"

Scrooge lowered his voice to a conspiratorial murmur, so that Kat had to lean even closer to him. If she breathed shallowly through her mouth, she could tolerate the stench to some extent.

"This thing with these dogs is a nasty story. It's about money. A lot of money. So, watch what you're doing. These people are not to be played with."

Kat grimaced. She had already suspected that much. It was always about money. What else would it be about?

"And why doesn't anyone know? Or is it just that nobody's telling?"

Scrooge looked into his cup as if reading coffee grounds. "I guess most of them really don't know anything," he finally replied. "And those who do know something, or at least suspect it, are afraid. You'd do better to keep your hands off it, too." The look from his eyes was direct and surprisingly clear.

She shrugged her shoulders and looked again at the picture of the injured dog. "I can't do that. I can't look away at something like this."

He nodded as if he had expected this answer. "You know, nobody pays attention to an old drunk. People discuss all kinds of things in my presence. Maybe I appear drunker than I am."

She let his answers run through her head. She still didn't know much. "And how does that help me now?"

Scrooge was shaken by a cough. When he had calmed down again, he said in a lowered voice: "Every month, people show up at the abandoned farm near the river. Keep your eyes and ears open. But don't ask too many questions. It's too dangerous." Suddenly he dropped his head on the tabletop and began to snore. Kat shook him irritably by the shoulder. But it was no use. Someone passed behind her and jostled her with full force. The flyers flew in all directions. Off-balance, she just managed to hold on as the stool she was sitting on began to tip. She turned around to see who had done it. But all she could see was the back of a man.

He was wrapped in a long coat and wore a hat. At the exit, he stopped. With a jerky movement, he ripped the flyer from the window and threw it down on the floor. She wanted to jump up angrily to confront him, but a hand tightened around her forearm.

"What the—" she started angrily, trying to free herself from his grip. Scrooge didn't bat an eyelash but didn't let her go, either.

"Wait until he's gone," Scrooge whispered urgently.

"Who?"

"The idiot who pushed you."

"You mean that was intentional?"

"You bet I do."

"But why?" She looked out the picture windows and saw a big red truck driving away.

"Because he doesn't want you stirring up questions. I'm sure you can guess why." He pointed to the flyer lying torn on the floor by the door.

Kat propped her head in her hands and groaned. "I thought I left people like that behind when I moved here from the big city."

"There are bad people everywhere. Maybe they're just desperate people who do bad things."

Simple, Kat thought. *And yet amazingly accurate.* She sighed and put twenty dollars on the counter. "Thanks for the information. Please treat yourself to some food."

Rich or not rich, the bill disappeared in a flash into Scrooge's sleeve. He stroked his wrinkled face. She was about to turn away when he grabbed her by the jacket. "Wait. Does the dog in the picture have a name yet?"

"No."

"I would call her Bella. I'm sure she didn't have much beauty in her life. She's not a beauty herself. At least not now. I'd call her Bella."

Kat wanted to protest. She twisted and turned the name in her head a few times. Bella. Not particularly original. But fitting. Scrooge was right. She nodded at him. "I will. And I hope your cat comes home okay from vacation."

"Yes, yes." He waved his hand as if to shoo her away. His capacity for small talk was obviously exhausted for the day.

Kat went to Miss Minnie to get the takeout for Sam. She hoped the poor man hadn't died of sudden starvation in the meantime. Her short trip to town had taken longer than expected. But that couldn't be helped now. Actually, this was a good opportunity to see how Sam would react to the situation. She thought cynically, with her father's outbursts in mind. When she caught herself thinking that she got angry. It was completely out of line that she always compared Sam, who had proven to be a good friend to her, to her wayward father.

She stepped out of the diner and headed for Nelly. Better she concentrated on finding out where this abandoned farm was. By the river? Was there only one river? She would ask Sam. Or Paula. And let Jake in on it. Or should she wait until she knew more?

CHAPTER SEVEN

Sam was up in the morning before Kat and glanced in at the spare bedroom where Nikki was standing up in the whelping box, spinning around.

"Is it going to be today girl?"

Nikki lay down with a groan and her distended stomach rippled.

"Kat!" Sam called. "I think you better come here."

The next few hours were turbulent. Sam called Nate, who promised to be there in half an hour. Still in her pajamas, Kat knelt beside the box and stroked the panting dog as Sam brought towels, a pan of water and antiseptic soap. As Nikki grew more agitated it was clear Kat would not emerge from the room until the vet arrived.

"Don't worry," Sam said. "The cavalry is on its way. You don't have to rely exclusively on me."

"I thought you said dogs had puppies all the time in Colorado."

"Sure. My family always had dogs. But I've never been interested in how they came into the world. Until now." He gave Nikki's ears a sympathetic nuzzle. "Maybe we should call Nate and tell him the puppies are coming sooner than we thought."

Kat grinned. "Don't worry. She can do most of it all by herself."

"I'm not so sure about that," Sam replied. "I certainly don't want to find out. I feel like giving Nate another call. And Paula. Between the two of them one should show up soon." Before Kat could protest, he was on the phone. It touched her to see this strong, handsome man so out of his comfort zone.

At that moment, a black cat wandered into the room. Her tail went up to say hello.

"Who's that?" Kat called to him, astonished. "Another new arrival?"

Sam dashed back. "Mr. Wilkinson told me she's been hanging around outside. When he comes home in that big old Cadillac, she jumps on the hood where it's warm. He lets her into his apartment sometimes. I figured it couldn't hurt to let her inside here now and then. The dogs don't seem to mind."

"You're even worse than me, and that's saying something."

Sam looked to the side. "That's Jinx."

Off Kat's incredulous stare he just said, "She needed a name."

"Do you think she was abandoned, too?" Kat's memory flew back to the conversation she had with Scrooge about his cat "being on vacation." Minnie had said his trailer was just a half mile away. Maybe this Jinx was his cat.

Sam shrugged his shoulders. "I don't think so. She looks too good for that. She's just an independent cat who decided the Wilkinson place was more interesting than where she used to be."

Jinx crept closer and carefully sniffed at Nikki. Then she meowed piteously and stalked to the door.

Sam let her out. "See what I mean?" Sam said.

At that moment the door knocker out front sounded. Kat scampered to see who it was. When she looked out, Paula, Leslie and Nate Bale were all standing in the entry.

Paula felt the hairs on the back of her neck stand up at the sight of Nate Bale. Leslie had begged to see Nikki before she gave birth, so Paula had decided to drop in unannounced. She looked at Nate out of one eye. His shoulders were as broad as ever. Plus that dark brown hair, always a little too long, gave him a slightly rakish look. Why couldn't he be bald and carry a beer belly in front of him? She suspected the discord that existed between them, and yes, for which she was primarily to blame, would be half as unpleasant to her if he were less attractive. Probably that marked her as a completely superficial person.

"What a coincidence that we turned up at the same time," Nate said.

Before Paula could answer, the door opened. It was Kat. "We were just about to call." She motioned them into the house. "But it seems you're both psychic and heard our thoughts."

The three stepped inside.

"You're just in time. Nikki's whelping right now."

"Ooo goodie," Leslie squealed and clapped her hands.

Paula steeled herself for what was to come, and they all trooped into Nikki's whelping bedroom. By the time they got there, one little pup had been born.

Nate crouched down next to the box beside Sam. "I wanted to call for help but I didn't want to scare the dog," Sam said.

"You did great," Nate answered. His dark eyes twinkled with amusement. "I see you are well prepared. As I've already told Kat, I couldn't think of a better midwife for Nikki than you." He smiled at Paula and rose.

Dumbfounded, she looked after him.

"I think another one's coming out!" squealed Leslie.

Kat met Sam's eyes. "This didn't go the way you thought it would. Am I right?"

Sam laughed and shook his head, staring amazed at the second little blob about to plop out of Nikki.

For once, Paula didn't know what to say. She was so happy Leslie was getting to see the miracle of birth. She just wasn't so crazy about sharing the moment with Nate Bale. Thankfully, Nikki seemed to be getting ready to drop her third, so Paula stayed focused and didn't have time to worry over Nate.

Nate washed his hands and forearms with soap at the kitchen sink and went back into the whelping room to say goodbye. He pointed his thumb at Paula, who was in the process of attaching a blue woolen string to the new addition's neck. More balls of wool in pink, red and green were beside her.

"Wow. You guys are professional." Nate drew closer to Paula, who held the puppy up for him to see.

"Isn't he cute?" Her eyes were moist.

Almost reverently, Nate took the little guy and placed him in the hollow of his arm. A smile stole onto Paula's lips. Nate and the pup made too cute a picture. Nate took him carefully and looked at him from all sides until he stuck her nose into the soft baby fur on the back of the puppy's neck. The scent of mother's milk and little dog filled his nose. Gently, he placed him back with his mother.

"This is Blue," Kat announced, stroking the pup's head with her index finger.

"Just Blue?" Sam asked. He pointed to the woolen thread around the pup's neck.

"Yes. Blue's future owner will give him a proper name. I just need to be able to tell them apart."

Paula nodded in agreement. "I do the same thing with animals I know won't stay with me. It gives a little illusion of distance. Even if I do end up howling like a castle dog every time I pass one on."

Sam let his eyes wander over the available balls of wool. "So we'll be welcoming Blue, Red, and Pink today?"

"Exactly. And in case we have more surprises, there's still green, yellow, and purple here." Paula lifted three more balls of yarn.

As if on cue, sounds came from the entry. The voices of Pat and Tyler could be heard coming home.

"In here!" Kat called.

Tyler walked in first and saw the happy occasion. "Hooray!" she crowed. "Anybody hungry? I have some of Jaz's sweet potato soup with me. She sent it home with us."

Pat pulled a bottle of wine from the bag he was carrying as well as freshly baked bread. "We're all prepared for a crowd."

"I'll see if Mr. Wilkinson's home," Tyler said. "He might like to join us, too."

"Nate, will you stay?" Kat added.

He nodded yes.

At that moment Nikki yelped and a fourth and final puppy joined the rest.

And that was when Kat realized an incredible thing— the ache she carried around inside ever since her friends left Seattle was gone. She wasn't lonely anymore.

Whelping day had been exhausting for Kat. Nikki gave birth to four healthy puppies, two boys, Blue and Green, and their two sisters, Red and Pink. It was as though Sam had fallen madly in love with all four. He helped Kat clean up after the little puppies. This made it harder and harder for her to stick to her principles. Everything suggested that Sam was not just a pretty package, but much more. She could not imagine that he would ever behave as brutally as her own father. But at the last moment, before she weakened, she sternly reminded herself that her mother probably never thought her father would act that way either.

Kat sighed and toyed with her cell phone. She owed her mother a call but in the mood she was in now, it wasn't the time. She might say something stupid. Her mother had never talked about what it was like when she and her father met. Should Kat ask her about it sometime? Until now, they had only discussed the subject in passing. And only when things were particularly bad. Otherwise, her mother had perfected the art of simply ignoring unpleasant things.

Kat pushed her unruly hair out of her face. She really needed to call her again anyway. Maybe it was time to shake up the status quo. At best, her mother would finally come to her senses and leave. If not, Kat would at least have answers to a few questions.

Until recently, she had been quite content to be eternally single. When she looked at the relationships around her, she was usually glad to not deal with all the beautiful and ugly emotions that seemed unavoidable in a relationship. But lately, she found her thoughts wandering into uncharted territory. What would it be like to share life with a man like Sam? The joy she felt at the thought was always clouded by fear that ran through her like a bolt of lightning.

Kat had lamented her woes to Jaz over the phone last night, standing on the porch in the bitter cold so Sam couldn't overhear. Jaz had only laughed and called her a drama queen. "The way I see it, you've got the whole roller coaster of emotions right now. Only without sex."

"Sex is overrated," she had replied.

"Then, my dear, you haven't had a good man in bed for a long time."

Jaz had sounded so sure, so downright satisfied, that Kat winced. It was true. The last time had been so long ago that she wasn't sure if it had been last year or the year before. Nor had the encounter been particularly memorable.

Sam's world had been turned upside-down and he didn't care. The home-zoo took him up completely. The puppies didn't move much, mostly they just laid around. But every once in a while a little blind worm, who looked like he was wearing pajamas that were too big, would crawl over to his mom and dock at the milk bar. This instinct-driven process fascinated Sam so much that he would drop everything and watch them every time. Nikki patiently endured the feeding, panting until it became too much for her, and she started cleaning the cubs from head to toe with her big tongue. For Sam, it was a true miracle that the little ones didn't just disappear down her throat, never to be seen again. Rocky played the worried uncle and stood next to the whelping box with big wrinkles on his face.

Sam was already aware that the wrinkles on Rocky's face were not an expression of his mood. But he could have sworn that they had been particularly pronounced since the little ones arrived.

"Always these all-nighters, huh, buddy?" he said to him, nuzzling the back of his neck. All the while, the pups were very quiet, only squealing to themselves from time to time when they were hungry. When it seemed like mom and kids were going to take a long nap, Sam decided to take the opportunity to walk Rocky around the house. The poor guy could certainly use a little fresh air.

On Sam's way out, a surprise awaited him in the kitchen. Bella was not lying on her makeshift sickbed, but standing on wobbly legs in the middle of the kitchen.

"What are you doing?" he exclaimed delightedly and took a step towards the dog. Bella backed away and huddled against the wall. He hadn't meant to scare her. Sam took two big steps away from the dog and made a big fuss about petting Rocky. Finally, Sam straightened up slowly, so as not to startle Bella again with an abrupt movement. He directed his gaze to the door and walked out with Rocky in tow. Deliberately, he blocked the door open a little. If Bella shed her fear and felt strong enough to come outside, she could do it without risk of being trapped. True, it was a little too cold to leave the door open. But he assumed the little ones were warm enough in their bedroom for the next fifteen minutes. It would probably take the frightened Bella a while before she dared to go out. That's how long he would wander with Rocky through the snow around the house.

When they returned fifteen minutes later, Bella was standing in the snow not far from the door, wagging her tail uncertainly. Rocky approached her at his casual gait. Sam held his breath as he watched the two. At first Bella cowered. But then she seemed to gather all her courage. Trembling, she stopped and let him sniff her. In the end, she even turned her own nose a little in his direction. Rocky remained completely calm and also soon turned away again. Sam watched in amazement as little Bella staggered after the huge dog on unsteady legs.

At the last moment, Jinx slipped through the door behind him and meowed loudly. Rocky ignored the cat. Sam lifted Jinx and cradled her against his chest. "You're feared, jungle cat. Let's go inside and see if there's anything for you to eat."

Agreeing, Jinx began to purr. Sam laughed softly and scratched her behind the ears. Rocky turned about and dashed past them into the kitchen. He sat in front of the cupboard where the dog food was stowed. Jinx did not settle for standing on the floor, but jumped from Sam's arms directly onto the kitchen counter, where she loudly meowed and demanded her reward.

Sam fed the demanding gang of predators. Each had their own bowl spread out over the kitchen so there was no crowding or stealing. He took some cooked rice and minced meat out of the fridge, as Kat had shown him, and put down some soft food for Bella.

He heard the front door open. Kat's voice rang out. "Are you here Sam?"

Sam rinsed his hands and dried them on a dishtowel. Both hands in his pockets, he strolled out to greet her. A broad smile spread across his face when he saw how trustingly Bella snuggled up to Kat. Kat looked up and beamed at him.

Sam returned her smile. "She was even outside with me and Rocky for a minute."

"I hope Rocky behaved himself. I know how wild he can be sometimes."

"He was the perfect gentleman. I don't think he takes Bella here seriously at all. Maybe later. When she's fully back on her feet." He looked doubtfully at the heap of misery at Kat's feet. Even though it seemed like Bella was out of the woods, it took quite a bit of imagination to discover beauty.

"You don't have to look at her so critically." Protectively, Kat cradled the dog in her arms. "Ignore him. The main thing is that you know you're beautiful," she whispered.

Amused at the two of them talking at cross-purposes, Sam shook his head. "I've noticed, by the way, that she's not big on men."

Kat felt a familiar anger creep up inside her as she imagined what had probably led to this. With difficulty she swallowed it and tried to concentrate on what Sam was saying to her. As she listened to Sam's thoughtful words, a warm feeling spread inside. He had such compassion. And kindness. Toward a broken dog she had dragged in. If she looked at it closely, she had also snowballed into his life unasked.

"What is it?" he wanted to know, looking at the expression on her face.

With a few steps Kat bridged the distance and kissed him. Directly on the mouth. Surprised, Sam stood frozen at first, but then his instincts awoke and he kissed her back. Later, much later, when they broke away from each other, Kat touched her lips in wonder, as if she didn't know what had just happened.

Sam looked as though he was wondering the same thing. He raised his hand and touched her gently on the cheek. "Friends, Kat? If this is what it feels like to be your friend, you can count me in from now on."

Her face colored red. She shut her eyes and then opened them a crack. No luck. Sam was still standing there, a satisfied, arrogant grin on his face. She groaned. Then she pulled herself together. "Don't think anything of it. Just a momentary lapse of reason." Abruptly she turned around and walked to her own room.

Sam tilted his head and looked at Bella, who watched her rescuer disappear with interest. "Don't ask me where she's running off to. But don't worry. I'm sure she'll be back."

Kat checked on the four puppies, patted Nikki on the head and scratched Rocky behind the ears. Then she put food for Sam in the oven. In other words, she did her best not to think about the kiss. To no avail, of course. What had gotten into her? She had been so on course with her "friend plan."

"Are you talking to me?" said a voice by her elbow. Startled, she jumped to the side. "Why sneak up on me like that!"

Sam laughed softly. "No one has ever told me that I'm good at sneaking up on people. Not at my size. Maybe on the ice I am." He wiggled his eyebrows exaggeratedly.

Kat laughed, and her tension eased a little. She must have been muttering out loud as Sam came in the kitchen. "I can imagine that." She pointed to the stove. "There's your breakfast in there. I don't know how warm it is yet, though."

"Thank you." He bent down and took the hashbrowns and sausage out of the oven. While making himself comfortable at the breakfast bar, he said, "Do you think you can handle this zoo by yourself? Because I really need to get back to Denver."

She looked over at him and watched him spread a generous portion of ketchup next to his fried potatoes.

"Sure. No problem," she replied lightly. "The animals are my responsibility. Not yours." She handed him a glass of orange juice. Before she could withdraw her hand, he had captured her wrist. Her skin tingled at his touch, reawakening the butterflies in her stomach.

"And what do you do in the event of another momentary lapse that results in a kiss? That's not just friends is it?"

She met his gaze and tried to maintain an uninvolved expression. Then she raised an eyebrow and said provocatively, "Then I guess I'll have to find another innocent victim, won't I?"

At Kat's words about finding an innocent victim, Sam had to restrain himself from growling. The idea of Kat kissing another man was repugnant to him. He had an impossible desire to throw her over his shoulder like a Neanderthal and drag her into his den. If she already felt the urgent need to kiss someone, she should take *him*. But suspecting that she would not appreciate the gesture, he pulled himself together. Patience, he told himself, patience, and took a deep breath.

"How long will you be gone?" Kat asked

"Why? Are you missing me already?"

She rolled her eyes. "Of course not," she replied indignantly.

"If you do, my number is on the list of numbers behind the bar by the landline. You can call me anytime." He winked at her.

She didn't seem to know what to say. Finally, she settled on a simple, "Thank you." He had really been a great help to her in the last few days.

Sam just shrugged like it was no big deal and wiped his mouth with a napkin. Jinx picked that moment to jump on his lap trying to steal the last piece of sausage off his plate. "Hey," he called, shooing her down. "We don't let uncivilized animals in the house around here."

Jinx retreated to safety on a windowsill.

"Did you find out if anyone missed the hellcat here? Or Bella?"

"Yes and no." Kat thought for a moment about how much to tell him. "Do you know Scrooge? The drunk guy who lives in a trailer on this side of Independence?" she added.

"Yeah. Everyone knows Scrooge. He practically lives in the diner in the winter."

Kat wrinkled her nose. "I wonder if Jinx probably belongs to him?"

"Could be. You'll have to ask him about it the next time you see him. And what about Bella?"

"Bella is a different story. Some people were very nice about the flyers I made. Lilly from the flower store, for example. Or your sister. Miss Minnie was more reserved. And others were hostile when I showed them Bella's picture and told them her story. That hit me pretty hard. Since I've been here, all I've heard is praise for Independence's tight-knit community. Everybody helps everybody, blah blah blah. I didn't notice much of that in Bella's case."

"They've been burned before. There was trouble a few years ago—some idiots who intimidated people with attack dogs. That was around when Tyler graduated from high school five years ago. So, Bella suffers because of it."

"My thoughts exactly!" Kat exclaimed. "But Scrooge was of the opinion that these people might be still around. They've just gone underground. He mentioned an abandoned farm by the river. Does that mean anything to you?" She looked at him hopefully.

Sam could tell she was in full investigator mode. If what she said was true, and these guys were still around, they were the wrong ones for her to play detective with. "I don't know," he said deceptively, without batting an eyelash.

Disappointed, the corners of her mouth tugged downward.

"Maybe Jake knows something," he added hastily. "The best thing you can do is pass on all the information to him." Sam made a mental note to call Jake later and make sure Kat stayed out of it. This was a job for professional law enforcement, not Pollyanna from Seattle.

Lost in thought, Kat nodded. "Will do. If there really is someone dogfighting in the area, it needs to be stopped."

Sam was of the same opinion. It just wasn't going to be done by Kat. But he wisely kept this opinion to himself. "If there was dogfighting going on there would be tickets and betting and a place where people would watch. Don't you think Jake would know about that?"

Kat was at a loss for words. If the dogs she'd rescued weren't being used to fight, then what could possibly be going on?"

CHAPTER EIGHT

"WHAT DO YOU MEAN you would have sent me the application materials by now?" Frustrated, Paula ruffled her hair. This administrator on the phone was exasperating.

"We sent them out over two weeks ago. You should have received them by now." The woman's voice sounded bored and arrogant. Almost as if she was wondering why someone who couldn't even keep track of her mail was even interested in becoming a licensed foster parent.

"But I didn't receive them," Paula protested. "Maybe they got lost at the post office," she added.

"I suppose," the woman replied ungraciously.

Paula closed her eyes and took a deep breath. *For Leslie. I'm doing this for Leslie*, she reminded herself. "Can't I do this online?"

"No. We are sending you hard copies because they have to be signed by a licensed notary and sent back."

"Could you please send me the application materials again?"

"Alright." The administrator sighed as if she had to deliver the letter herself, and on foot.

Paula rolled her eyes toward the ceiling. Bureaucrats. Everything was too much for them. "Thank you so much," she said sweetly and ended the call. Hopefully it would work out this time. She wanted to finally get this application over with. Leslie had been in a permanently bad mood for two weeks and spoke only when necessary.

Not even the animals could coax her out of her shell. Paula hoped that the prospect of having an official home here would give the stability she needed. If that didn't work, she was all out of ideas. She had tried to approach Leslie about her bad mood but she had avoided the conversation. Teens had perfected evasive maneuvers these days.

Paula leaned back in her chair and rubbed her temples. She just didn't know what to do. Leave her alone? Insist on having a conversation? Raising horses and dogs was definitely easier. She had more experience with them. Maybe she should ask someone for advice. Her own mother came to mind and a smile stole onto her lips. Mom would know what to do. She reached for the phone again and dialed her parents' number.

When Leslie came home a few hours later, Paula intercepted her right there on the porch.

"Come on, get in the car. We're going to see my mom."

Caught off guard, Leslie forgot her bad mood for a moment. "We're going to Brenda's? Do you think she has cookies?"

"I'm sure she has, and if not, I'm sure you can bake some."

"Great," the girl rejoiced.

Paula followed her outside to the truck, irritated that the prospect of visiting her mother caused such joy. Maybe she should bake more often, too, she thought sullenly. That seemed to be the key to teenage bliss. Or maybe she just wasn't cut out for this mother-daughter thing. Until Leslie showed up, she'd never felt a pressing desire to have children, either. She pushed the unpleasant thoughts away. After all, it wasn't about her, it was about Leslie. And if her plan to draw the girl out of her reserve worked, all the better. She counted on her mother to tease out of Leslie what was on her mind.

"Let me try it once," her mother had said. "Not because I can do it better, but because I'm not that close. It's often easier to talk to someone on the outside."

Paula was not convinced that this was the solution. But in the absence of alternative ideas, she had agreed. Making sure they were strapped inside the truck, Paula pulled away. It was going to be a relief to share worries about a child with her own mother. Which was probably why it usually took two to produce a child, she thought glumly. She was so engrossed in her thoughts about her own inability as far as child-rearing was concerned that she missed Leslie animatedly recounting her day and listing all the things she wanted to tell Brenda. It was only when she fell silent that Paula noticed the sudden silence.

She looked over at Leslie. Immediately, the teen averted her eyes and clammed up. Just great. Now Paula felt twice as bad. When the girl finally opened up and let her in on her life, she missed it because she was too busy wallowing in self-pity. She put her hand on Leslie's thigh.

"Sorry. I was distracted. That's why I didn't hear what you were trying to tell me."

"It's okay. It wasn't important." Leslie continued to stare out the window.

"Of course it's important. You matter to me." To reinforce her statement, she squeezed her leg. Leslie giggled.

"Are you ticklish?"

"No."

Paula squeezed again. "Yes!" Leslie shrieked, giggling. "Stop it."

Paula withdrew her hand and smiled, too. "So. Tell me again. I'm all ears, I promise."

As she turned into the driveway at her parents' house, at least she knew Leslie's low mood wasn't from school. She said she loved everything about her school. The teachers, the subject matter, her new friends, and there was probably even a boy, Michael, who she thought was cute. Everything was reassuringly normal.

"Bye. And save me some cookies," said Paula.

"You're not coming?"

"I have a few errands to run. I'll pick you up in a couple of hours. If you have homework, I'm sure you can do it here."

Leslie nodded eagerly, her hand already on the door handle. "Will do. Bye."

And away she went. Paula sighed and shook her head. Project Leslie was in play. She glanced at the dashboard clock. It was time to get a dose of cute puppies. She hoped Kat or maybe Pat was home at the Wilkinson place. She grinned thinking of them, wondering how long it would be before Kat and Sam stopped sneaking around each other. Her brother Sam seemed blown away. Kat was harder to gauge. She seemed determined to ignore the sparks as much as possible. Paula was curious to see how well that worked.

Her truck took the hill up the butte easily. As Paula parked out front she saw an all-too-familiar car and groaned. Of course it was *him*. How could it be otherwise? Of all times for Nate to make a checkup, it coincided with her own visit. If it wasn't for bad luck she'd have none. She just couldn't figure Nate out. After acting like an idiot in the past with Nate, he had every right to be frosty but civil toward her. Instead, he was downright friendly. What's more, he seemed to know her surprisingly well, for having dealt with him only a few times. Very confusing.

She got out of the car and walked to the gorgeous front of the Prairie-style home. The big door knocker resounded through the house. "Anyone home?" she called out.

"We're here," Kat's voice rang out. "Come on in, door's open." She sounded cheerful. Paula turned the door handle and let herself in. Walking through the house, the first thing she spotted was Nate's broad shoulders. He was in the back bedroom, weighing puppies on a kitchen scale. He had set it on a bedside table while Kat dutifully entered each puppy's weight on a spreadsheet. Nikki stood next to the table, resting her head on the tabletop as if to make sure her pups weren't harmed in the whole procedure. Rocky was lying on the floor in front of the bed. The little injured dog was snuggled close to him. Amused, Paula raised an eyebrow. "Someone seems to be doing better," she noted.

Kat beamed. "It sure does." She accepted the last puppy from Nate and placed him back in the box, where he tried to climb over his brother. Nikki immediately went to them and started licking the four rascals clean.

Nate turned and gave Paula a lazy smile. "Hey."

"Hey." Embarrassed, Paula quickly averted her eyes. "How are the color-coded canines doing?"

"Glad you're here," Nate remarked.

Paula looked over at him in surprise. That was really nice of him. But the safest thing was to ignore him. Thankfully, Kat didn't elaborate on his comment either. After an awkward pause he cleared his throat. "I'll be off, then. The puppies are thriving. Miss Bella is doing well, too."

Kat got to her feet. "I've been wanting to ask you both," she shifted her feet uncertainly. "Do you know anything about an abandoned farm by the river?"

Nate got a funny look on his face. "I've never been there. But I'd stay away. I've heard there's riffraff hanging around. Why do you ask?"

Kat shrugged her shoulders. "Oh, no reason. The place came up when I was asking around about Bella."

Paula chimed in. "Have you asked Jake?"

For the second time in a few days, Kat noted that people were advising her to leave the search to the sheriff. Problem was, the sheriff had more pressing problems. While she could understand that she was still growing impatient. She wanted to find out more before the next dead or badly injured dog showed up on the property.

Nate took his leave and she and Paula were finally alone. Blue and Red chewed on the soles of Paula's boots, while Pink and Green cuddled up in the whelping box.

"What's going on with the old homestead by the river?" asked Paula once Nate was gone.

"Long story."

Paula pointedly looked at her bare wrist where there was no wristwatch. "I have time."

So, Kat told her everything, from the frustrating conversations with people to the curious story Scrooge had told her. When she got to the part where he had pretended to be dead or drunk as a skunk, Paula narrowed her eyes.

"Did you see the man who bumped into you?"

"Unfortunately, only from behind."

"You couldn't draw a picture of him?"

Kat shook her head. "No. Definitely not. But maybe I could recognize the coat. Will you tell me how to get to that farm?"

"You really don't want to leave this with Jake, do you." It wasn't a question, it was a statement.

"Jake is busy. And I really don't know if there's anything at the old farm or not. Just a quick look might tell me more." She left out the part about dogfighting. That might be too much for Paula. She didn't want her running to Jake behind her back.

Paula frowned. "Okay, I get it. You don't want to leave everything to a man. I can tell you how to get to the farm. But take backup with you if you really want to look around there. My shotgun and I are at your disposal."

Kat gave her a warm smile. Paula gave her directions as Kat loaded all the puppies into the whelping box and penned them in. Then she whistled up the dogs. Nikki was glad to leave her mothering duties behind for a moment and jumped out of the box, wagging her tail. Bella hobbled along as best she could. Rocky brought up the rear.

"Want to walk with us?" Kat said to Paula.

"Sure."

Finally, they were outside. Kat stretched her face toward the sun. The biting wind of the last few days had died down a bit, so the weak winter sun actually had a chance to send down warming rays. If the weather stayed like this, maybe some of the snow would finally melt. As beautiful as it was, she was getting tired of it.

"Do you have any idea yet how you're going to set up your business?" Paula, who was walking next to her, snapped her out of her thoughts.

Kat grimaced. "Honestly, with everything that's going on with me right now I haven't had time to give it much thought. "At least I get free advertising driving around town." Kat laughed as the dogs dodged and nudged one another. The two women stopped to watch the canine antics. Finally, they started moving again.

"What do your plans look like? Anything happened businesswise yet?"

"I had a nibble and an invitation from a hotel manager. I need to call her. Meanwhile, Bella and Nikki showed me there are far too many animals who have no one to speak for them. Or to give them sanctuary."

"You want to open an animal shelter?"

"Not really. I can't imagine keeping animals in kennels. I would just like to take the animals in temporarily, nurse them back to health if necessary, and find them new homes. I'm aware that there are many animal shelters. I'd just like to do my part for Independence."

"Seems like you already do."

"Exactly. That brings me to the second part of my plan. I'm going to start writing a blog. Bella's story, for example. Or Nikki's, too. That way I can reach out to the public and raise awareness about these issues. Maybe others will be willing to take in an animal temporarily. It's a good way to find new owners."

Paula was impressed. "You thought this through pretty well. What about the money? I'm not even talking about food right now, although that becomes an issue when you get to a certain number of dogs, I guess."

She coughed and looked to the side, where three of the four puppies were trying to climb each others' backs and chew their ears off. "They sure are hungry."

"Exactly. And I don't want to know how much Bella's vet bills will be."

Kat wrinkled her nose. "Nate said he'd give me a special price. Still, it won't be cheap." She shrugged. "I don't know yet. Crowdfunding? Donations? Who knows? I'd just like to try it out."

"How are you settling in, anyway?" Paula asked.

"I'm having a harder time at that than I would have thought."

"Don't you like it here?" asked Paula in dismay.

"Sure. Sure." Kat pointed to the breathtaking scenery around her. The Rockies rose out of mist behind them. "Who wouldn't like it here? The scenery is great."

"Then it's the people."

Kat shook her head. "It's not that either." She dared a glance at her new friend, worried that she might have upset her. But Paula's face expressed no anger. Just open interest.

Kat relaxed a little. "With you and the rest of your family, I get along very well. I got along well with Jaz and Pat before. The other people, as far as I know them at all, are mostly okay, too."

"But?" echoed Paula.

"I don't know either. Maybe because of Jaz's and Pat's stories that I've heard about Independence, I've just idealized this place a lot. And now that I live here, I realize that like everywhere else in this world, it's very human."

"Remember, you're new here. Not like Tyler, who's lived here all her life. Even Jaz kind of had a home advantage. She spent a lot of her summer vacations at her grandmother's house."

"And how long does it take to belong?"

"Oh, just about thirty years," Paula replied with a twinkle in her eye.

Kat groaned. "Great. So only half an eternity."

"Just think of it this way. Thirty years from now, you'll be one of the old-timers here. In the anonymous big city, thirty years from now, nobody will know you."

This made Kat laugh, and Sam, who also possessed this talent, came to mind. "Thank you, that's what I needed. Someone to give me a little shake, make me laugh, and make me understand that the whole world doesn't revolve around me. Your brother is good at that, too."

"My brother? Is that so? What else is he good at?"

Kat tried to put on an unconcerned expression. But in vain. She couldn't stop a telltale smile from stealing onto her lips. "I don't know."

"Liar," it came back lovingly from Paula.

"We can talk about Nate, what do you think?" Kat's voice was sugary sweet.

"I have to get back soon," Paula said, changing the subject not exactly unobtrusively. Kat grinned knowingly as Paula continued hastily, "I left Leslie with my mom. She's been in such a bad mood lately." She frowned. "Or rather, I have the impression that something is bothering her." She tilted her head as something occurred to her. "Do you remember the day you went to get the whelping box?"

"Sure I do."

"Just before you came to our door, something happened. Since then, it's like she's changed."

Concerned, Kat eyed her new friend while she picked a stick out of the snow for Rocky and threw it. "Do you think she's being bullied at school or something?"

Paula frowned. "I don't think so, actually. We talked about school on the way to my parents' house today. It all sounded positive. And convincing, too."

"Difficult. Maybe she'll tell your mother something."

"That's what I'm hoping for, to be honest. That's why I left her there for a few hours. I'm getting to the end of my rope. For a long time it was going really well and I felt like she was getting better and better. And all of a sudden, it's all gone."

Kat, sensing Paula's concern, reached over and lightly squeezed her hand. "Hey. Parenting is never linear. With dogs, it isn't. With horses, it's not. So I guess with kids, it's not either."

"Cheer up. Things will turn around. It's just a phase." Kat hugged Paula goodbye and watched her go as she headed down the exit ramp to the main road. How lucky for Leslie that her path had led her to Paula. The girl may not have known it yet, but Paula would fight like a bear to protect her.

Kat's for Dogs, Seattle

"Come on! Come in! Time for treats!"

Caitlin called to the dogs in the run from the doorway of the salon. Just another few hours and their owners would be on the way to take them home for supper. Things were going well and Caitlin enjoyed her new autonomy as the manager of Kat's for Dogs, all on her own. She noticed a note had been slipped under the door while she'd been in the back. She walked over and picked it up as the dogs streamed back inside, collars jingling and nails clicking on the floor.

Caitlin opened the note. It was printed in a careful hand.

Thank you for taking care of my dog. I love her but I just can't afford to keep her. Thank you again, so much.

A dirty, much-folded ten-dollar bill fell out of the note. Caitlin caught it before it fluttered to the floor. It broke her heart to think of this person, probably homeless, taking from their food money to give the salon ten dollars toward food for Nikki. Especially when she wasn't even here.

Caitlin resolved to add some of her own money to the ten and purchase a large bag of pet food to take over to the food bank. People down on their luck, either temporarily or permanently, needed to feed their pets, too.

The canines around her feet reminded Caitlin that she'd promised treats. "Hold your horses," she grumbled going for the canister of goodies, realizing how lucky they all were to have treats right there for the taking.

INDEPENDENCE, AN HOUR LATER

When Kat got home, Mr. Wilkinson was standing in the window of his new apartment on the back, gazing down with Jinx in his arms. Both the cat and the man looked happy with each other's company. Mr. Wilkinson broke into a wide smile. Kat returned the same.

Inside, she found Sam was just leaving for Denver. Tyler wanted him to stay for dinner but he insisted he had to get back to the team. So, Tyler suggested leftovers with a good bottle of wine for the rest of them. "We'll have enough if we all share some lasagna, some lamb stew that I got in Breck, and a big salad. And wine, don't forget the wine. How does that sound?"

It sounded pretty good to Kat and Pat, so they ate around the kitchen island using paper plates so there were no dishes to worry about. They continued with the wine and conversation into the evening.

Next day, Kat packed Rocky into the RV and drove back over to Paula's place. Her mind was back on her probe into the farm. If she was going to slip over there and do some recon, Nelly was not the right vehicle. It was just too conspicuous. She hoped Paula would let her borrow the truck for a few hours. Nikki and Bella were home alone with the puppies so she couldn't stay away long. She had locked the whole bunch in the basement for the morning with the Little Buddy heater carefully placed where they couldn't get at it. The puppies were getting more enterprising by the day. She didn't want to risk them turning Sam's living room upside-down while she was gone.

The scenery on the way to Paula's was spectacular. Kat motored past snowy clearings with frozen ponds where skaters circled and skidded, and cross-country skiers carved tracks as they went along. Snowmen raised stick arms to the sky. Hikers in snowshoes stopped to chuckle at Nelly's fantastic paint job as she passed by.

Kat was lucky. Paula was at home.

"Wouldn't you rather wait until I have time to come with you to the farm?"

"That's sweet of you. But I want answers. I've waited long enough."

"Hasn't anyone responded to your flyers?"

"No. They've sort of disappeared, too."

"What do you mean?"

"They are gone. Only two or three stores still have them up. All the ones I put up outside have been torn down."

"Did you tell Jake about this?"

"About torn flyers? Please."

Paula looked at her in dismay.

"I'm not going to sit idly by and wait for the next dead dog to show up. Although I doubt one will show up on my property again."

"What can I do for you, then?"

"I want to borrow your truck. Mine sticks out too much."

Paula nodded decisively. "It does that for sure. Alright. Take my truck. But if you're not back here in two hours, I'll send in the cavalry. And believe me, Jake won't be pleased if he finds out you've gone off on your own."

"He's not the only one," Kat replied, "Sam agrees I should stay out of it."

Paula took a deep breath. "I can't decide which one of you is right now."

Kat laughed. "Probably both of us. But I know one thing about you Paula, you'd never let Jake stop you."

"Even in fairy-tales heroines have to help themselves," Paula replied dryly. She handed over a set of keys.

"Exactly." Kat picked them up and went outside to transfer Rocky into the truck.

After several attempts, Kat found the right turnoff Paula had told her about. She stopped the truck on a small hill. Below, the partially frozen river meandered through the small valley. Where the river curved was the farm. Even from this distance, she could see that the buildings were in bad shape. There was a farmhouse, a shabby barn, and a long low structure that could be used for equipment storage. No human beings were around. Her exploration could begin. She got Rocky out on his leash and then hunted around and grabbed a stick. She now had two pretty good defenses to use, just in case.

She decided to hike around to the other side and see what the view revealed from there. On the northern side the ground was cleared and free of snow. She could see tire tracks. Vehicles parked here. Watching carefully, she made her way down the hill. Rocky obediently stayed close at heel. When she reached the bottom, she turned back to see where the truck was parked. She realized with a sinking feeling that if she had to run, she would never reach it in time. On the other hand, the only way to spot that there was a strange truck up there was to deliberately look for it. Most people didn't.

Once she had circled a bit and saw no movement, she expelled a tense breath. So far, so safe. Becoming bolder, she walked closer to the main house. Moving up to the door she peered through a grimy pane. Inside, there wasn't much to see. A table, a chair and a filing cabinet where the living room should be. A computer and a telephone were visible on the table. Odd. As dilapidated as it looked, the door was fastened with couple of sturdy new locks. It didn't match the rest of the house's appearance at all. But she couldn't get anywhere here unless she broke a window, and lock picking was not one of her talents. She left it alone and went over to the barn.

Outwardly, it was a barn, but when Kat stepped up to a window she discovered wire cages attached to the wall. Rocky sniffed around and grew more excited by the minute. Everything was filthy. The bare floors appeared to have been only superficially cleaned. Dark stains spotted the ground in several places. Kat squinted at the stains as closely as she could. Without the magic ingredient Luminol, which she knew only from watching crime shows on TV, there was no way to determine if it was blood. Rocky seemed to sense that this wasn't his ordinary walk and did not leave her side.

She went to the large barn door where a chain hung uselessly. The lock was missing. Was she lucky for the first time? She pushed the gate open a crack with her shoulder. Inside it was dark. To let in a little daylight, she pushed the gate open wider and waited for her eyes to adjust to the low light. A makeshift arena was constructed of rough boards in the center of the room. There were many stains in that area. A few feet away were benches. A place for spectators, although not many. This wasn't a place for public dogfights, there wasn't the seating. At both ends of the arena were gates where people and animals entered and left the main arena space. She walked toward one of the gates. A tuft of hair was stuck to the hinge. A little further to the right lay bloodstained feathers. So this was not just dogfighting, but cockfighting as well. Kat pushed at the feathers with her stick, full of pity for the innocent animals.

As if in a trance, she circled the arena. A metallic taste spread through her mouth. She simply didn't understand how people could consider it a recreational pleasure to watch animals tearing at each other. She was about to enter the "arena" when Rocky let out a low rumble. She froze and listened. Sure enough. The sound of an engine. Hastily, she made her way to the exit and slipped out of the barn. What was she supposed to do now? Hide? Or hope that the vehicle was approaching from the back and make a dash for her own? She exited the far end of the barn through a rickety door and closer to the third, low building away from the noise. As she did a clamor of barking started up from the third building. So that was where the dogs were kept.

Rocky nosed her leg, pushing her to walk away. Off she went for Paula's truck. As fast as possible on the icy ground, she got to the hill and stumbled up a narrow path. Surely she was going to be seen. Her heart was thumping but finally she reached the truck. Fueled by the adrenaline rushing through her body, she pushed Rocky inside the vehicle and jumped into the driver's seat. Breathing heavily, she closed her eyes for a second. Get a grip, she scolded herself. Now was not the time to have a nervous breakdown.

She forced her eyes open and looked for the engine she'd heard a moment ago. Only when she let her eyes wander a little more into the distance did she spot it. A red truck. The distance between the car and the barn was greater than she had originally thought, and the driver was obviously having to hold it to the road as it humped and bumped over potholes. That could explain why she wasn't spotted because the driver had to pay very close attention to the road.

The truck drove directly toward the low building where the barking had come from. She prayed that the driver still had not lifted his eyes to see her and started the engine. Slowly she backed the truck up until she was sure it could no longer be seen from below. Rocky whined. He sensed her tension. "We're getting out of here, Rocky." The big French mastiff seemed to agree wholeheartedly. As they got on their way he heaved a sigh and rested his head on her lap.

Driving the road back to Paula's place, Kat almost didn't see the trees decorated with snow whizzing past her eyes. She was too busy recalling the farm. There were animals on the property, there was an arena for fighting animals. But no place for an audience. How strange was that? Then the thought struck her: What if this were a breeding and training place for fight dogs? What if they were supplying fight dogs and roosters to others who actually held the illegal public fights in other parts of the country? Even the world?

Paula's homestead was just up ahead so Kat pulled into the driveway and stopped with the engine running. She pulled out her phone and searched "fight dogs" and "fight dog breeders." Nothing. Then she searched "dog breeders + Colorado" and the site she was looking for popped up. There was no identifying outside shot so the farm could be recognized. But there were interior shots of large fighting breeds in cages, with an emphasis on mothers with puppies. There were shots of adolescent males, obviously in training. This place supplied the illegal trade with animals who were brought up and trained to be vicious fighters. One shot was of a dog inside a crate labeled AIR FREIGHT, LIVE CARGO.

That's when Kat realized what had happened to Bella. She was a training dog for the young fighters to attack and easily overwhelm. The success would make them bolder, more confident. Poor little Bella had been made a chew toy for bigger, stronger dogs who would grow up to fight. It was sickening.

Kat clicked another picture so it grew larger. In it, a hand grasped a rooster by the feet so that it hung upside-down. She felt nauseous when she saw sharp blades attached to its legs to make the fighting even more bloody and deadly. In a couple of pictures there were a few women whose faces were blurred out wearing short, tight outfits and posing beside the cages.

A knock on the window made her flinch. Startled, she cried out before her brain registered that it was only Paula standing next to her door. Paula stepped backwards as Kat opened the door.

"You scared me now," Paula said, rolling her eyes. "That banshee scream took at least ten years off my life. What's the matter that you're so nervous?"

"I'll tell you in a minute. Here are the keys. Can we go in? Is Leslie here?"

"Leslie is in school."

"Good, because I don't want her to hear what I have to say."

"That bad? Well, come on in. I'll make coffee."

In the kitchen a few minutes later Paula put a cup in front of Kat. "Go ahead. Tell me what you found out."

Kat slid her cell phone across the table to Paula. "Here."

Paula squinted at it. "Looks like a place to fight dogs." She swiped the screen. "This one looks like big dogs in breeder cages. But this could be anywhere. Did you get a picture of anything at the farm that's clearly recognizable on the website?"

"I didn't have time. They're pretty crafty about not giving the location away. But it sure looks like the same place."

"So you were right all along with your feeling."

Kat blew on the surface of her hot drink. "Sure looks like it. Believe me, I would have been happy if my suspicions had turned out to be wrong."

"At least now you can take it to Jake."

"M-hm."

"You will, won't you?!" Paula's voice sounded stern.

Kat ducked her head, but then said defiantly. "Honestly, I'd like to do my own research first. I want photos, maybe even a video to show Jake so he'll believe me."

"Are you out of your mind?"

"Maybe. But I just don't want these guys getting off scot-free and moving their whole operation to the next county. Because that's exactly what will happen if Jake drops over for an interrogation but doesn't have a warrant to search the place." Kat pushed a curly strand of hair behind her ear. "Understand? I'd lose my chance to help these animals."

Paula thought about her words. She nodded reluctantly. "I see what you mean. Only, how are you going to do it? Are you sure you weren't seen?"

"Pretty sure. When I go back it'll be without makeup, in one of Pat's jackets, maybe, and black pants. Or I can put an outfit together from the thrift store. No chance of anyone recognizing me by sight."

"Send me a picture before you go. I want to see that. And I want regular situation reports."

"Photo you get. Situation reports are getting harder. I need to work fast." Kat was grateful that Paula didn't press her further to let it go after all. She actually supported her.

"Thank you."

"For what?"

"Well, for your help. Jake and Sam would have tried to talk me out of it."

"The two of them would forbid it. But since I can roughly imagine how prohibitions go down with you, I'd rather help you. That way I can at least reduce the risk of something happening to you."

Kat laughed. "You know me pretty well already."

"I'm just going to assume that you're similar to me. So far, this tactic is working quite well."

Kat emptied her coffee cup and put it in the sink. "I've got to get going, then. The other dogs are home alone. Why don't you bring Leslie by sometime in the next few days? The puppies are growing at the speed of light and getting frisky."

A shadow passed over Paula's face, but then she nodded. "I'm sure she'd enjoy that."

Kat put a hand on Paula's arm. "Is something wrong with Leslie?"

"It's probably nothing. Don't worry about it."

"I might not. But it's obvious you care. You know, this friendship thing works both ways. Can I help?"

Paula shook her head. "Thank you. But you need to get back to Nikki and company now. I'll tell you next time, I promise. Maybe by then the problem will dissolve into nothing, too."

While Kat went home to take care of her dogs, Paula busied herself in the kitchen baking chocolate chip cookies. If her mom was to be believed, these helped in all circumstances. Still, she doubted it would be enough to get Leslie to speak up about what was troubling her. Although Leslie did not divulge a lot while visiting with Paula's mother, her spirits had lifted. Paula had inquired if her mom, Brenda, got a handle on what the teen's problem was. But Brenda hadn't really been able to shed any light on it.

"I don't know what's bothering her. She probably just needs time to get up the nerve to believe she can stay with you."

"I'm already doing everything I can to make it official. If that stupid application form hadn't gotten lost in the mail, we might already have the first hurdles behind us."

"Does she know that?"

This question struck Paula like lightning. While she had talked to all sorts of people about her intention to officially apply as Leslie's foster mother, she had never talked to Leslie herself. Maybe Leslie didn't want this. Maybe she had overheard snippets of conversation that led her to draw the wrong conclusions. No wonder the girl was unsettled. With the experiences she had already gathered in her short life, it was practically pre-programmed for her to assume the worst.

Suddenly Paula knew what she had to do. She would ask Leslie for her opinion and ask for her help. Strangers had decided her life, all her life until she had taken it into her own hands and run away. In Paula's opinion, all the adults had let the little girl down. Perhaps she would appreciate Paula's attempt to include her in the decision-making process. Paula wasn't above helping out with a little bribery in the process, either. Cookies and horses were her secret weapons and bait.

Fifteen minutes later, Leslie came home from school. Barns and Roo jumped around her excitedly as she walked in the entryway. "Cut it out, Roo." She scolded the dog in a kind way when he tried to play rope pull with a strap from her school backpack.

Paula walked out to greet her with a smile. Leslie was always consistently friendly with the animals.

"What smells so delicious in here?" Leslie asked, slipping out of her heavy jacket and boots. She neatly hung the jacket on a hook and placed the boots to dry. Apparently she had forgotten her bad mood for a moment.

"Chocolate chip cookies." Paula answered. She trotted back to the kitchen and pulled the chair away so Leslie could sit down.

"I'm not a baby anymore," she grumbled.

"Whatever you say. You don't have to eat anything. But I'll need your help later, and it may well be that we won't be back until late." Paula patted a pair of saddlebags that were slung over the back of a kitchen chair.

Suspicious, Leslie turned, "On horseback? Where are we going?"

"We need to check the goats in the east pasture. I want to make sure the wind hasn't uprooted a tree. If one falls on the fence, it won't hold up. And then we can look for the goats all over the woods and beyond." Paula tucked some cookies into a napkin and placed them in one of the saddlebags.

"Oh," Leslie replied, eyeing them with a puzzled look. "You really want me to come along?"

"Sure. You've been practicing your riding on Rufus. It shouldn't be a problem for you to keep up."

"What? It's no problem for me," snapped Leslie.

Paula raised an eyebrow. Her patience had limits, too. She didn't see why she should let a teenager dig at her when she had just presented a great idea. On a positive note, Leslie no longer seemed to fear that she'd be chased off the ranch at the slightest misstep. Still. Enough was enough.

Leslie seemed to realize she had gone too far and hung her head. "I'm sorry. I'll be happy to come."

"Fine," Paula said in a calm tone, as if nothing had happened. "If you're sure you don't want anything to eat, you can change into riding clothes. Don't forget the long johns. It's still freezing out there."

Leslie stood up, but at the last second grabbed a cookie to go.

In the middle of the stairs, Leslie paused. "Who are you riding, anyway? Lucky's not even ready yet."

"I was thinking of Dolly," Paula teased.

"Dolly? She's way too small!" Leslie said indignantly. "Ha-ha. Very funny. Now tell me."

"I borrowed a horse from a friend. Blondie. A mare."

"I didn't even see her when I came home." With these words Leslie raced up the stairs.

It looked like Paula's secret weapon, the horse, was having an effect. Paula sighed as she filled a thermos flask with hot chocolate.

With ears pricked up, the horses trudged through the deep snow. Barns and Roo, the blue-heeler dogs, followed in the horses' hoofprints. Paula and Leslie rode in silence, drinking in the scenery of woods and snow with the Rocky Mountains in the background.

Halfway to the destination, Paula cleared her throat. She really hoped she didn't screw this up. Somehow she felt it was now or never. Either they managed to talk to each other or they were doomed to failure.

"Listen, I've been wanting to talk to you about something for a long time."

Leslie, sensing from Paula's tone that this was something serious, was immediately on guard. "Oh yeah?" she asked suspiciously.

"Talking is actually the wrong expression," Paula hurried to say when she noticed how the girl started to put up protective walls. "You've been here with me for almost half a year." She dared a quick sideways glance at Leslie.

The girl looked expressionless, staring straight ahead.

At least she wasn't galloping back to the ranch yet, Paula noted. "I'm glad you're here every day. But as I'm sure you've picked up, it's not so easy for you to stay here and go to school."

"You mean because of laws and stuff?" Her voice sounded very soft.

"Exactly," Paula confirmed. "But because I want you to be able to stay here forever, I've started talking to people at Child Protective Services."

"Why is that?" Leslie asked, horrified. "They'll take me away from here, I'm sure. Oh no." Tears ran down her cheeks.

Paula searched in her jacket pocket for a handkerchief. "Here. Take this and please, please, listen to what I have to say. You don't have to be afraid. I'll take care of you. Really. And for heaven's sake, stop crying. You'll freeze in a block of ice if you don't."

The last sentence got a watery smile from Leslie. Paula steered Blondie closer to Rufus and leaned over to give the girl a quick hug. "Keep smiling. There's nothing to cry about."

Leslie nodded bravely but said nothing.

"Right now, they don't know anything about you. But if I want to take in a foster kid, I have to be certified."

"You mean like taking an exam?" Leslie asked incredulously. That couldn't be right. All her previous foster parents would have failed completely.

"Yes, I have to take a test," Paula replied seriously. "And when I've done that, I'd like to make sure you can stay with me. As long as you want to. Assuming that's what you want, too."

Leslie's face worked with emotion. "But what if they take me back? To the last place? I couldn't stand it."

"Leslie," Paula said softly. "We make a decision we both like. Difficulties can be solved much better if we work together."

"You would really let me have a say in this?"

Paula nodded. "Of course. It's your life, after all. However, we have to abide by the law."

The girl, who had straightened up more and more in the saddle at Paula's words, collapsed again. "Then we don't have a chance. Why can't everything stay the way it is? I'll help more too, I promise. I'll do my homework. Study for all the exams."

It almost broke Paula's heart to listen to it. "Oh, Leslie. You're already doing all that."

That earned her a puzzled and somewhat guilty glance.

"You've been in a bad mood lately, but you know what? I still want you with me. For all I care, we could leave things the way they are. But unfortunately there are other people involved. For example, I can't expect the principal, Nadine, to break the laws over letting you go to school if you're not mine."

"Why not?"

"Look, if something happens to you, for example, during sports and you have to go to the hospital. Then the insurance company wants to know who has to pay for it. Your insurance or the school's insurance. If they find out you're not properly registered, we have a problem. But if I apply to be a foster parent now and make it official, we'll be okay. We won't have a problem."

Leslie's face looked like a thundercloud.

"Do you even want to stay here? Me being your foster family?"

Leslie didn't answer right away. Many thoughts seemed to flash through her mind. Finally, she turned to Paula and looked directly at her, "Only if you don't become like everyone else."

"Like what others? The other foster families?" Since the girl had told almost nothing about her past life, Paula could only guess. But now was not the time for prying questions. She simply stopped her horse, looked her in the eye, and told her the one thing she knew one hundred percent to be true. "Nothing changes for me. ID or not, you belong to me, to my family. To the horses, and to Roo and Barns. You're one of us now."

Roo and Barns picked that exact moment to jump around the horses yelping excitedly as if to say, "Let's go on!"

Leslie laughed. A loud, liberated laugh. "Yes! That's what I want!" she said.

"Race you to the tree!?" Paula challenged, and off they went. The young girl and the old horse. Two crazy dogs in tow.

CHAPTER NINE

Sam was on his way back to the luxury hotel where he and the team stayed while in Denver. He was supposed to change into dress clothes for a benefit gala that evening but he couldn't muster up any real enthusiasm. Images of Kat kept popping into in his head. That luxurious curly hair, her tall curvy figure. How was she doing with Bella or cleaning up after the puppies? Whew. He hadn't known small dogs could make such a mess. Raising puppies was a full-time job. And for some reason, he couldn't wait to get back to them and the whole zoo. He must have lost his mind, he realized, shaking his head in amusement. Despite this realization, he dialed a number on the cell phone.

"Hi, Sven," he greeted the Blizzard goalie. "Can you do me a favor?"

"Maybe," the goalie replied suspiciously. Sam was known for his pranks. That's why Sven became cautious about making immediate promises. "What's it about?"

"I really need some quiet. Can you cover for me tonight at this benefit gala?"

"What's the matter? Are you sick?"

"No." Sam replied, irritated.

"Usually you volunteer for these events the main thing is publicity, isn't it?"

Am I really that much of a fame junkie? Sam asked himself involuntarily. When he thought about it closely, the answer was yes. Not that he found anything wrong with that. He only had a certain amount of time to get the most out of being a professional hockey player, and he was doing it. Publicity was money and he needed to make it and save it wisely. Athletic careers were short. But he noticed his priorities shifting. Spending the evening with Kat and the dogs sounded a lot more enticing. Besides, he didn't want her to discover photos of him and Carla, his date, on the Internet tomorrow and draw the wrong conclusions. Kat would never understand that Carla was a front, a professional model set up to decorate his arm for the evening at a high-profile event. It was just business. Anyway, he had the feeling that Kat was looking for reasons why it could never work out between them. He didn't want to deliver a reason on a silver platter the first day he was away.

Sam gave an exasperated growl into the phone.

Sven, who was not exactly easily intimidated, barked back, "Don't get so upset. I'll do it. On one condition."

"And what would that be?" Sam shot back, not hiding his impatience.

"I want your date for tonight, too."

Sam chuckled. "Sure. I'll let Carla know. I'm sure she'll be happy to be seen with you tonight."

Carla was a friend of Tyler's who worked as a model when she wasn't at university. She was studying medicine and needed to pay for her studies. She had a lot of fun fueling the rumor mill with guesses about which Colorado Blizzard player she was dating. As far as Sam knew, she was just good friends with all of them. But then, the tabloids didn't need to know that. It was a win-win situation for everyone. Carla had better jobs in the modeling business if her name was always in the conversation, and the hockey players knew who to ask when they needed a good-looking date. Sure, none of the players lacked female companionship. But most brought complications. Carla didn't.

"Yes! Don't tell Carla anything, I'll just pick her up instead of you."

Sam put a thoughtful frown on his face. Carla certainly didn't care which of the players accompanied her. Unless... "Did something happen between you two?" he asked.

"I can't hear you. Bad connection." Sven hung up. Sam shook his head. His friend had just pulled the oldest trick since the invention of the cell phone. Then he shrugged. Sven and Carla could solve their own problems. His mouth twisted into a broad smile. He was free to go to his beautiful house in the mountains and surprise a certain dark-haired beauty.

Sam was disappointed to find Kat wasn't at home. Pat and Tyler were also out somewhere. But because Nelly was in the driveway he figured Kat was probably out for a walk. He kept going to the window to keep an eye out for her. It wasn't his usual style to dote on a woman. Especially a woman who, after the first kiss, had jumped at the chance to run away from him. Most women fell over their own feet trying to please him. Accordingly, his efforts were usually kept to a minimum. It looked like he was going to have to try a little harder this time.

Kat proved the accuracy of his assumption as she let herself in through the basement and came up the stairs. The jingling of collars told him Rocky and Bella were with her. Nikki left her puppies in their box to come out and say hello.

"What are you doing here?" Kat asked. "Don't you have a practice game tomorrow?"

Sam raised both eyebrows in surprise. "Is somebody following the Colorado Blizzard schedule?" he asked teasingly. Maybe things were simpler than he thought.

"Don't worry. I'm not turning into a hockey ho. Paula mentioned the game on the phone yesterday."

"I'm relieved," he replied dryly. "Back to your question about what I'm doing here. I live here."

"Right. I remembered that earlier, too, when I saw your car." She had the decency to blush.

"It's your home too," he replied, slightly irritated.

"Yeah, yeah," she waved it off. "You know what I mean."

Yes. Maybe. Something like that. As well as a man knew what a woman meant. He didn't always know that even with his sisters. And he had known them all his life.

"Did you miss me?" he ventured, teasing again.

"Why should I?" she answered. "You're the perfect roommate. Never around. I have my peace and quiet and don't always have to remember to bring fresh clothes to the bathroom before showering."

Ouch. Roommate. What was she trying to say? Imagining her walking around the house wrapped only in a towel didn't help clear the fog in his brain either. Worse, he knew what she looked like doing it. He swallowed.

Kat noticed it and suppressed a satisfied grin.

He could tell she was pleased to know that he liked her.

The puppies rushed into the room, diverting attention. Red and Green started playing tug-of-war with one of the puppy toys strewn about. They already had their pointy baby teeth and the damage they could do was considerable. Rocky took his uncle role very seriously and gave Pink her daily bath with his big slobbery tongue. The little girl squirmed but she stood no chance against his determination. Blue was a typical mama's kid and the mouse of the group.

"I'm so glad you're home," Kat said, a little self-consciously. "I was just getting ready to meet Jaz at the diner. Afternoon coffee and girl gossip. Do you mind being at home alone with the dogs?"

He was disappointed but swallowed his feelings so they wouldn't show. "Of course not. We're friends, after all." And then his voice dropped. "Although, I didn't know a kiss between friends could feel like that."

Kat lowered her eyes. "Which is why we shouldn't repeat it."

"That was a damn good kiss!"

She sighed and nodded. "Exactly. That's the problem. If I ever did it again I probably couldn't stick to my once-and-never rule."

What rule is this?"

"No hookups, no one-night connections in Independence. It's not that kind of place."

"None? Never?" He stared at her in disbelief.

"Sex yes, relationship no," she summarized.

"But that's contradictory. That's not what you just said!"

"This is a story for a dimly lit bar and alcoholic beverages. Plus, I think your reaction is pretty ironic. It's not like you're known for years of relationships."

He grinned. "You're right there again. So we can kiss anytime without danger."

"Excuse me?" She stared at him while the butterflies in her stomach cheered.

He shrugged his shoulders and picked up a puppy off the floor. "I'm obviously incapable of relationships. You jumped to that conclusion the minute you met me, right? Therefore I'm completely harmless to you."

She blinked as wheels turned in her head.

"Think about it," he said with a wink. Walking past, he leaned in. His breath slid over the tender skin on her neck. "I can assure you, it's more fun not to be 'just friends.' It's called 'friends with benefits' for a reason."

She gritted her teeth, determined not to let on what effect his words had on her. She let him exit the room. "We can do dinner if you want," she called out casually.

"Bring us home something from the diner," he called back. "You can pay this time."

Driving to the diner to meet Jaz, the cell phone blipped. Kat looked at the screen. Her mother was calling from Poland! She pulled over to the side of the road to take the call. Her mother rarely called, since it was so much cheaper to place calls from the States and not the other way around. This must be important.

Kat put on a cheery voice. "Mom! You're coming to visit? How nice to hear from you."

"I don't have long, *luby*. But I might be thinking of a trip." She broke off and Kat thought she could hear a muffled sob.

"Are things bad again, Mom? What's going on?"

"Not so bad. Not yet. But I'm afraid."

"Just pack your suitcase and go to the airport. There you show your passport and get the ticket. You can be here in a day or two."

"Be quiet, you know it can't be done. Your father would never let me. But I just wanted to hear your voice. I love you so much."

"You don't have to tell him," Kat urged her mother. "Leave before he gets home."

"What if I come back? What then?" her mother asked anxiously.

Kat bit her lower lip. *Then stay forever*, she wanted to answer. But that would only have shocked her mother even more.

"I have to go, Kathrina," her mother whispered into the phone. The connection cut off.

Why didn't her mother see that she was better off without this tyrant of a husband? Kat just didn't understand. She could rent the both of them a nice apartment as soon as things resolved here in Independence. Kat could afford to pay for her mother's living expenses. She wouldn't have to fear her volatile husband anymore, and she wouldn't have to work. It sounded like she might be ready to make a move. All the more reason for Kat to get a move on with the other problems at hand.

She checked her cell phone for the time and realized she was early. Jaz would still be at the studio. Good, then she could drop by and whisk her away on time. Jaz sometimes had a tough time pulling herself away from yoga students.

Kat reached the studio, opened the door and entered. Two people working at the far end of the space turned around.

"Kat!" they both called out. It was Pat and Tyler, working on the main floor while Jaz taught yoga upstairs.

"Hi you guys, what's up?"

"I was just explaining a punching technique to Tyler," Pat explained. As he walked toward her Kat saw they stood in front of a red punching bag hanging from the ceiling.

"I see that," she grinned. "It reminds me of when you used to give Jaz and me self-defense lessons. I'm no stranger to that bag."

"What are you doing here?" Tyler asked. She had worked up a sheen of moisture on her forehead and her blonde hair was pulled out of its bun in a few places. She looked happy.

"I'm here to meet Jaz. We're going to catch up over coffee at the diner."

"Carry on!" Pat said. "We'll see you at home."

Kat waved cheerily to the two and hurried up the stairs. Halfway up, she paused. From here she could see the whole room through the banister. She was lucky. The class seemed to be coming to an end.

She waited patiently until the relaxation phase at the end of the lesson was complete. Then she climbed the last steps and greeted Jaz.

"Hey there!"

"Hey there, yourself," Jaz answered, nodding and waving at departing students.

"I'm so excited to have a girl talk with you, an adult conversation. At my house the youngsters have taken over."

"Even though they can't talk, huh?"

"I swear they grow a bit every time I turn my back on them."

Jaz bent down to pick up two forgotten yoga mats. She passed one of them to Kat.

"Would you mind rolling those up for me, please? We can get out of here faster. Maybe Tyler and Pat will join us, too."

"Right. Want me to let them know downstairs?"

"Please. Then I'll finish cleaning up here and be down."

After informing Pat and Tyler to her delight, both agreed to come she stepped out of the building. No sooner had she passed the large window on the first floor than a hand reached out and yanked her by the arm around to the side of the building.

"Are you crazy?" she said. "This is assault!"

"I just want to talk to you," a man said in a rough voice.

The man with the red pickup truck. He smelled of tobacco and leather, and tequila, probably from last night.

He stood very close, so close she was pinned against the wall even though he wasn't touching her. He leaned even closer, making the hairs on the back of her neck stand up.

"I have a message for you."

Her frightened eyes searched his face.

"Don't play detective. It's not the game for a newcomer like you."

To make his words clear, he pressed side of his hip against her so she could feel the steel of a concealed gun.

She swallowed hard. She hardly dared to breathe. Her brain raced to remember directions from self-defense courses but her brain seemed frozen. Scream, she should scream.

"Got it?" he said.

Kat, too scared to nod, just widened her eyes in panic, hoping it would be enough.

"We wouldn't want you to suffer the same fate as those mutts in the woods." He pushed her away and she stumbled into the street.

"We're ready," Pat called. He was just exiting the door of the yoga studio. "What happened, did you trip?"

Kat regained her footing. The man was gone.

"Clumsy me," she lied. And even as she lied it made her feel like her mother. Covering for a man. But because she hadn't thought it through, it felt safer to stay mute. She didn't want Pat to take a bullet if he gave chase. So she didn't say anything.

When arrived at the diner, Miss Minnie rushed up with her apron swishing from the effort. "The gang's all here! What a happy surprise."

Kat watched as Jaz got lost in a Minnie-hug that placed her in the depths of Miss Minnie's expansive bosom. She'd be lucky to still get air. But the hug must have felt comfortingly good. Suddenly, Kat missed her mother like she hadn't in a long time. She blinked to prevent her eyes from overflowing. Crying was not on the agenda.

Minnie let Jaz go and turned to hug Kat. But first, she caught the expression on her face. "What's wrong?" she said. And in a split second she jumped to a conclusion. "Are you crying about what's going to happen to those puppies your dog is carrying?" Not waiting for an answer, she continued, "Don't worry, sweetie, you'll find good homes for them in this town." She smiled encouragingly. "Now come on to a table and get something good to eat."

While they were waiting for the food to come, the trio of Jaz, Tyler, and Pat talked yoga and houses. Kat's eyes went around the room. She spied Scrooge on a swivel stool at the counter. "Excuse me," she said.

The others barely noticed her leave. As she walked up, Scrooge seemed to be meditating over a glass of beer. But when she got close, without lifting his head, he said, "I hear you have my cat."

"Jinx?" she asked in surprise.

"Is that her name now?"

"Yes." Kat grew flustered. "How did you know?"

"I know everything that happens in the woods, remember?"

"She came to us. I'll be happy to bring her over," Kat said, trying to back pedal.

The old man waved it off. "That's alright. Don't get flustered. It doesn't matter to me what her name is. I don't want her back either."

"No? Are you sure?"

He studied her. "Why should I? She's found herself a new home. I have to respect that."

Oh. Well. That was one way to look at it. She didn't even think that attitude was wrong. "Should I just keep her?"

Scrooge nodded. "I think so. If that's alright with you."

"Sure it's fine with me. Would you like to visit her sometime?" Not that she desperately wanted this old drunk to visit her at home. But she had to offer it to him.

"She visits me whenever she wants. Seems you don't know cats."

"Well, I—"

"And what happened to you, anyway? You seem—he searched for a word—perturbed."

This was her chance to confide in someone who knew the reality around here. It was now or never. "The guy from the farm knew I went out there to look around. He just threatened me behind the yoga studio."

"What did he say?"

"He told me not to play detective. That's how I knew he'd spotted me."

"He's probably right. What were you trying to do? We have a very good sheriff in this town, you know."

"And if the law goes out there and asks questions, it will tip those guys off. All the animals they have now will disappear and they'll move on someplace else."

"I see. It's a good solution for Independence but a bad one for the animals."

"That's it exactly."

"Those guys should be stopped but you can't put yourself in danger. No more going it alone, understand? Who else is going to take care of Jinx when you're gone?"

"I can take care of myself," she protested.

"Don't be stupid," he replied bluntly. He ran the back of his hand over his mouth. A bit of spit stuck to the lapel of his stained jacket.

She slumped a little and exhaled. "I know. Believe me, I realized that in the last hour."

"Promise me you'll get help?" The answer seemed important to him. He even put down his beer glass.

"Yes. I promise."

"Good girl," he replied, lifting his glass again and draining it in one go. "Then I'll also tell you that once a month they bring in a limo full of sex-for-pay gals, and guys with party drugs from Denver and have a high old time. It's usually on the last Saturday of every month. That's the time to snoop around, when they're busy. With the right support, you can dig up a real rat's nest."

Somehow Kat felt that this story was getting bigger and more unpredictable. She stood up. "Thanks for the info. I'll keep you posted."

He waved it off. "No need. I'll find out the same way. The fewer people who see us talking together, the better."

She returned to the table with a fake smile pasted on to cover her anxiety. Plates of meringue pie had just arrived so nobody noticed.

After eating, Jaz leaned back in the chair and patted her stomach. "Whew. I'm glad I don't live right next door to this place. Otherwise, I wouldn't be able to fit through the front door in no time."

Kat snorted. "Like you'd ever have to worry about that. The fact that you're not already half chocolate is a miracle."

Jaz grinned. "Chocolate doesn't have calories. At least mine doesn't."

Miss Minnie stopped by with the check.

"I'm supposed to bring dinner home for Sam," Kat said. "What's the special today?"

"Pot roast, potatoes, and carrots," Minnie answered, "He will love it." She leaned toward Kat conspiratorially, "Say, how are things with you and Sam anyway?"

Kat's ears grew hot. "What do you mean with me and Sam?" she asked a bit dumbly.

"Well, you know," Miss Minnie said, rolling her eyes meaningfully. "Because I've got my money set on next week."

"Next week for what?"

Miss Minnie laughed so hard her double chin quivered. Ignoring the question she continued, lowering her voice a little. "And it would make me very happy if I won again. Mr. Wilkinson has been ahead in the last three bets." She patted Kat's arm again. "If you could arrange to not fall into bed with Sam until next week, I'd appreciate it." With those words and a wink, she turned and disappeared through the swinging doors to the kitchen.

When Kat parked Nelly in front of the house an hour later, she discovered she was actually hungry for the takeout Minnie had sent with her. She'd missed out on the goodies that came while she was talking to Scrooge and had barely touched her lemon meringue pie. Exhausted from the events of the last few hours, she didn't quite know whether she was happy to see Sam or not. Mostly she was looking forward to a hot bath with a glass of wine.

First, she had to take care of the dogs. Walking in the front, instead of expected chaos, she found heavenly peace. The puppies were lying in a heap on the area rug under the enormous coffee table, sleeping. Nikki was lying next them with her eyes closed as well. The floor looked clean. Sam was sitting on the sofa with a laptop on his knees. Very domestic, the whole scene. He looked up as she stepped into the living room, smiling so broadly that she couldn't help but smile back.

"Hello."

"Hi. How are things going?"

"The little rascals behaved themselves. And you? How was the girl talk?"

Embarrassed, she ducked away under his gaze. "It kind of extended to Pat and Tyler." She felt guilty not including him. "But I brought dinner so I hope that makes up for it." She looked around the room again in wonder. "Thanks for cleaning up. It looks like elves got in here on an afternoon assignment."

"It wasn't a big deal. I took the adult dogs out. Only briefly, though. I didn't know if the puppies were allowed out yet."

"That's great. Then I don't have to do that anymore. Thanks." She frowned. "Say, where have you been hiding Bella, anyway?"

He grinned and pointed to the other end of the sofa. There, the mongrel had curled up into a little ball and was almost invisible next to the dark cushion. "I was amazed when she jumped onto the sofa. I haven't dared to move since."

Kat crouched down. Then she called out, "Bella, come here." The mongrel dog raised her head and literally flew into Kat's outstretched arms.

The humans shared a soft chuckle.

"Are you hungry yet?" Sam asked.

"I will be after I clean up. Mind if I take a few minutes? I'll put the takeout in the oven just to keep warm."

"I can do that. You go."

The bathtub beckoned and the wine was already calling her name. "That sounds wonderful." With those words, she walked over to the bar, poured herself a glass of red wine from an open bottle, and disappeared with it.

When Kat came down an hour later, Sam noticed her face had more color. She was wearing fleece pants, warm woolen socks, and a sweatshirt. But wasn't that his sweatshirt?

Noting his questioning look, she blushed. "You're right. It's yours. You left it before you went to Denver and I needed something warmer. Do you forgive me?"

She enchanted him again, looking so soft and vulnerable. Knowing that there was so much courage and strength behind that beautiful facade only increased his respect and affection for her. That was the limit. He put the laptop aside and went to her with long strides. He didn't kiss her, just pressed her head against his chest. For a moment she felt tense in his arms. Then she accepted his embrace and relaxed. For while they remained standing like that. Only when Rocky nosed between them did they laughingly let go of each other.

"Someone's jealous, I guess." Sam bent down and nuzzled the dog.

"Poor guy. No one ever strokes him," Kat remarked sarcastically and affectionately at the same time.

"I know. He's been telling me that all along," he joked.

Kat looked down at the two of them. Sam's strawberry blonde hair went with Rocky's reddish fur perfectly. Sam kept surprising her. It felt like her heart didn't stand a chance. While that realization still stirred the old familiar panic in her, she realized with surprise that she felt something else. Hope was rising. And instead of efficiently stifling it before it could grow, she let herself go with the feeling. Maybe she should just wait and see which feeling would win in the end. The incident today made her realize that life was too short to always play it safe.

Sam raised his head and met her gaze. He noticed she wasn't retreating from him, like before. On the contrary.

Her gaze was open and curious. He hadn't been sure if his embrace would be welcome, but he wasn't able to hold back.

Looking at her, he wanted to start planning their life together right then and there. Kind of crazy. But he had never been so sure about a woman before. It seemed like he had just been marking time waiting for her. Had she come to the same conclusion? Judging by her look, something decisive had changed today. He had no illusions that it was a 180-degree turn right away. But it was a beginning.

They spent the evening with a foreign film *Pretty Best Friends* about an unusual friendship that developed between a millionaire and a recently released felon who needed a job. Sam found he had to laugh so much in places that he almost couldn't stop.

"I told you it was a good movie." Kat grinned mischievously and leaned against his shoulder.

"True. Most of the foreign films I've seen so far have been dark affairs with confusing plots. And then there are those subtitles."

"You can't read them?" she asked incredulously.

He dropped his head against the back of the couch. "Life is so much easier when people think you're stupid."

"I'm sure it is. But you can't fool me. Good night." Then she stunned him by leaning over and kissing him briefly, but firmly, on the mouth. "It wasn't an accident this time," she whispered in his ear.

Before he recovered from surprise, she stroked the dog's backs one last time, and disappeared.

Sighing, Sam sat up. Women really were a mystery.

Kat sat on her bed, far too excited by her own courage to sleep. When she wasn't thinking about the incident with Mr. Pickup, and the dog breeding going on at the farm, her thoughts were circling around Sam. When she got her thoughts in order and realized that there wasn't much she could do until that big party happened at the farm, she reached for her e-reader. A good book would take her to another world. Only after she knew that the good guys would actually win against the bad guys did her eyes finally fall closed.

CHAPTER TEN

THE PEACEFUL MOOD did not last long. Full of trust and good feelings for Sam, Kat got up early and made eggs, toast, and coffee. Sam was up, too. He had to get back to Denver. Things were going so well that Kat decided to tell him what happened yesterday with Mr. Pickup, her name for the driver of the red truck. She expected Sam's support. Unfortunately, he didn't see between the lines like Scrooge did. Sam had very clear ideas about what she had to do. He stormed out of the kitchen for a bit and when he came back, he held a note under her nose.

"What's that?" she asked, frowning. Without looking at the list closely, she went to the coffee machine and filled it with fresh water, as they had already drained the first pot.

"I drafted a checklist for you." He held out the piece of paper to her again.

"A checklist?" she asked incredulously.

"Yeah, you know, go to the police station, make a statement, don't go out on your own anymore, and definitely don't play detective."

She looked at him keenly. Many words tumbled through her head including ones her mother would not allow. Finally, she just said, "Coffee. I need more coffee before I argue with you."

"What's there to argue about?"

"Because you're organizing my life right now. Emphasis on MY!"

He gave her a foul look. "What does it matter? You're in danger, so we have to find a solution."

"Wrong," she replied. Her voice was frostier than a January night in the Rockies. "I have to find a solution. Not us." She tilted her head and looked at him questioningly. "I'm sorry if my kiss last night somehow gave the wrong impression that you should take charge from now on."

"That has nothing to do with it," he insisted.

"Oh no?" It was clear from her face that she didn't believe the two things were unrelated. "Seems to me you think I'm a weak woman desperately in need of a knight to sort things out."

"Yesterday, you were glad Pat showed up, weren't you?"

Her eyes flashed as she approached him. "Of course. Which is why I'm going to be more careful in the future and take necessary steps to make sure this doesn't happen again. But for that, I don't need a list someone else made for me." With the last words, she vehemently poked her index finger into his chest to give her words more emphasis.

Now he seemed completely confused. To add icing on the cake, Nikki and the puppies made an entrance.

Kat threw her hands in the air. "Pah. I'm just wasting my time here! Go boss someone else!" Kat turned on her heel and walked out.

Sam looked after her. Even her back seemed to be seething. She wasn't the only one boiling with anger. He would strangle that guy, Mr. Pickup, with his bare hands if he caught him. Loud cursing and a few frustrated kicks at the kitchen chairs made him feel better. He only stopped when he saw Bella trying to squeeze under the breakfast bar out of sheer terror.

He scratched his head. Why was Kat so stubborn? He only wanted to help. She was an outsider, didn't half know the trouble she could get herself into. He felt anger building up inside and decided to use the energy for something practical. He grabbed a bucket and rag, and began cleaning up the pups' messes. Within minutes, Red and Blue had him engaged in a game that involved the rag and his pant legs. "Knock it off, you guys. I have to get out of here," he scolded them kindly. Bella watched with interest from a safe distance. Rocky had followed Kat and was gone.

Finished with his task, Sam put the cleaning utensils back under the sink and dried his hands. The work had distracted him a little, but when his gaze fell on the list again, he noticed how the anger returned. Not wanting to get into another fight with Kat right away, he decided to go for a jog. He still had time and it would work off some frustration. There had been virtually no snow in the last few days. The daily dog walks meant the paths in the immediate vicinity of the house were well-trodden enough that this was possible.

As Sam went through the house to his room, he stopped in front of Kat's door. After a moment's hesitation, he knocked.

"What?" she said tersely, from inside.

O-o. She still sounded like she was about to rip his head off. No matter. He had very similar feelings.

"I'm going for a run. Because of the snow I won't be very fast. What dogs should I take with me?" He was eager to take Bella with him but wasn't sure if she was up to the effort.

Kat yanked open the door and stared at him in disbelief.

Now it was Sam who let out an irritated "What?"

"Rocky. He's happy."

"Okay. Well then. See you later," he replied curtly.

Kat looked confused. "Why are you doing this?"

"Going for a run? Now you're the one micromanaging ME."

"No. I mean, we just had a fight. Now you're taking care of the dogs." She searched for the right words. "You're not responsible for them, and we just had words."

"What does one have to do with the other? The dogs have to go out, don't they?"

"Yessss." Her voice trailed off. She had no experience with arguments in a relationship. Not that she thought they were in a relationship. Absolutely not. But in her childhood home disagreements had only ever resulted in her father trying to beat his opinions into her mother. She'd learned to avoid arguments whenever possible, even if it meant fitting in. Or, like a cornered dog, she would bite immediately if she feared someone was getting too close. Because she didn't know anything else to say she settled for, "In that case, I'd be happy if you took Rocky with you. I'll take care of the rest."

"Good," he replied curtly and disappeared into his room.

This last sentence was enough to drive Kat crazy again. Why did he have to go and ruin the good impression with just a few words? She couldn't decide whether the man was a dominant asshole or a good friend. Men! She went to her door and jerked it open. "I have a plan, you know," she called down the empty hallway.

All she heard was the front door slam as he exited the house. Kat took stock of her situation. What she needed to bring this whole thing to a close and set Sam's mind at ease was proof of what was going on at the farm. Then she could take that proof to Jake and get him take action, not just give a warning. And to get proof Kat know what she had to do. She needed to go *undercover.*

On one of her outings to town she'd seen a thrift store. It was time to pay a visit.

Jaz dismissed the last student. The yoga studio was doing better every day, ahead of projections. Most of her classes were full and she still had people interested in starting new ones. Mornings, especially, were going well. She'd hit the mark with her class for mothers, where moms could bring their children. More than one of the mostly young women had come up to her and expressed their gratitude. It warmed her heart every time she realized that she could do something meaningful for the community here.

Jaz had received so much support in the time after the violence of last summer with her ex-boyfriend, that it was nice to be able to give something back. Sure, she was making a living doing it, too. But she intentionally made the lessons for mother and child cheaper than the others. For one thing, the extra noise the children made meant there was never the same soothing quiet as in the other lessons. For another, she knew all too well that young moms often didn't have much money to spend.

She glanced at the clock on the wall. It was just before noon. She had a few hours off and would have time to surprise Jake at the station and invite him to lunch. Humming a song to herself, she tidied up the last of the yoga mats and pushed paperwork into a neat pile on her small reception desk. She could always do the rest later, when she got back.

"Rambo?" she called.

Her poodle was with her in no time, looking expectant. Lunchtime was his favorite part of the day. It promised a walk and plenty of attention from people they met. The sheriff's station was a little way off the main street but it was a good day for a walk.

They were across the street from the station and about to walk onto the property when a woman stepped out of the building. Jake was close behind her. Jaz waved, but Jake didn't see her. A closer look revealed there was no wonder he was following that woman out. She was an impressive figure in large sunglasses, a big fake-fur hat, high-heeled boots, tight pants and a leather bustier under her jacket that gave a generous view of ample cleavage. *A biker chick?* Jaz thought. *And didn't she know the temperature was just above freezing?* The woman laughed at something Jake said and threw him a kiss with her hand. He smiled warmly and gave a wave. She must have parked on the other side of the building because she headed around the side. Jake looked after her. Jaz felt hot jealousy course through her veins. Was Jake admiring that rear view?

With a lump in her throat Jaz didn't know what to think. Sure, the interaction between the two looked quite harmless. Except Jaz thought she knew most of Jake's friends. Why hadn't he told her about this chick? Was this one of his many ex-girlfriends? In any case, Jaz lost the desire to have lunch with him. Abruptly she turned around and walked back towards town. Rambo reluctantly followed the pressure of the leash.

Jaz pulled out her cell phone and pondered which of her friends she should call. Female support was needed. She decided to call Kat. Unfortunately, she did not pick up her phone. Paula? After all, this was about her brother. On the other hand, maybe Paula knew who the beautiful stranger was. Indecisively, Jaz bit her lower lip. Rambo, meanwhile, picked up a branch off the ground. He nudged her with it. Then he took a step back and waited. They were in an open space and it was safe to let him off the leash. She took the stick and let it fly. Rambo darted after it with ears flying and tongue hanging out.

At least one of them was happy.

"Paula! What did I do that was so wrong?" Sam said with frustration into the phone. He was just driving into the outskirts of Denver. "Do you have any idea what was so bad about my list?"

"Sam, now be honest. What do you think would have happened if you had told me point by point what to do first thing in the morning?"

Silence on the other end of the phone line.

"That's not what's at issue here, Paula!"

"Yes, it is. Because it's the answer to your question."

"You mean she would have taken it better if I had waited until noon?"

"Really now," Paula reprimanded him, "You grew up with two sisters! What did that teach you?"

"That you always do the exact opposite of what you're told?"

Paula rolled her eyes. "I was thinking more about the fact that we women also like to make our own decisions and are quite excellent at it. We're not in the Middle Ages here."

Sam muttered something that sounded suspiciously like "too bad."

Paula laughed. It did her successful brother a world of good when a woman he was interested in didn't roll over on her back as soon as he made a peep. She was looking out the window when she heard the roar of an engine. Nelly was chugging up the driveway.

"She said she had a plan," Sam continued. He sounded annoyed and worried. "Not that she shared it with me."

At that moment Kat stepped out of the Vanagon. At least Paula assumed it was Kat, because she couldn't really recognize the woman. But the musical "hi" gave her away.

Paula snorted into the phone with Sam still on the line. "You can say that again—she has a plan. And what a plan it is."

"What do you know about it?"

"Nothing. Listen, I have to go. A little tip on the side: questions and subtle suggestions go down much better than ready-made to-do lists."

"But..."

Paula hung up. Otherwise she would certainly have given herself away. And that probably wouldn't have been what Kat needed. With a crazy smile Paula yanked open the door. "Rocker girl? The way you look, you could make me look for my dream girl and forget about the dream man."

Kat grinned broadly. "Hot, isn't it? Jake got quite the eyeful when I showed up at the police station like this."

"What were you doing at the station?"

"I wanted to see if my undercover look fooled him. I posed as a Polish tourist with the full accent and everything. He never caught on."

"And you did this *why?*"

"To know if I could fool the guys at the farm. Mr. Pickup knows me by sight. And I need to infiltrate a party. They have them once a month and one's coming up."

"And you're really going to go through with this now? Despite the warning yesterday?" At that moment, Paula could understand Sam's concern.

"Sure. Now more than ever! I'm going to get the proof I need to give to Jake."

"You're sure no one will recognize you?"

"I'm sure. You recognized me because you know Nelly."

"What are you going to drive in?"

"Can I borrow your truck again?"

"No. You might be recognized."

Kat's face fell. "I'm going to need help with this, aren't I?"

Paula saw this as an opportunity to change the subject. "How are things going with Sam?" she asked innocently.

"He's back in Denver now but he came home yesterday afternoon unexpectedly. He's a big help with the dogs, he's doing great."

"So living with my brother is going smoothly?"

Kat screwed up her face. "Smooth might be a bit of an exaggeration. Just this morning he delighted me and then drove me insane right after. You know what he made? A list. Brushing my teeth and breathing weren't on the list for me to do. Probably an oversight on his part."

Paula secretly wished her brother good luck and suppressed a grin. He was going to need it. There was no way he would approve if he knew Kat was planning to mingle with the farm guys and their guests dressed like that, as casual as he was about most other things.

"Has Sam seen your disguise yet?"

"No. And he won't. I'm sure he'll object to a hundred things again if he does."

"He probably meant well." Paula thought Sam hadn't been very clever when he presented his list to Kat. But she also knew he was genuinely concerned and wanted to help. While she was perfectly capable of recognizing her brother's faults, she wouldn't trash him with Kat. "You have to understand that he's a very successful hockey player. Team captain. He's used to tackling and solving problems."

Inside, the phone rang. "Come on in," Paula said, inviting her into the house with a wave of her hand.

With swinging hips, Kat strutted past her into the kitchen and leaned against the counter.

Paula reached for the phone and took the call while gesturing for Kat to grab something to drink.

"Paula, you won't believe what happened!" Jaz was on the other end of the line. She was almost crying.

"Jaz, what's going on? Kat's here right now, by the way. I'll put the phone on speaker so she can listen in, okay?"

When Kat heard her Jaz's voice she raised her eyebrows in alarm.

"It's Jake!" Jaz sobbed.

"What about Jake? Go ahead and tell."

"I saw him with another woman today." Noisily, Jaz blew her nose.

"No! In what way was he with another woman?"

"Flirting at the station. You should have seen her. I'm telling you, a dream girl!" She sobbed again. "And they were very intimate with each other."

A thought occurred to Paula. She covered the mouthpiece on the receiver and whispered to Kat, "Were you with Jake before noon today?"

"Yeah, why?"

Paula waved it off and turned her attention back to Jaz. "What did this beautiful woman look like?"

"She wore great boots, a bustier that should be banned." Jaz had to stop talking to blow her nose again.

Paula's eyes traced the clothing on Kat's body, nodding off each item. "A fake-fur hat and sunglasses?"

"Exactly," Jaz cried. After more blubbering there was silence on the line. Then Jaz asked suspiciously, "Do you have an idea who that was?"

"I do," Paula said, stifling a laugh. "In fact, she's right here."

"What?" Jaz asked feverishly. "Kat? Was that you?"

"I'm working on an undercover outfit and wanted to see if it would fool Jake."

Kat and Paula both laughed out loud. Finally, Jaz joined in. "I take it you weren't there to steal my man," she said when she had calmed down.

"No. Definitely not. The one at my house gives me enough headaches. One is quite enough."

"What's this all about?"

"I can't tell you yet."

"I completely overreacted," Jaz let out.

"A little bit," the two women answered in unison. Then Paula continued, "Please don't take offense at this now. But buy yourself a pregnancy test in the next few days."

"Tell me, are you crazy?" Jaz said in disbelief. "Is everyone going crazy now?

"Think about it. It's not at all like you to freak out like that just because Jake is talking to an attractive woman. Something must have caused that behavior."

"And you're guessing hormones?"

"If it isn't, it's very easy to rule it out," Paula replied, unusually diplomatic.

"I still think you've just inseminated too many cows without seeing any action yourself again."

"Just get tested. Okay?"

"Okay. And send me a picture of Kat. I want to see this outfit with my own eyes."

A little later, Kat drove home with mixed feelings. She didn't feel like arguing with Sam. She wanted to enjoy time with him when he was home. Maybe they could call a truce? Wisely, she had changed clothes at Paula's. Her face was without makeup, her hair tied back in a practical ponytail, and she was wearing jeans and a T-shirt again. Just her everyday clothes.

Pat watched with Pink in his arms as Nelly turned into the driveway. Behind him, Rocky burst into a welcome howl. Even Bella stood up and sat down with a happy expression by the door.

"Hey," he said kindly as she came in the entry.

"Hey yourself," she replied with a smile. "Where's Tyler."

"She's here. Up talking to Mr. Wilkinson. It'll probably be a long conversation," he joked. Mr. Wilkinson was not known for being short on words.

Kat cell phone blipped. She looked at the screen. She frowned. "It's Sam. FaceTiming me," she said.

"Go and take it," Pat said agreeably.

Kat accepted the call and walked quickly to her room, Rocky and Bella trotting behind.

"Hi Sam," she said pleasantly.

"About that list." On-screen, Sam's throat moved as he swallowed. "I'm sorry. I didn't mean to squash your plans like a steamroller."

Kat sat on the edge of the bed. "It's okay. It annoyed me, but I can understand why you did it. It could have been the same for me."

"Really?" he asked, surprised.

"Yes. I would have said it a little different, though," she said pointedly.

Sam looked to one side. "Women have more talent for that, I guess." He wiggled his eyebrows at the last word and shifted in his seat. Kat noticed the move flexed his pecs which were clearly visible under his faded long-sleeved shirt.

She quickly averted her eyes and swallowed. "That's ancient history, then. We don't need to talk about it anymore."

"Wait," Sam said quickly as if she might hang up. "Come out to Denver for dinner this evening."

"What?"

"It's only an hour's drive give or take. Let's go out on the town."

"But I have nothing to wear."

"Borrow something from Tyler. She's got some Vegas stuff with her somewhere, I'm sure."

"We're not exactly the same size."

Sam waved the protest away. "Please?"

"Where are you? I don't know Denver."

"You don't need to. I'll send a car. Have dinner with me."

She stared into the phone. "Dinner with me? Like on a date? After I just told you we're not going to work out?"

He shrugged his shoulders nonchalantly. "It's no big deal. You have to eat anyway. We might as well do it together."

She didn't know whether to be annoyed or flattered.

"Things might be different without a hundred dogs to distract us," he continued. "We might learn something about each other we didn't already know."

That was exactly what Kat feared. On the other hand, his invitation sounded very tempting. What harm could it do? "Alright, then. But just dinner. That's it. And no telling anybody, either. I don't feel like adding to the local Independence betting pool and rumor mill."

She could tell he was letting his gaze glide over her body. It made her feel hot.

"And you're sure you want to make rules this early in the evening? Maybe you'll think differently in a few hours."

She stopped short. There it was again. That pure arrogance. "Don't talk like that. Otherwise I'll stay home."

He bit back a laugh. "Just don't. I'll call Tyler and ask if she'll feed the dogs and care for them as a favor to me."

"In addition to letting me wear her clothes?"

"I can have a car there in an hour. Can you be ready?"

"I guess so."

Tyler was only too thrilled to help with the wardrobe dilemma. It was decided that Kat could wear a slim black top over black tights with her high-heeled books and a sparkly jacket over top with sequins. The jacket had a swirling multicolored design. It would fit so long as she left it unbuttoned, and it looked better that way.

Kat left her hair long and curly, "big" hair in the western style, and accepted an attractive makeup job from Tyler.

"You should do this more often," Tyler quipped.

"You think it would look good in my dog-grooming van?" Kat replied.

"You know what I mean," Tyler said, not letting her off the hook.

Outside, the setting sun bathed the mountain peaks in pink light before it faded and dusk took hold. An hour later a stretch limousine arrived outside. Tyler, Pat, Mr. Wilkinson and the dogs all gathered to see her off. Even Jinx appeared for the occasion.

"Bye! Have fun!" said Pat and Tyler.

"Don't do anything I wouldn't do," hollered Mr. Wilkinson. "What happens in Denver doesn't stay in Denver!"

Kat entered the luxurious leather back seat of the limo. The driver smiled at her in his rearview mirror and she realized with a start that she didn't know where they were going. He saw her reaction and said, "Don't worry ma'am, we're headed to the Hotel Clio."

"You know where that is?" she said uncertainly.

"It's in Cherry Creek North."

Her face went blank.

"I think you'll like it there," he said with a smile.

Kat smiled back and settled into the plush leather seat. They drove up the interstate which led into the mountains in great curves. This evening was going to be interesting.

The driver called Sam to let them know he was five minutes away. Sam hurried to the lobby to greet Kat. No way was he going to let her wander the hipster halls of the Hotel Clio unescorted with the entire Blizzard hockey team running loose.

He watched as the driver hopped out, ran around the limo, and opened Kat's door. When her shapely leg dropped out first, wearing a black, high-heeled boot, he felt his head nodding in approval as though it had a will of its own. Sam strode past the doorman and signaled to the driver, "Wait a minute." He held out his hand and helped her out. A slight breeze ruffled her curled hair and the light caught the sequins of her jacket, making one spectacular entrance.

Kat's eyes looked huge and bright the way Tyler had made them up. She scanned the lobby, taking everything in. Even though they were still outside, the hotel's huge glass doors gave a perfect view of the graciously appointed foyer. Most striking was the marble floor in white and dark grays that gave the impression of a flowing river. It contrasted with earth tones of designer chairs, sofas, and oak furniture. Subtle gold accents caught the eye here and there.

"Wow," Kat said softly.

"Wow yourself," Sam replied. He could hardly take his eyes off of her. "You can have a welcome cocktail," he added. "That's what they do at this hotel. But maybe you'd rather go see the town first?"

Kat looked at him with wide eyes sparkling. This was such a contrast to Independence, she could hardly get over it. Frankly, almost nothing looked this smart and new in Seattle. "Whatever you think," she said.

"Let's go then," Sam said.

Kat gave a last look at the colorful artwork gracing the walls under the hotel lobby's vaulted ceiling and got back in the car.

The minute they entered the club called Temple Denver, Sam felt uncertain about his choice. First of all, too many eyes were swiveling to look at Kathrina. It made him uncomfortable. When he was alone with the guys, the place seemed the ultimate in cool. Lit in ice blue and pink, the walls soared upward dozens of yards, showcasing a gigantic screen flashing images to a pulsating soundtrack. A VIP concierge led them to a balcony table overlooking the dance floor with a bird's-eye view of all the action. But Kat's expression was stunned, not impressed. Even more so when a cocktail waitress wearing a slip of a dress in silver satin welcomed Sam by name and purred, "What are you drinking tonight, Mister Carter?" The way she said it sounded like an instant invitation to bed.

"You know what? I changed my mind," Sam said. He threw a hundred dollar bill on the table and stood up. "This was a mistake," he said to Kat. "I know where we should go."

The concierge hurried over. "Is something wrong?" he asked. "What can I do to serve you?"

"Nothing," Sam answered. "I just got an emergency business call is all. We'll be back again, and thank you very much."

The concierge smiled, relieved, and escorted them out. The limo driver was waiting as they emerged from the club. He opened the back door so Kat could slide in and Sam jumped in the other side.

"Take us to the Blue Island," he directed. To Kat he said, "Do you feel like seafood?"

"In the Rocky Mountains?" she said incredulously.

"Yes, it's right here. The restaurant has their own seafood farm on the east coast. They raise their own and fly it in fresh."

"Sure," she said enthusiastically.

The restaurant was elegant but relaxed. The music was sophisticated and playing at just the right volume. Sam could see that Kat was comfortable here. He watched as her eyes roved over the natural-wood paddles arranged on the ceiling, the curved "cold seafood" bar, and ergonomic booths made of wooden slats painted blue. It was modern with a natural feel.

"Let's sit at the cold bar for drinks and appetizers," Sam suggested.

Kat sat down and picked up a menu. "Look, they get supplied by a shellfish farm in Long Island, just like you said."

Liking the new, relaxed Kat, Sam told a few anecdotes from his life as a hockey player. "It's great to be part of a team and play excellent games together. But I'm starting to have to think about what my life will look like after hockey."

"Why is that?"

"I'm not getting any younger."

Kat snorted. "You're in great shape."

He grinned. "Sure. It's just that twenty-year-olds are fifteen years fitter. It won't be today or tomorrow, but I'd like to quit while I'm still healthy." He grimaced. "It would be awful to quit because I'm forced to. You may have heard that's what happened to Tyler."

"I heard her knee forced her out of dancing as a ballerina in a Cirque du Soleil-style show in Las Vegas."

"Then you know the crisis it threw her into. It really hit home for me. Not only because she's my sister but because we're both professional athletes. I vowed to myself that I would start planning my future."

"Do you have a concrete idea yet?"

He brushed his blonde hair off of his forehead. "Honestly, no. Just a few vague ideas at first. But when you said the other day that you weren't in a rush to start a business here... that you're not even sure the demand is there, since you've got the Seattle revenue, it occurred to me that I don't need to stress about it. The right thing will come along."

"Did I tell you a hotel manager gave me her card?"

"No, what for?"

"To come and talk about offering my services to guests of the hotel who want to bring their pets."

"Nice. Hope you get it."

Kat frowned, remembering some of the risqué pictures she'd seen of Sam on the Internet. "Haven't you been in front of the camera as a model for underwear?" She waited with interest for his answer.

Sam smirked. "Figures you'd come up with that. The answer is 'yes' and I'd do it again. Those advertising contracts pay well. But as a way of life?" He shook his head.

"You won't you miss the whole media circus?"

Sam noticed she had slipped the question in so casually. "You mean, do I miss the parties with lightly dressed models and photos the morning after in the tabloids?"

"Yes."

He kissed her on the cheek. "No."

The conversation paused while they were served platters of smoked trout dip and steamed crab legs dipped in a garlic butter and wine sauce. A minute later a figure loomed beside them.

"What are you doing here?" a deep voice said ominously.

Kat gasped while Sam looked up quickly and a tall, fit man still in his twenties boomed out a hearty laugh.

"Cole!" Sam exclaimed. He jumped up and gave him a bear-hug.

"Kat, this is my brother Cole."

"And this is my friend, Avery," Cole said, standing aside so they could see an attractive woman with long blue-black hair, a reminder of Native American heritage, and exotic dark eyes. "Avery and I met at Quantico, way back," Cole said in a low voice.

Kat had heard the word "Quantico" before. That was where FBI agents went to train. Were these two FBI?

"Nice to meet you both," Avery said, shaking hands. "I understand you're staying in my grandfather's house right now."

"Mr. Wilkinson is your grandfather? What a pleasure to meet you," Kat replied.

"Are you here alone? Would you like to join us? We're just getting started with dinner."

Sam looked questioningly at Kat. She smiled in agreement. In a jiffy they were sitting at a table for four with Avery and Cole.

"That's a stunning necklace you have on," Kat said to Avery, noting the brilliantly colored choker in red, yellow, and turquoise around her neck. It set off the slim black dress she was wearing.

"Thank you, it was made by Ute artists, she said."

"Ute? I haven't heard of that," Kat said.

"The Ute Indians," Cole explained. "The Utes are the first people of Colorado and Utah."

Avery nodded. "The Utes still embroider porcupine quills in ancient patterns." She lightly touched her throat. "This one is vintage, though."

"I haven't seen anything else like it," Kat exclaimed.

"How big is the Ute population in Colorado now?" Sam asked.

"Less than 10,000," Avery said simply. "I'm half Ute on my mother's side." Redirecting the conversation she said, "Have you been to this restaurant before?" Avery sipped her cocktail from its oversized glass.

"I have," Sam answered, "and the Arctic Norwegian grilled salmon is my favorite. It comes with a New Orleans-style crab cake and asparagus."

"Sounds so good I think I'll have that, too," Avery replied.

"I'm not a big seafood eater like Avery," said Cole. "Think I'll go with filet mignon medallions with béarnaise sauce and parmesan potatoes."

"Mmm," Kat murmured. "I'm going for the ricotta gnocchi served with jumbo sea scallops."

"We have a tough decision to make about the wine list," Cole said. He and Sam began debating the finer points of various vintages.

"What do you do?" Kat asked Avery politely, while the men argued over the wine list.

"Right now I'm learning all about drone technology," Avery answered.

"I've heard the word, but I confess, I don't really know what that is," Kat answered. "I run a dog salon and grooming business. High tech isn't really part of it." She laughed to take the edge off any embarrassment.

"Drones are small flying machines. They can go anywhere that's legal and they can take pictures and bring them back. They're very handy for law enforcement."

The rest of the dinner passed in a blur. The information about drones crowded Kat's mind and all she could think of was how useful a drone would be in investigating the farm and its dirty business. She made small talk, telling stories about Mr. Kleeves with his bulging eyes and volatile temper, and the new puppies. But a part of her mind was on her own investigation. *Somehow, some way, she had to get a drone.*

CHAPTER ELEVEN

THE DRIVE BACK TO THE HOTEL passed in silence. Kat's head was spinning. Sam had entertained Avery and Sam with funny anecdotes from the life of a hockey player and surprised her once again with how well he could laugh at himself. He was a charmer, sometimes unbearably arrogant, and he knew his effect on women. On the other hand, he had a witty sense of humor, was helpful and warmhearted. She credited him with keeping to her rules. His looks had made her understand that he desired her. But he hadn't made ambiguous remarks or tried to touch her. The man was simply dangerous. She sighed.

Sam glanced at her from the side. "That was a deep sigh, though. I hope I wasn't the reason.

"I had such a nice time," she said genuinely. "Thanks again."

He would have preferred to be able to exchange her gratitude for something else. But he was careful not to say it out loud. He didn't want to immediately ruin the good foundation he'd laid. The limo pulled up to the glamorous entrance of the Hotel Clio.

"It's still early," he said. "We have the limo till midnight. Want to spend an hour in the bar? Coffee and a liqueur? Or just a hot chocolate?" He knew he'd grabbed her attention with that.

The limo driver helped them out and went to park. Sam and Kat stood in the fresh, cold air. Stars were clear in the sky.

Kat studied the myriad points of light. "I'm amazed every time at how many there are."

"Too much light in Seattle?"

"Probably. Plus, we're closer here, even though it's Denver."

He laughed softly. "They still impress me, too. And I grew up with them." He noticed she was shivering. "Let's go inside."

Nodding in agreement, she said, "But just the hotel bar. I'm not going up to your room." She didn't trust her traitorous hands. Right now they desperately wanted to feel Sam's muscles.

"Don't look at me like that," Sam said, drawing closer like a tiger on the prowl.

"How am I looking at you?" she asked, taking a step back. But at the same time, Sam's attitude fascinated her, so her gaze kept returning to him.

He noticed that she was alarmed and stopped. He ran a hand over his face. "You're looking at me like you're about to jump. Hungry."

At his words, Kat's gaze lowered to his mouth. Her own tongue took on a life of its own and darted out to moisten her dry lips.

"Now you're doing it again," he whispered, taking another step toward her.

She raised her hand to stop him. "I'm sorry. You're right." She took a deep breath as if deciding to be transparent. To him and to herself. "I am attracted to you. Very much so. The chemistry between us is beyond anything I've ever experienced."

When she saw him make an effort to get closer, she hurried to say, "But physical attraction isn't the only thing."

"No?" He studied her closely.

She lowered her eyes and studied the grain of the hotel's fancy brickwork on the driveway. "At least, not for me. I feel like this between us could be a lot more."

"Good. Because that's the impression I get, too."

"No. I never get involved in anything more. I can't." She turned away. Her hands trembled. She fervently hoped he would understand.

Sam tried to process what he'd just heard. He hadn't seen this coming. Usually it was the other way around. Most women were already planning the wedding before the first date with him. *If you don't have to make an effort, it's not worth anything,* he could hear his mother saying. It was time to change tactics. He wasn't such a good hockey player for nothing.

He took a step back and said lightly, "No going up to my room. Just hot chocolate in the bar downstairs. It will be a nice end to the evening."

"I'd love that," she said, smiling. "Just excuse me while I freshen up."

She was in the restroom combing her hair when the call came.

The chocolate was ready and Kat still hadn't come back to the table in the bar. Sam frowned and mentally went over the past ten minutes, trying to figure out if she might have been upset about something. When he couldn't think of anything, he ran the rest of the evening through his memory, but still couldn't figure it out. Besides, she had made it quite clear beforehand that she wanted hot chocolate. Kat was a complex personality. But she was also very direct. If she didn't want something, she didn't hide her opinion. Something wasn't right.

Outside the ladies' room door, he stopped and listened. Someone was crying. It sounded like Kat.

"Are you okay in there?" he said.

There was the sound of high heels walking across bathroom tiles to the door. It cracked open but he couldn't see her very well.

"Hey, what's going on? Did something happen?"

Kat couldn't answer, she was crying so hard. "My mom," she groaned. "Hospital." She dropped the phone. It skittered through the crack and out to where Sam was standing.

He picked it up and raised it to his ear, hoping the person on the other end would have more information. "Hello? Who is this?"

The voice belonged to a woman. She kept asking for Kathrina. Was that Kat's name? He hadn't known that at all. Just as he hadn't known that she apparently had Polish roots, if he correctly interpreted the words that bubbled up to him from the phone. The hockey team had a few Polish members and he'd picked up a phrase or two over the years. But unfortunately, nowhere near enough to carry on an entire conversation. He rummaged in his brain for the appropriate words and let the woman know that Kathrina would call her back. At least, that's what he hoped he'd said.

"Come on, I think we'd better go to my room," he said.

Kat nodded and joined him in the hall, keeping her tearstained face down.

In the room, Sam put the phone on the bed and went to the bathroom to get a glass of water and a washcloth. Back in the room, he wiped the tears from Kat's face and cursed himself for forgetting tissues. She didn't resist, but just let him take care of her. As the tears continued to flow, he awkwardly pressed the washcloth into her hand. Then he sat down at the head of the bed and pulled her to his chest. For a brief moment, her body went into a defensive posture. But then she gave in and leaned against him.

Never before had a man taken such care of her. Despite all the worry about her mother, she was just glad not to be alone. Slowly, her breathing calmed, and the tears dried up. Ashamed of her breakdown, she closed her eyes. Pressing her head to his chest, she murmured, "I'm sorry. You must think I'm getting hysterical."

He continued to stroke her hair soothingly. "Not at all. You just got some terrible news, didn't you? Your mother? Is she in the hospital? I'm afraid I didn't understand the woman on the phone. There are some Polish guys on the team but I only know a few words."

Even in her upset she caught that he had spoken Polish on the phone. "Don't pretend. I heard you, after all."

Glad to see her fighting spirit flash, he smiled. "I hope I didn't tell her I wanted to marry her."

Kat let a little smile spread across her face. She was grateful for him trying some humor. She snuggled a little closer. Apparently her heart had decided to trust him, even if her brain hadn't read the memo yet.

"That was my parents' neighbor on the phone. My mother was just taken to the hospital." Her voice broke and she swallowed hard to prevent another burst of tears. "M-my parents have a dysfunctional relationship."

When she didn't speak further, Sam asked, "What does that look like?"

"It means my father uses his hands on her. There are better times where he leaves her alone. And then there are worse times where the slightest thing is enough to make him go off." Her voice was toneless.

Sam said nothing at first. Only the sudden tensing of his muscles betrayed how much this statement was affecting him. He forced himself to breathe regularly and bring his anger under control. "Did he ever do it to you?"

"No. Mom intervened every time. Or sent me into hiding ahead of time. I suppose that's something, after all. I'm grateful to her for that. But she refuses to save herself." Kat wrinkled her nose. "He's obviously gone too far this time. He pushed her, and she banged her head on the corner of a table. The neighbor overheard the argument from next door. When my father stormed out of the house, she checked on my mother and found her covered in blood. That was when she called the ambulance."

"That's good, isn't it?" Sam had no idea what to say to this terrible story. He would have loved to fly to Poland right then and there to beat up the father. He forced himself to relax his cramped muscles.

Kat shrugged in his arms. "Depends on whether she presses charges against him and finally leaves him. Otherwise, it's business as usual once she gets back home. I've been trying to talk her into coming back to the States for years. To no avail." She began to cry again. "I wish I had tried harder. In the last few weeks, I've hardly had any contact with her. I was so angry because she wouldn't let me help her."

Sam's face showed a sudden understanding. It seemed to Kat that everything made sense to him all of a sudden. He understood her refusal to get involved with a man. Her need for independence. The realization showed on his face.

"Oh, Kat," Sam said, and hugged her a little tighter.

She had no more energy, was completely exhausted. She felt safe and protected in Sam's arms. Her resistance to him melted away. How had she ever lumped him in with her father? His loyalty to his family and friends, his willingness to help and his compassion had been evident the very first night he offered her a roof over her head. And that was despite his anger at being disturbed. Her refusal to get to know him better suddenly seemed ridiculous to her. Life was far too short to let fear rule it. Because that's exactly what she was doing.

In this way, she continued to live the cycle of violence in which her mother had been trapped for so long. In this way, she allowed her father to exercise his tyranny even from a distance. With this realization, she felt as if a weight the size of the Rockies fell from her shoulders. On impulse, she lifted her head and kissed Sam on the mouth.

Caught off guard, he kissed her back. The taste of her tongue mixed with the salty tears. Though he couldn't get enough, he somehow mustered enough willpower to pull away. He wanted to be kissed for the right reasons. Gratitude didn't count. Until he was sure her motives were the right ones, he would support her in other ways.

She stared at him with wide eyes, as if she were seeing him for the first time. Which, in a way, was true. Embarrassed, she turned away and reached for the washcloth as she realized what she must look like. Tears, snot, and mascara were not a good combination. She probably looked like a raccoon on drugs. No wonder his reaction hadn't turned out too enthusiastically. But that thinking belonged with the past, she decided. It was time to silence the inner demons and stop resisting the attraction he had for her. But maybe he'd change his mind? Not that she could blame him now that he knew all the sordid details of her life. Nervously, she kneaded the tissue in her hand.

"What do you want to do now?" He interrupted her train of thought and placed a reassuring hand on hers.

She shrugged her shoulders. "I could fly into Warsaw, I suppose. I don't know if she'll listen to me this time, though. Besides, I don't really want to run into my father." Dejected, she hung her head and buried her face in her hands.

Sam shifted his weight beside her. "Call back the helpful neighbor. Find out what hospital she's in. And then we'll figure out what to do together."

For once, she was grateful that she didn't have to make any decisions. The irony crossed her mind how she had fought tooth and nail this morning against him interfering.

She called back and got everything she needed from the same woman who had initially answered the phone.

"Kathrina," Sam said when she hung up, "Something has to change. Today he could have killed your mother."

Kat rubbed her temple. "I know. But she won't do anything. What am I going to do?"

"You have to convince her! Your father is out of control."

"Okay. I'll give it a try." Even though she had no idea how to go about it. After all, she had spent the last few years trying to change her mother's mind.

Sam was on the other side of the big room by now, in an alcove with a desk. He was talking softly on the phone. His facial expression was very concentrated. Finally, he ended the phone call and sat down with her on the sofa.

"Listen, I'll make you a deal."

Kat nodded silently.

"Micah is a teammate of mine. He suffered an injury two weeks ago and is in rehab in his home country before coming back and joining us. Like your parents, he lives near St. Petersburg. He is trying to find out more about your mother's condition and will call us. As soon as she's better, we'll draft a plan to bring your mother here. Micah will help us. He's a sports star in Poland and can be quite persuasive." He *tisked* softly. "I hope you don't mind that I let Micah in on this."

Relief overwhelmed her. "Thank you, thank you, thank you, because otherwise I'll never know about my mother's health. As for the rest, we'll see." She let everything go through her mind again, worrying about where she would house her mother once she came to the States. But common sense told her she was worrying too much ahead of time. She would cross that bridge when she got to it. She put a hand to his cheek. "You are a wonderful man. I'm sorry I didn't want to admit it until now."

Now it was Sam's turn to look aside, embarrassed. "Just don't tell anyone. Otherwise I'll have to listen to the ridicule on the ice for weeks."

Micah called a few hours later with good news. Her mother had been lucky. The laceration was stitched and she had suffered a mild concussion. In addition, there were bruised ribs and a few contusions. Micah had arranged for a private security guard to watch that her husband could not make an unannounced visit. When Kat protested, worried about the expense, Sam reassured her. "They're all buddies of mine. They owe me a favor. She's not safe otherwise." What he didn't say was that he wanted to avoid Kat's father showing up and apologizing so the mother would go back to him. This cycle had to be broken. Micah had seen it happen all too often, unfortunately. Not with his own family, but those around him.

Micah also had bad news. As expected, her mother refused to press charges, insisting that it had all been a chain of unfortunate circumstances. "It will be difficult to convince her to leave your father," Micah said. "But I have a plan. Is it okay if I put a little pressure on your father?"

Kat answered snidely. "Sure. Anytime."

"Good, I'll get back to you when I have news."

Exhausted, Kat handed the phone to Sam who said goodbye and ended the call. "I don't think you want to go home tonight, do you? I should call the driver and let him go."

Kat nodded in agreement. Emotions had a tedious habit of draining her completely.

"I can loan you a T-shirt to sleep in."

In the bathroom Kat brushed her teeth with one finger. When she came out, Sam was throwing a sheet over a big chair. The bed was empty.

"Good night," he said.

She reached for his hand. "Will you sleep with me? Please?"

He stared into her eyes and said, "Yes."

He made himself comfortable next to her and soon she heard his regular breaths. Kat realized she was exactly where she wanted to be.

The next morning, Kat awoke and snuggled close to Sam. For a moment she lay very still, enjoying his closeness and feeling his steady heartbeat against her body. Also, she didn't feel cold as she usually did in the mornings. The man was a first-class heater.

The memory of the previous evening and her mother made her sad. On the other hand, the liberated feeling she felt yesterday continued. After all, it had brought Sam to her in bed on a purely friendly basis for now. To start a love affair in the middle of the explosive, emotional mix would certainly be too much. Gently, she stroked his blond hair. As soon as the dust settled and her mother was finally safe, she would do everything she could to win Sam over.

Quietly, she got up and dressed. She scribbled a note: *Goodbye and thank you for a magical evening. Please call when you get up.* On the nightstand was the card for the limo service. She memorized the number, slipped out of the room, and pulled the door shut behind her. Downstairs in the lobby she called the service. In just about an hour she was home.

Letting herself in, the house was quiet. Rocky and Ranger padded out to greet her, nails clicking on the hardwood floor. An empty wine bottle and plates of food littered the coffee table. Evidently Pat and Tyler had spent last night at home, just the two of them. They deserved a little romance alone after everything that was going on and they were still in bed. It was still only seven-thirty in the morning.

Kat let the dogs out and then hurried to distribute food. The puppies could already get noisy if they thought food was coming to the bowl too slowly. Jinx waited patiently. She knew as soon as the dog pack was fed, it would be her turn. While the cat ate, Kat stroked her silky fur.

"It's strange that you were Scrooge's cat. You've come quite a long way since then."

Jinx just flicked her tail indifferently and didn't give an answer.

Kat cleaned last night's leftovers on the coffee table and cleaned the bowls. Bella seemed in a good mood, gently playing with the pups. Kat would soon have to look for future owners for the little ones. Until now, she had always pushed the thought of that away. But time flew by.

Kat listened for any sounds of stirring from Pat and Tyler. But no. Everything remained quiet. Everything that could be done had been done around the house. It was about time that this dogfighting breeder was finally put out of business. It was time to go see Scrooge.

Calling Rocky and Ranger with a soft whistle, she scribbled a quick note to Pat and Tyler that she was taking the two dogs for a walk, and slipped out. With Ranger's training as a former K-9, he was great protection. Although Rocky didn't have his training, he provided youth and energy. Nothing in the woods would be a great match against them, including Mr. Pickup. Wrapping a scarf around her neck, she pulled on her snow boots and headed out.

Scrooge's trailer was about half a mile north along the borderline of Mr. Wilkinson's property. Half a mile was just a nice walk for Kat and the two dogs at their level of fitness but in the snow that was another level entirely. The dogs handled it well but Kat was red-faced and perspiring by the time the trailer came into view. Steam poured from a pipe on the roof, signaling Scrooge was at home. She walked to the door and tapped.

"Hello? It's Kat from the diner. I drive the pink and white RV around town? You know me."

There was a rustling from inside and in a moment the door cracked open. Kat heard a grunt of recognition.

"What are you doing here, girl? Wait a minute and I'll come out."

Scrooge emerged in a moth-eaten parka and a toque over his scraggly gray hair. The dogs sniffed at him deeply.

"I found out a way to get the proof I need for the sheriff," Kat started excitedly.

"Eh?" Scrooge snorted. "What's that got to do with me?"

"I just wanted to brainstorm my strategy with you."

Scrooge hissed and bobbed from the waist up. He sounded like a steam kettle. She realized he was laughing. "Brainstorm your strategy is it? Go on, I'm listening."

Kat was on the verge of getting huffy. It wasn't pleasant being laughed at. "A drone would do the trick," she said flatly.

Scrooge stopped laughing and narrowed his eyes at her. He turned on his heel and yanked open the door of the trailer. "Come inside," he said gruffly. "Knock the snow off your feet." He threw her a stained towel. "That towel's clean and washed, it just looks bad," he explained. "Dry the dogs off and bring them in, too."

A minute later Kat was inside the surprisingly neat trailer. Breakfast dishes were washed and drying on a drainboard. The dogs sank gratefully to the floor and started snoring. Scrooge put water down in a bowl but they ignored it. They'd been eating snow the whole walk.

"You found out about drones did you?" Scrooge cackled.

The thought went through Kat's mind that she should be a little frightened, but she wasn't. It was as though Scrooge was an old friend already. The neat appearance inside the trailer inspired trust as well. An orderly home usually meant an orderly mind. Which was not exactly how anyone thought of Scrooge, but evidently they were wrong.

He went to a cupboard and pulled something out. It was about two feet long with wings and a propeller, and what Kat recognized as a camera on the front. Scrooge also held a little box with lights and a joystick jutting out of it. "If you wonder how I know everything that's going on in these woods, this is how," he said simply.

Kat looked at the device. "This flies?"

Scrooge nodded. "Yep, and the stick controls it. I can tell it to fly left and right, higher and lower. And I push this button here to take a picture."

"When can we take this to the farm?" Kat blurted.

"It's early. Those guys like to sleep in. Let's go now."

With a high-pitched whine, the little drone flew close to the third building on the farm. Inside, a few dogs ruffed, but mostly their ears were perked, listening. This was a new sound to them.

Up on the ridge, Scrooge and Kat lay on their bellies in the snow. They had parked Nelly many yards away so the RV was invisible. Then they had literally crawled through the snow to the bluff where they could see over the farm. Scrooge had the black box with the joystick in his hand and was manipulating it so the drone flew close to the windows to take pictures.

"These aren't going to be beauty shots but at least you'll see inside," Scrooge said.

The little drone flew back and Scrooge took the camera off so they could see the digital pictures. Some caught too much reflection, some showed only the darkest part of the barn. But in one shot, a pit bull and puppies were clearly evident. The mother had a distinctive white stripe that ran down her face.

"That dog is shown on the website," Kat said excitedly. "She's on the 'prime breeding stock' page."

"You got the first part of what you need," said Scrooge. "Now you need something that ties it all together. Something that identifies this farm as the one they're talking about on the website."

"They don't show an outside shot of the farm or anything," Kat said. "What do you suppose I could use to do that?"

Scrooge thought a minute and scratched at the whiskers on his face. "A picture of an invoice would work if you found something on the desk inside the house. Anything they show on the website like an address or a shot on the website that matches something in the interior buildings. The picture of the mother pit bull is a good start. But you need a few of those. The sheriff has to be able to say, 'Okay, that's the physical farm and you've proved it with this picture, and this picture, and this picture.' That's solid proof."

Kat nodded, taking in the words.

"How are you getting to the party tonight?"

"Tonight?!!"

"My intel told me they moved the date up a day or two. Likely because they knew you were snooping. They're pretty crafty those guys."

"How do the, um, ladies from Denver get here?"

"Usually dropped off in a limousine."

Kat nodded. "I can do that."

As Kat arrived home, Micah called.

"Sam gave me your number," he explained. "Your mother is better. You can talk to her yourself."

"Have you convinced her yet?"

Micah hesitated with the answer. Her heart sank.

"Almost. But it will turn out right. Give me time. She's only been here since yesterday."

That was true. Kat assured him she would be patient. Talking to her mother on the phone, she was surprised to hear her mother rave about the charming hockey player.

"Just think, he brought me flowers," she gushed. Kat was almost heartbroken that such a small gesture gave her such great joy. Her father didn't give gifts. Anyway, it was comforting to hear her mother with a note of happiness in her voice. Talking more, she seemed to regard her stay as a cure, as though everything was now fine and no other precautions were needed.

Kat got Micah back on the phone. "You have to try harder, please," she pleaded. "She talks like she's going back to him. I couldn't stand that."

"Don't worry. It's not going to be difficult right now."

"Why do you think?"

Micah fussed a bit before answering, "Your father has temporarily left Warsaw. He was convinced to take some time off."

She could read between the lines well enough to understand what he meant. "What did you do to him?"

"Visited him," was Micah's curt answer.

Probably just as well. Kat didn't know if she could have handled the details. She really hoped Micah could be as convincing with her mother. Sam had said, "If anyone can do it, it's Micah. The guy could sell sand in the desert."

Kat had answered, "But where will we put her if Mom comes here?"

"You worry too much," Sam said, kissing her on the forehead. "Let's get her here for a visit first and worry about that later."

Leslie let herself into the house after school and cast a glance at the mail. Shoot, Paula had already picked it up.

No chance to go over it for something from child services. She heard a small noise coming from the direction of the kitchen. At first Leslie thought it had to be one of the dogs but if the dogs were out there, they would have come running to the door to greet her. More likely they were out back with the horses.

The noise came again. She listened more closely. The sound was crying. She padded down the hall in her sock feet toward the kitchen. Paula was sitting at the kitchen with papers spread before her. She was weeping. Leslie felt a pang go through her heart. "Paula," she said. "What's wrong? Why are you crying?"

Paula jumped and wiped at her face. "I'm not crying," she said.

"Yes, you are. Don't lie," Leslie said.

"You caught me," Paula said. "I'm just so frustrated with this paperwork. I can't be your foster mother until they find your parents. And they can't find your parents because your name doesn't match anybody." Paula pushed back from the table in fresh agony. "We're going to be in limbo forever with nothing settled. I can't stand it!" She burst into fresh tears.

Leslie felt the blood run out of her face. Paula never cried about anything. She was the strongest woman Leslie had ever met. And now Paula was crying over her. Right then and there Leslie knew she had to do something. But what?

"So what if we're in limbo?" Leslie said. "It doesn't hurt us does it?"

"Yes, it does," Paula said, turning red-rimmed eyes toward her. "It means you miss out on certain benefits.

But that's not the worst. The worst is that you'll always be temporary, and if someone from your past pops up, they could take you away." Paula looked beaten. It hurt to see her this way.

Leslie walked a little closer and put her hand on Paula's shoulder. "Are you sure you want to be my foster mother?"

"I want to be your adopted mother, Leslie! Fostering you is just a step toward that."

"Maybe you should try another name with the services people, then," Leslie said. "Try Leslie Sterling instead of the one you've been using. Leslie Anne Sterling."

Paula turned her eyes upward. Leslie recoiled a bit. Was she going to call her a liar for using a false name? Was she going to throw a fit over all the wasted time this had caused?

Instead, Paula smiled as though the sun had just come out. "Leslie Anne Sterling," she repeated. "Yes, I'll try that."

It was eight p.m. at the Wilkinson house. By this time, the limo service knew Kat's address, and she had no trouble ordering a car to pick her up in an hour. The charge had to go on Sam's account, and yes, it was a little secretive, but she had every intention of paying him back. It was all for a good cause. Before getting out of the back of the stretch, she drew her lips blood red one last time. Then she straightened her shoulders, fumbled for the door latch to open it and got out. She summoned her inner spy persona. Sexy, tough, and not taking any crap from anyone. Just what she needed right now. Hopefully, some of Avery's FBI agent skills had rubbed off. In her tiny purse was her trusty cell phone to take pictures of anything that could possibly help link the farm to the Internet dog-selling business.

She left her own dogs behind with a heavy heart. Nikki had to stay there anyway to take care of her offspring. Bella could not go near that place. And for Rocky she was simply afraid. She didn't doubt for a second that these people would be able to shoot a dog. *That goes for humans too*, the know-it-all voice said in her head.

She shook off the oppressive feeling, tightened her shoulders and wrapped a faux fur jacket around her bare shoulders. The leather bustier wasn't really warm. She shivered and wondered if the chance of dying of hypothermia tonight was greater than being shot.

Paula and Leslie were watching TV when a call came in from Sam.

"Where are you?" Paula asked.

"Still in Denver, Sam answered. "Say, have you heard from Kat?"

"Not for a day or so," Paula said, probing her memory.

"I can't get through to her. I keep going to voicemail. I'm trying to find out why she would order a limousine to take her to some rural route address."

"A rural route as in the boonies?"

"Could be. The car service just called me to authorize the charge."

"If it's a rural route it might be the farm."

"What farm? Not the farm with the fight dogs?"

"She must have gone undercover. I didn't think it was happening until next week, but—"

"Undercover?" Sam said suspiciously.

Paula was surprised. "You didn't know about this?"

"No! I didn't know about it. Otherwise I wouldn't be sitting here right now while Kat is off trying to play spy with some criminals."

Paula could hear him get up and throw something aside. "Now wait a minute—"

But the phone went dead.

Paula looked at Leslie across the table. "I did a great job with that," she muttered.

Leslie gave her a friendly pat. "You didn't know."

"I also assumed she'd let him in on it. Then again, I can understand why she didn't. Our brother has a tendency to want to solve all problems. But sometimes we have to face certain problems ourselves." Paula suspected that he would have locked Kat in the broom closet if he had known about her plan. She was feeling a little uneasy about it, too.

"What's so funny?"

"Nothing, except Sam will probably have a heart attack when he sees what she's wearing. Even Jaz didn't recognize her."

"Wow, that's saying something."

"The disguise is really good. I'll give her that."

CHAPTER TWELVE

Without any problems, Kat mingled inside the party. The heavy guy at the door didn't even speak to her. He took one look at the departing limousine and waved her inside. Loud music boomed from the speakers. It smelled like man sweat, cheap perfume, grease from a grill, and stale cigarette smoke. It made her feel sick. But she suppressed the feeling and concentrated on what was happening around her.

She strolled around the room once, which was not so easy with so many people. There were rough looking men, but more city types than farmers. Apparently, it took help from Denver to run this operation. Probably on the business side. Kat took her phone from the purse and pretended to place a call. Giggling and smiling while talking to no one, she snapped pictures of the party crowd. Maybe Jake could use them later.

She put the phone away and continued slipping through people. The guys here had grabby hands. It was not so easy to fend them off and maintain the flirtatious personality. More than once she was tempted to punch an offender. There was a makeshift bar set up at the far end consisting of a card table covered with beer bottles, hard liquor, and mix. A trash can full of ice sat beside it. She walked up and smiled at the bartender.

"Haven't seen you here before," he remarked.

"You know how it is," she said, trying not to stumble over her words. "New girls all the time."

"And we're happy about it!" he chortled. "What'll it be?"

"Ginger ale."

"Ginger and Southern Comfort it is," he said, splashing hard liquor into a cup and topping it off with a few ounces of soft drink.

He handed it over and she clutched it tightly.

Kat continued to navigate the room. Soon, she noticed a hallway leading to the back of the house. Although doors were shut all the way down there was no one guarding it. Kat walked all the way to the end of the hall and opened the last door. She slipped inside and turned on the light. The room was full of crates. Stacks and stacks of animal crates lined the room. Made of wood with airholes on all four sides, they were stamped with the words Air Cargo/Live Cargo. Kat snapped pictures and slipped her phone away. She had seen these before on the website!

The door burst open.

"WHAT ARE YOU DOING IN HERE?" the heavy man bellowed. He was acting as security at the front door when she'd arrived. A gun was tucked into the belt of his pants.

"I-I was looking for the bathroom," Kat answered, shaking.

He calmed down somewhat. "It's not in here," the man said, and motioned her out.

Walking down the hall, followed by the guard, Kat's mind raced. Were those cargo crates what she needed as final proof there was an operation selling dogs here?

Maybe she had enough proof. She was just about to pull her phone out to call the limo to come for her when everyone started heading for the back door. It looked like they were going outside even though they were still holding drinks.

A tented tunnel was erected from the back door to the second building where Kat knew the fight arena was located. Plywood flats had been laid on the ground so the women could walk over in high heels without sinking into snow, and heaters blew warm air in both ends. This way they didn't have to cover up their small outfits with coats.

It was a short walk and they all filed out the other side into the second building. The place was full of people and animals and there was almost no place to sit. How was she going to get out of here?

Betting was going on and bills changed hands. Kat found a post to lean on in the semidarkness, her eyes probing for an easy exit. It was also an opportunity to gather as much evidence as possible.

Suddenly, tension in the room rose and two roosters were released into the ring. She pushed her way forward to get a better look. As soon as she caught sight of them, she wished she hadn't. To hide her disgust, she took a big swig from her drink. It burned like fire all the way down. She closed her eyes and held the condensation-covered plastic cup to her throbbing temples. Three rounds she suffered through. Then the one rooster was dead. Blood and feathers adorned the dirt.

More and more bets were made. The tone became rougher as more alcohol flowed. Women in revealing outfits clung to the arms of their "boyfriends for the evening."

Others meandered through the crowd looking for one. The noise increased in intensity as the dogs were brought in. Kat braced herself for the sight. They looked a lot like Bella. She could see the fear in their eyes and it broke her heart. The metallic smell of blood was in the air. She breathed shallowly through her mouth and struggled to suppress the gag reflex. Her pulse was pounding like crazy.

She had just calmed down somewhat when a huge man with the logo of a biker gang on his jacket grabbed her butt. She grabbed his hand and pushed him away. She couldn't very well break his nose, even though that's exactly what she felt like doing.

"Don't be coy, sweetheart," he murmured in her ear. The whiff of alcohol was overpowering.

She grimaced in disgust.

"You bitch," he hissed. His other hand went to her throat. She raised her arm to block him and braced for impact. A different hand reached between them and stopped the fist in midair.

"She's mine," growled a familiar voice behind her. Surprised, she let go of her attacker's thumb. Sam! What was he doing here? She hoped he wasn't putting the whole investigation in jeopardy. Was he out of his mind?

Her attacker seemed to recognize ferocity in Sam's gaze. He raised his hands and backed away, never taking his eyes off the two of them. "Better watch out for next time," he growled, spitting at their feet.

Sam grabbed her by the elbow and steered her toward the door. She resisted, but in vain. If she didn't want to make a big fuss, she had to follow him. He seemed to be seething with anger.

"Let go of me," she hissed to him through clenched teeth as he continued to drag her behind him.

"In your dreams."

"People are looking. You're putting both of us and the whole investigation in danger."

Sam snorted. "Believe me, honey, I'm not the danger here."

"Don't call me honey!" She tore herself away and faded into the crowd.

From the other side of the room, Kat counted six dogs and five roosters in cages. They were there because they were going to fight tonight. There had probably been six roosters to begin with, she figured, remembering the fate of the rooster. She had snapped pictures of all of them even though the lighting out here was extremely poor. All she had to do was get out safely. But now that she had everything she needed, she couldn't leave Sam. She made her way back.

Sam was standing to one side. He was facing her, but she could have sworn he was concentrating on something that was behind him. And why was he holding his hands in the air? Strange. Probably he wanted to lecture her again about how reckless she was acting. Getting closer she recognized Mr. Pickup standing right behind Sam, pressing a shotgun into his back. That's why Sam was standing so strangely.

Without making a sound Kat ducked behind some people and looked around. Back by the animal cages there was an ancient shovel and old boards leaning against the wall. She made her way there and grabbed the thinnest of the boards. This one would work. The animals in the cages followed her movements with wide eyes but made no sound. She silently thanked them before heading off to get Sam out of trouble.

Nimbly, she covered the distance to the corner. Mr. Pickup was directing Sam to the door. She had to stop him from getting Sam outside alone at all costs. He could shoot freely there. She wouldn't stand a chance against that shotgun one on one. But she had to time this just right because they had to exit so no one inside could see what she was doing. She broke into a trot, slipping past people and caught up to Mr. Pickup's heels. He pushed Sam out the back way and before the door had fully closed, Kat was through it, too. In a flash, she leaped forward and swung the board in precise strokes, just as she had learned from Pat in countless training sessions. Knees, head, kidneys. The man fell over like a felled tree. A little startled that it had worked so well, she poked the man lying on his stomach on the ground. Was he dead?

The man groaned, very much alive.

"Leave him!" Sam hissed. "Come on, RUN!"

He grabbed her by the hand and they took off across the snow.

"Where are we going?" she yelled.

"My jeep is parked off the road. Come on, fast!"

Running through the snow in the dark Kat stumbled and almost fell.

"It's right up ahead," Sam urged. "You can do it." He took a firmer grip on her hand and pulled her along.

Gradually, the shadowy shape of the jeep parked on the side of the dirt road came into focus. Sam jumped in the driver's seat as Kat scrambled in the other side.

"You got pictures right?" he asked, breathless.

"I got a lot," Kat wheezed, trying to catch her breath. "It should be everything the cops need."

"Quick! You text your pictures to Jake. He'll need them for probably cause."

"Probable cause? What's that!?"

"It means a good excuse to enter the house and the arena."

Kat fumbled with her bag.

"You start texting and I'll call and explain."

"He'll think I'm nuts!"

"No he won't. I called Jake on my way over here. I knew there might be problems. He's waiting for my call."

Less than an hour later they were parked in the jeep at the top of the ridge. Police car after police car arrived at the farm, squealing sirens, red and blue lights flashing. People walked out of the arena with their hands held high. Paddy wagons marked *Breckenridge PD* wheeled in to take people away.

"Jake must have called Breck for backup," Sam observed, as a black and white SUV pulled in behind them. An officer got out and walked toward the jeep. Sam pressed the button to open his window. Cold air rushed in and Kat huddled into her faux fur a little more.

"Hi Toby," Sam said out the window as a flashlight shone in his face.

"Sam Carter," a voice said. The flashlight turned off and they were lit by the soft glow of the dashboard. "Jake will be busy while all these people get processed. What is your name, ma'am?" he asked, motioning at Kathrina.

She told Deputy Toby her name and he nodded.

"Jake says for both of you to follow me to the station. I'll take your statements and then you can go home. Be warned, it's probably gonna be a long night."

By three-thirty a.m. Kat and Sam were finally through at the police station. They walked hand in hand back to the jeep. Sitting in the dark with Sam beside her and the adrenaline still rushing through her veins, Kat was almost painfully aware of his presence. Their eyes met. The air between them seemed to become electrically charged. Sam cleared his throat.

"Yes?" She looked at him expectantly.

"My place or yours?"

Kat laughed abruptly. Her nervousness subsided a little and she became bolder. "I need something to help me decide."

Lovingly, Sam put a hand on the back of her neck and leaned over. His lips approached hers. She closed her eyes. Then he wrapped her long dark hair around his hand and playfully tugged at it. Surprised, she opened her eyes and looked at him.

"Do you have any idea how hot it is to watch a beautiful woman take on the bad guys?"

Kat pulled him close and smiled. "You talk too much. If you wait any longer to kiss me, this carriage will turn into a pumpkin."

Sam laughed softly and kissed her. Thoroughly. So thoroughly that the windows were completely fogged up when they separated, breathing heavily. She reached out to the dashboard and turned the air fan on 'high.'

"Home?" she asked when she could see through the windshield again.

He nodded. "Home. I'm definitely too old and too big to continue what I have in mind in the car."

Desire and passion were in the look she gave him. Once home, they staggered out of the jeep and into the house, only to be reminded by seven wet dog noses that they hadn't quite finished. They took it with humor.

"Are you feeding the little ones?" Sam asked. "I'll go out the door with the rest."

Kat nodded, marveling once again at how smooth it was with Sam. They fit each other really well. With a practiced hand she prepared food for the puppies. The corners of her mouth twisted into an ironic smile. Here she had her first chance at wild uninhibited sex with a Norse god, and who was interfering? Her dogs. But at the very moment these thoughts flashed through her mind, she realized she wouldn't have it any other way. Dogs had always been a part of her life and always would be. She had to admit Sam seemed to be coping quite well.

Sam walked with the dogs until they reached the first trees. His expression said that he enjoyed the feeling of being out with friends even if they had four legs. The three adult dogs sniffed and explored and got down to business. Bella had decided that Sam was harmless and chose him as her play partner. He threw her a ball which she returned again and again. When she showed signs of fatigue he hid the ball so that she could rest again.

After one last look at the surrounding peaks, kissed by moonlight, he followed the dogs back into the house.

In the kitchen he crept up behind Kat and put his arms around her waist. Was she really ready to dive headfirst into the Sam adventure? Intuitively, she knew there was more at stake than just a few hours of fun together. "Ready, set, go?" she quipped, trying to mask the nervousness that suddenly flared up again.

Sam grabbed her hand and pulled her against him until their bodies touched from head to toe. Gently, he began to spread kisses over her face. Pausing at the corner of her mouth he whispered, "No chance of a race. I'm going to touch every inch of you. Discover and enjoy. Together, we're dynamite."

Her breath caught at his promise. Sam lifted her up in one fluid motion. When she wanted to protest because she was definitely too big and heavy for that, in her opinion, he silenced her with a kiss. Distracted by his lips on hers, she only vaguely got that he was carrying her somewhere. With his shoulder, he pushed open the door to his room and laid her on the bed. Almost ran a hand over her body. Along the line of her cheek, down to her neck and collarbone, until his fingers dipped into the valley between her breasts. She stretched toward him but when he made no move to quicken the pace, she pulled him down to her. At last his iron control seemed to waver. Together they did everything they could to find out how explosive they could truly be.

It couldn't be morning yet, could it? Kat opened her eyes. Three pairs of dog eyes, two brown and one yellow, stared back at her. It was a lazy Sunday morning and she let her eyes wander around the room, looking for a clock. Somehow, her room looked different today. She blinked a few times to shoo away the cobwebs in her head. That's right, she wasn't in her room. She was in Sam's room. A strong man's arm was wrapped around her waist. She listened within, waiting for the panic attack that liked to announce itself at moments like these. But she felt nothing but great satisfaction. And a desire to wake the man up right now to find out if last night had been a one-time event or if it could be repeated at will.

Rocky seemed to suspect the direction her thoughts were taking. He put a paw on the bed. Bella, who was coming out of her shell more and more, tried to do the same. In her eagerness she overshot and landed all fours on the bed, right on top of Kat and Sam.

This woke Sam and there went the plan for sneaking out unnoticed, letting the dogs out, and sneaking back in while the man was still asleep. A romantic and leisurely time waking up would have to wait for another morning.

Embarrassed, she tried to pull Bella off the bed. But Sam stopped her.

"Don't bother. I'm awake anyway. It's great when she finally dares to come near me, too."

Kat's heart melted a little more. Dangerous, wonderful man. "I have to let them out," she responded. She threw off the covers and sat up.

He grabbed her hand and pulled on it so she came to lie half on top of him. Unsure what this new game was all about, Bella laid her mangled ears flat against her head. But she bravely held her ground and did not flee. The tip of her tail wagged like crazy.

"Don't run away, warrior princess. Good morning first."

Kat blushed. "Good morning."

Sam kissed her squarely on the mouth. Two seconds later she lost herself in the kiss. Every distracting thought evaporated. Even the dogs faded into the background.

Of course, this did not escape the dogs. Rocky took the initiative and grabbed a corner of the comforter. He began to walk backwards, slowly and steadily pulling it off the bed.

Kat noticed, despite the phenomenal kiss. Her lips curled into a smile. She sensed Sam chuckling as well.

"Should we have mercy on them?" Kat said.

"Yes, otherwise there'll be a mastiff in bed with us. The bed isn't big enough for that."

Next to the bed his phone blipped. He squinted at a text. "Mom wants us to come for brunch in a few hours. Looks like the whole family will be there."

When they arrived at the Carter homestead, where Sam's mother and father resided, most of the guests were already there. Stan and Brenda had downsized to this place once all the kids were out. The walls were finished with redwood. Modern Mexican tile was on the floor.

Everything showed Brenda's talented touch from Ute Indian artwork on the walls to woven blankets in bright, primary colors, thrown over the wooden furniture. A bronze reproduction of Remington's classic Mountain Man sculpture sat on the fireplace mantel.

Brenda and Stan welcomed them with warm hugs. "We're so glad you're all okay," she said. "What a wild night for everybody."

Jake appeared in the entryway. "Look who's here!" He didn't look a bit worse for wear.

"I'm surprised you're up at all," Sam said, thumping him on the shoulder.

"I never went to bed," Jake answered, making everyone laugh. "We threw the book at those guys. Along with the illegal animal fights and all the rest of that, they brought in some of those prostitutes from out of state. So we got them on human trafficking, too."

Smiles and cheers went up.

Jaz's dog, Rambo, greeted Kat enthusiastically. He stuck his nose out the open door and looked for his best buddy.

"Oh, you poor thing," she said, petting his curly poodle fur. "Jaz, your dog is sad that I didn't bring Rocky."

"Why not?"

"We went outside with the puppies for the first time today. You saw for yourself how seriously he takes his role as uncle. So he had a lot of work to make sure none of the pups got lost in the snow. That's why I left him at home. He's in a deep sleep in front of the fireplace."

"Rambo doesn't even have to make a fuss. Leslie has already entertained him for half an hour with hide-and-seek games."

Leslie, who was in the process of setting the table, ducked her head in embarrassment.

"I'm sure he was happy to hear that. Leslie, you really need to come by again. The puppies are totally cute. You haven't seen them in a while now."

"You must have totally grown a lot," Leslie dared to say. It still amazed her when people spoke up and were obviously genuinely interested in what she had to say. With Paula, she had almost gotten a little used to it. But the others? Strange as it seemed, it still made her feel good. As if she were someone special.

"I guess you could say that. I can't wait to see which one turns out to be your favorite."

"What's for brunch?" called Sam into the kitchen.

Jake came over and gave him a good slap on the back. "Are you annoying Mom again?"

Sam jumped as though he might have forgotten something. "Mom, have you met Kat yet? Kat, this is Brenda, our mom and the boss at our house."

"Thank goodness it's not me," Stan let himself be heard from the kitchen.

"No, I don't know Kat yet," Brenda answered. "But I've heard a lot about you. The grumpy professor in the kitchen is my husband Stan and the father of my children."

Kat shook hands with the striking woman. She wore her auburn hair in a chin-length bob. Her moss-green eyes sparkled with warmth and intelligence. The color of her eyes was the same as Sam's and Kat knew immediately that she was looking at his mother. "I'm glad to meet you, Mrs. Carter."

"Oh," she waved it off. "Please call me Brenda. It makes me feel old."

"You *are* old, Mom," Sam teased her, but moved away from her reach for safety's sake. Her pinches were legendary.

Brenda narrowed her eyes. "And this from an aging hockey star, of all people."

"Ouch!" Sam grabbed his heart theatrically, as if he had been fatally shot.

For Kat, this banter among family members was a completely new experience. She was a little tense observing the hustle and bustle around her. Despite the well-aimed words, she sensed the cohesion of the family.

Jaz stepped over and put her arm around Kat's waist. "Pretty overwhelming to see the Carter family all in one place for the first time, isn't it?"

"You can say that again." Kat nodded at Rose McArthy who had just arrived with her friend Nadine. "Tell me, did you plan this?"

"I had this brunch in mind for a while but you might say last night's excitement spurred me on."

Kat blushed and lowered her eyes. "Well, uh, what can I say?"

"That you're my girlfriend, of course," Sam answered for her.

"I would have gotten to that in a minute."

Jaz made a shooing hand gesture. "Give us some peace to make girl talk."

"I'd better get out of here then. I'll blush if I don't." He winked at Jaz and kissed Kat on the mouth before disappearing with Rambo.

Kat rolled her eyes. "Arrogant as ever."

"Except now you find it adorable," Jaz observed.

"That might be a little exaggerated." But she heard how weak her protest sounded.

"All things considered, since you look like a cat that tripped over the milk jug, I'll assume you're satisfied."

"Very much," Kat replied, unable to prevent a dreamy undertone.

Jaz laughed. "You're worse than Jake and me."

"With you, habit has already set in. I'm in the early infatuation phase."

"Enjoy it," Jaz said. "Come on, breakfast is ready. I hope you like *huevos rancheros*. I made the salsa fresh myself."

During the meal, Kat, Sam, and Jake took turns recounting the events of last night. Each brought a different perspective to the story. Sam emphasized again and again how proud he was of his warrior princess. When the egg course was finished, and Brenda and Stan were dishing up coffee cake and more hot java, Jaz spoke up. "I also have a little anecdote to share. The day Kat was at the police station in her hot outfit, which she calls her 'disguise,' I wanted to surprise Jake for lunch."

Stunned, Jake stared at her. Obviously, she hadn't told him the story yet.

"You can imagine my face when my friend and former notorious womanizer," she gave Jake a meaningful look, "smiled and paid attention to a hot chick dressed in skintight leather pants and a bustier that showed more than it hid. In freezing weather, no less."

A nervous chuckle went around the table.

"I saw red," Jaz continued. "I was so horrified that I turned around on the spot and went back to the studio without letting Jake know I was there." She paused for effect.

Everyone looked at her eagerly, waiting for the story to continue.

"Sometime later, despite attempts at meditation and breathing exercises, I still hadn't calmed down. I actually wanted to talk to Kat, since she's not related to the bastard, but I couldn't reach her. So I called Paula to have a good cry on the phone."

Paula couldn't resist the chance to jump in on the story. "What she didn't know was that Kat had shown up at my house in the meantime. In full gear, trying to convince me to lend her my truck."

Jaz tapped the table with her fork. "I wasn't done yet. I called Paula and told her my woes. In the middle she started laughing and describing to me in great detail what the woman had been wearing. My first thought, of course, was that she had already seen Jake with the stranger. When she realized I was close to tears, she quickly set me straight. You can imagine my relief. It didn't last long, though. Her next question was, "Why am I so overly emotional? Was I pregnant?"

"Does this mean I'm going to be a grandmother?" Brenda stood up and clapped her hands enthusiastically.

Jaz and Jake nodded with delight.

Everyone erupted with congratulations. Kat hugged her and whispered in her ear, "I hope you put me down for the godmother job."

Jaz squeezed her arm. "Would you really do that? I was going to ask you anyway!"

"And when are you getting married?" suddenly Brenda let herself be heard.

Jake and Jaz exchanged a look. "That's still under negotiation," Jake replied.

"Let the kids decide that," Stan said. Everyone looked at him in surprise. It was quite rare that he spoke his mind so decidedly. "I know my son will do the right thing. The main thing is to keep everyone safe and sound." And that was the end of this delicate discussion.

Paula nudged Leslie with her shoulder. "Want to share our news, too?"

Leslie looked nervously around, then nodded.

Paula rose. "

"Let me guess," Sam teased them. "You rescued a dog-slash-cat-slash-horse?"

"No, youuuuu. Children are present so I won't call you what you deserve!" returned Paula. Reassuringly, she put a hand on Leslie's shoulder. "We filled out my foster care application today. Under the name of Leslie Sterling. If everything goes smoothly, Leslie will be a

Carter—officially—within the year. And if she wants to change her name again, that's her prerogative." Leslie smiled shyly.

"That's just great," Brenda exclaimed, jumping up to hug the little girl. Wide-eyed, Leslie turned to Paula for help, but she just laughed. "You better get used to this. Welcome to the family!"

Hand in hand, Sam and Kat left the Carter homestead and took the jeep on a leisurely drive home.

"Maybe we could stop at the diner?" Kat asked. "I'd like to see if Scrooge is around and fill him in on last night.

"Sure."

As they made their way from the parking lot to the diner, Lilly from the flower store arrived at the same time. She held the door open for them. "Here comes our heroine."

"Heroine?" Kat gave Sam a questioning look. He just shrugged his shoulders.

"The whole town is talking about how you helped the police bust the gang."

The whole town was talking about it and calling her a heroine? Hadn't the same people sniffed at her flyer and been uninterested? Except for Lily from the flower store. Slightly confused, Kat followed the other two inside the restaurant. Loud whistles and cheers greeted her. Several people came up and patted her back. Someone pressed a glass of champagne into her hand.

She looked around for Sam. Supportively, he put his arm around her shoulder. The gesture did not escape the attention of the guests present. Mingled with the voices of congratulation were comments from those who had bet she and Sam would end up together. Kat's confusion turned to irritation. Her eyes flitted to the exit. Sam stroked her back reassuringly. But after the emotionally draining twenty-four hours she'd been through, this was too much.

Scrooge, sitting at his usual place at the counter with a half-empty beer glass, watched the scene and Kat's reaction to it. He signaled to her to come over but it was too late. Gall rose in Kat's throat. What hypocrites they all were! Except for Minnie who had put up a flyer only to have it torn down. She switched her champagne glass to her other hand and reached for an abandoned coffee spoon on the counter. She clinked the side of the glass with it. She would have preferred to use a large gong. But she had to make do with what was at hand.

"Everybody, listen up."

People fell silent or into whispers. The crowd waited anxiously to hear what she had to say.

"Thank you very much for the nice welcome and your support." She couldn't keep the disappointment and hurt out of her voice. A few of the people gave each other uncomfortable looks. They probably thought she had lost her mind.

"The people who actually helped me, I can count on one hand. Praising me after the parasites have been removed from your town is easy. You have a great sheriff with a dedicated staff. But bad men ran a bad business under your noses because I couldn't get anybody to pay attention to the evidence I found. Together, you are strong. I know, I am new here. And some people will think that I have no right to speak like this. But you have to know that it could have been easier and solved earlier if you had cared a little more." With these words, she turned on her heel and walked out of the diner.

Mutterings of, "What does she think she's doing?" were quickly silenced. Sam shook his head and followed Kat. She was leaning against the wall outside when he found her. She felt sick at her own outburst. But didn't regret it. Sam stood next to her and silently supported her.

"I don't know what came over me either. I'll probably be run out of town. You should think twice about whether you really want to be associated with me."

With one fluid motion, Sam pressed her against the wall and kissed her. When he stopped, he rested his forehead against hers. "Don't say that. I'm very proud of you. It takes a strong personality to stand up for a cause like that. I love that about you." Touched, she pulled him closer. She could get used to that. Someone who was loyal and was there for her.

"Let's go home and have a drink," he said.

"Best idea I've heard today," she answered.

CHAPTER THIRTEEN

KAT WAS TAKING A NAP in her bedroom and Sam was enjoying a beer in the living room when his cell phone rang. He picked it up.

"Hello, Sam."

It took him a moment to identify the voice. Jaz's grandmother Rose. What did Rose McArthy want with him? "What can I do for you, Miz Rose?"

The older woman laughed. "Let me get right to the point. Your friend made quite an impression with her speech at the diner."

Sam kept his voice soft. "If you're looking for an apology, that might be a long time coming."

"She was right on every word she said."

"Why, thanks for the vote of confidence. That means a lot coming from you, Rose."

"I'm a bit of a town ambassador as you know. Wilkinson and I hold that position together, and a lot of people were very unhappy with how things went. They want to let Kat know how they feel. They want to make it right."

"Sounds like a good idea." He cast a glance at the hall. Kat was still sleeping behind a closed door.

"We were hoping you might have an idea of what we could do to please her. We don't want to just put a glass of champagne in her hand."

"That worked out so wonderfully last time," he replied dryly.

"Exactly. We were thinking more of a project where we could support her. What are her plans? Is she really staying in Independence? Does she really want to open a dog salon here?" Rose trailed off.

Sam thought for a moment. The fingers of his left hand drummed against the beer bottle.

"You know what? I'm just enjoying a drink and I have some time to think. As soon as I have an idea, I'll get back to you."

"Do that. And hurry up with thinking. We don't want to let much more time pass."

Sam laughed. "I can imagine that with you and Nadine involved." The two women were very energetic and efficient no matter what they were tackling.

He said goodbye and hung up. So the residents of the city wanted to make nice. To Kat. He liked the idea. Making nice to his girlfriend. He smiled. Kat sometimes reacted a little prickly to being called that. But it was just for show, as he knew very well. She had trouble reconciling that word *girlfriend* with herself. Emotionally, she was as involved as he was. She showed him that every day, whether they saw each other or not. Her witty texts and the pictures of the dogs she sent every day were a testament to that.

Sam looked up as Blue, the little rascal, wobbled into the room. He had grown so much! Blue already specialized in shoes. Exclusively in Kat's shoes. Sam suppressed a grin. Kat had tried everything to make his shoes a treat for Blue, but no dice. Blue preferred chewing Kat's.

Bella's physical injuries had practically all healed. She had also reduced her shyness in front of strangers and situations. Kat really had a special gift with the dogs. The four-legged friends all seemed to relax the minute she was around. Even Pirate, his parents' sometimes slightly neurotic Parson Russell terrier, turned into a tame lapdog in her presence.

So, to please Kat, whatever the town was planning, it had to involve the dogs. The four-legged friends just seemed to accumulate. And then he suddenly knew what Independence could do for Kat.

A Week Later

Sam went down the hall with a morning breakfast tray and coffee. In order to open the bedroom door he had to lift it with one hand, high out of reach, because the dogs had followed. All seven of them. And all seven noses were quivering.

Sam went into the room. Kat was not disturbed by the patter of twenty-eight paws trying to get in. She was sound asleep under a quilt with a pale blue blanket on top. Sam walked over quietly and sat down on the bed. The dogs came in and sat obediently, watching. After a moment Kat opened her eyes in a sleepy daze.

"Good morning, Sleeping Beauty."

She smiled at Sam, rolled onto her side and squinted past at the pack of dogs.

"I see you brought reinforcements."

Sam eased back until he came to lie next to her on the mattress.

"Little did I know how hard you would be to wake," he teased her. He rolled onto Kat and kissed her.

"Mmmm. That way you don't need any reinforcement at all. But you have an advantage over me."

"What's that?"

"You already brushed your teeth." Embarrassed, she turned her head away.

Sam reached for a peppermint candy on the nightstand and popped it into her mouth. "There, now you have no reason not to kiss me."

"What's the rush?"

"Because your four-legged friends are about to take my place."

Paws, wet noses, and wagging tails swarmed on and off the bed. Kat struggled out from under them.

"I don't know why you brought my breakfast here in the first place," she grumbled, "I can't eat it in bed without half of it being stolen."

"True. But it's the thought that counts, right? I'll carry it back to the kitchen for you. Come out when you're dressed. We have to leave in an hour."

Kat stretched and yawned heartily. "Go?" she asked, frowning. "What time is it?"

"It's half past seven. We have to leave here at half past eight."

Before she could ask him where they had to go at half past eight, he grabbed the breakfast tray and disappeared. As soon as the dogs noticed that the food was no longer in the room, they let her go and trotted after Sam.

"Abandoned and deserted for scrambled eggs and bacon," she said to Nikki, who was the only one who had stayed with her. "Except you. You're already the best."

Nikki, knowing full well that she had just scored with her mistress, laid her head on the edge of the bed and blinked up from under long eyelashes. Kat petted her and massaged her floppy ears for a moment.

"There, my dear. As much as I'd love to lounge in bed for another half hour and cuddle your fur, I'm afraid I have to get up." More to herself, she said, "Even though I have no idea what's so urgent on a Saturday morning."

When she came out to the kitchen Sam whisked her plate from the warming oven and set it on the counter. "Before we leave we should get a few details straight."

"Sure," she said, settling on a kitchen stool and picking up a fork. "You mean details about the other night?"

"I mean more about us."

"Are we an *us*?"

Kat shook her head, but she couldn't really be mad at him. She took a deep breath and took the plunge. "Alright." She rolled her eyes. "Then it's official now. You're my boyfriend and I'm your girlfriend. Let's see how long that lasts." The last comment was pretty snarky. But she couldn't help it. In moments like this her old insecurities resurfaced.

Sam gently took her chin in his hand and turned her face toward him. He could see how much courage this concession cost her. He found it a little scary how much she meant to him, considering the short time they had known each other.

She stared into his green eyes. She saw understanding in them, but also determination.

"If I have my way, it will last a very long time. Be prepared to still bring dogs home to me fifty years from now."

This made her laugh and calmed her wildly beating heart.

"You almost convinced me." She couldn't resist leaning over her plate, lips puckered for a kiss. He leaned in and pecked her. "Now eat up."

Kat ate a few bites and slid off the stool. In her own bedroom she dressed quickly; jeans, a T-shirt, and a blue wool sweater that made her eyes sparkle. She ran a wide-tooth comb through her curls before tying them into a loose knot at the nape of her neck. A little bronze eye shadow, some mascara, and a spritz of her favorite perfume, she was done. Having no idea what Sam had planned, she could only hope that her outfit was appropriate.

Minutes later they were on their way. A warmer winter day had arrived in the Rockies in the last few days. The sun shone, the ice thawed. At least on the plain, if not yet on the mountain tops.

"Where are you taking me anyway?" Kat wanted to know and snuggled closer to Sam in the jeep. For the first time in her life she was in love and even happy about it. She would never have expected that.

Her hockey player just smiled mysteriously at the question. "Patience. We'll be right there."

"Patience is not one of my strong points," she grumbled.

Finally, he parked in front of the community center because there were so many cars in front of the diner. She frowned. For the second time she asked, "What are we doing here? We just ate."

"You're going to like it. Trust me." He held out his hand. Hesitantly, she took it. Trust was still not her strong point. But slowly she was getting better at it.

There were more guests than ever in the diner. Sam held the door open for her and smiled at the few people who were in the way until they let them pass. Miss Minnie took over from there. She made her way to the door, arms spread wide.

"Our guest of honor," she exclaimed.

Kat looked around at Sam. But he had joined his siblings and parents near the door and winked encouragingly at her. Great. *As if that would help*, she thought glumly, and let Miss Minnie glide her over to the counter. There she sat down on the only vacant stool. It had obviously been kept free for her. She let her snow jacket slide off her shoulder and put it over her knees. It was uncomfortably warm in the diner because of all the people. Many acquaintances along with strange faces surrounded her. She accepted a coffee that Miss Daisy, Minnie's sister and accomplice in the kitchen, held out to her. Kat figured at least she could hold on to the cup and look busy.

"Listen up, everyone," a mature female voice announced. "Our guest of honor has arrived." It was Rose McArthy. "I'm going to let Nadine, my friend and your school principal, do the speechifying for me."

A chuckle went around the room and conversations fell silent.

Nadine addressed Kat directly. "Kathrina Orlow. We want to officially welcome you to Independence."

Already warm with embarrassment, Kat nodded. But Nadine didn't let herself be stopped. With a wave of her hand, she continued. "You hadn't been here a week, I don't think, when you made a terrible discovery. You found a dead dog and wanted to know what had happened to it." Nadine paused meaningfully and looked at each person in turn.

"Not content with a flimsy explanation of a coyote gone wild, you found a second dog a short time later. This one was still alive. Without hesitation you took this dog home and nursed her back to health. Aside from a few citizens, you were mostly ignored in your efforts to get to the bottom of what happened to the dogs. Had it not been for you, we would have continued to tolerate the presence of people in our community conducting an illegal business and making us cast nervous glances over our shoulders. Thanks to you, our capable sheriff and his team, we don't have that anymore."

Kat would have loved to disappear into a mousehole.

"When the danger was over, we were all too happy to give you a high five." Nadine turned directly to Kat again. "But as you quite rightly made us understand, that's easy. And also rather hypocritical. We took your words very much to heart. Independence needs people like you. People who show civil courage and fight for what is important to them." Nadine paused and took a breath. "That's why we have decided that all betting proceeds that were related to the dogs, or to you and Sam, should go to the *Safe Haven*."

Safe Haven? A safe haven? For who, for what? Kat looked around in wonder.

Nate Bale, the veterinarian, interrupted Nadine. He whispered something and handed her a piece of paper. As she studied it her eyes widened in astonishment. Then she looked up as Nate said, "I have wonderful news. The amount of five thousand dollars has been matched by an anonymous donor. That means *Project Safe Haven* will receive ten thousand!"

All the people began to clap. Kat joined them hesitantly. It all sounded wonderful. But what did it have to do with her? What anonymous donor would possibly do this? Confusion reflected on her face as Nadine addressed her again. "You're probably wondering what Project Safe Haven is all about."

Kat cleared her throat. "An animal welfare organization or something like that?"

"Right. Except it's not just any animal rights organization, it's yours."

"Mine?" Kat's mouth gaped open before she snapped it shut, thinking she probably looked like a fish gasping for air." What do you mean, mine?"

"A little birdie told us you'd like to set up some kind of sanctuary for stray or injured animals."

Kat risked a quick glance at Sam. He innocently returned her gaze. He must have copied the innocent expression from Rocky.

"An animal sanctuary is something we lack in Independence. Until now, we've always relied on the generosity of individuals. Paula, for example, has taken in more than one stray."

In the crowd, Paula gave a cheery wave.

"She even took me in," Leslie chirped, unexpectedly brave.

A few people chuckled in amusement. Kat saw Paula lovingly put her arm around the teenager and gave her a squeeze.

Nadine smiled at the two as well. "Exactly. There are others in Independence who have done this and I'm sure will continue to do so. But it will be a big help to have a place to go. I'm sure you'll find a way to combine private help with the help that an organization like this can provide."

Slowly, Kat found her speech again, even though the thoughts in her head were racing. "Are you saying this money is meant to set up a sanctuary? To pay vet bills? To pay for food?"

Nadine laughed. "You're already thinking along the right lines."

Kat blushed.

"Then the money is in good hands. We're glad you'll be with us for a long time to come."

Kat grinned. "Deal. Thank you all. Here's to our Safe Haven!"

Kat suddenly spotted Scrooge by the door. Their eyes met. He raised his walking stick in salute. Then he turned and disappeared through the door to the outside.

At that moment, she knew who the anonymous patron was.

But before Kat and Sam could make a glorious exit, Minnie came back.

"Are you interested in helping place those puppies in good homes?"

Before this, Kat couldn't get any help and now she was overwhelmed with it. But it was important to stay gracious. "Of course, Minnie. I would love some help. Paula says she's found new owners for Red and Pink. They're almost ready to go."

"You know Lily at the flower store? I believe she was one of the few who put up a flyer for you?"

"Yes, she did."

"She has a Dalmatian already, Pebbles. But she'd be interested in a puppy. There's a couple in Breckenridge who expressed an interest also, and Nate Bale said he'd ask around with his clients."

"That's incredible, Minnie. Sounds like you've given me a jumpstart."

EPILOGUE

KAT AND SAM STOOD in the arrivals area of the terminal where international flights were landing. Kat clung excitedly to Sam's arm. Reassuringly, he pressed a kiss to her temple. Kat felt something of his unwavering calmness pass over to her. Loving Sam didn't make her weaker, it made her stronger. That much she had come to understand. Despite their obvious differences, they were a perfect match in all the ways that mattered. Spontaneously, she turned toward him and kissed him on the mouth. The butterflies in her stomach came to life as she felt his lips on hers. The now familiar tingling sensation grew stronger, and she pressed closer to him. Finally, he stopped her and pushed her away a little. "Not that I'm complaining, but I'd like to shake my future mother-in-law's hand before she sees me kissing her daughter in the middle of airport arrivals."

Kat playfully swatted at his arm. "Future mother-in-law. You must be dreaming."

"I suppose so. But as you know, I'm very persistent in pursuing my dreams," he replied with a smug smile.

She shook her head in amusement. Then she became serious again. "Thanks for coming with me."

"Did you think I would leave you alone to meet with Micah for even a second? It's too dangerous for me." He joked to lighten the mood a bit.

"I still can't believe she's actually coming." Tears shimmered in Kat's eyes. Even though she was getting better at dealing with her past, the old wounds still ran deep.

"You'll be able to hug her in a few minutes," Sam reassured her.

Kat wasn't so sure about that. Over the years there hadn't been much room for sincere conversation. They had only ever told each other the good things, so as not to worry the other. Everything else had remained unspoken. She really hoped it wasn't too late to change that. But would her mother also see it that way?

At that moment, her mother stepped through the automatic sliding door. Involuntarily, Kat's heart leapt. She hurried toward her mother who was clinging to the arm of a tall young man with a mischievous smile on his face.

As soon as her mother spotted Kat, she gave a cry and ran with arms open. As Kat hugged her mother, she felt all the fears of the past weeks fall away from her. A great relief spread through her being. They would make it. The worst was already behind them.

Kat and her mother had tears running down their faces. Micah greeted Sam, who steered them all to a quieter corner while the women talked excitedly in Polish between laughing and crying. Micah translated a few sentences. "Kat says she has an appointment with a hotel for her dog grooming business. Her mother is crying with joy."

Sam gave Micah a friendly punch on the shoulder. "Thanks. I owe you."

"Seeing the two of them like this is thanks enough. I've gotten to know the woman quite well over the past few weeks. It warms my heart to see mother and daughter united. It wasn't easy, I can tell you. Polish pride is like a wild animal. It's not easy tame."

"Believe me, I know what you're talking about," Sam replied, but the look on his face revealed that he was deeply happy with the woman who had chosen him.

"Don't pretend," Micah countered. "I can tell by looking at you that it was worth it. If she's half as great as her mother, I'll believe it right now."

"Paws off," Sam warned, only half joking.

"Yes, yes, calm down. Say, can you teach me to speak Polish? I'm going to need to keep up with these two."

"Good idea," Micah grinned. "But for now, let's get them home."

They followed the two women who were talking animatedly while walking towards the exit and a new life.

THANK YOU FOR READING!

READERS LIKE YOU are my daily motivation to write.

If you enjoyed my story, it would mean a lot if you could leave a review on your preferred book platforms. This actively supports my writing, as it is one of the few ways for me as an author to draw attention to my craft.

If you are a NetGalley member, you can review advanced reader copies of my upcoming titles before they are released.

CONNECT WITH ME

I LOVE HEARING FROM my valued readers, so please reach out to me directly via email or social media:

 MAIL@VIRGINIAFOX.COM

 @FOX_VIRGINIA

 BOOKSVIRGINIAFOX

WWW.VIRGINIAFOX.COM

JOIN ME!

Sign up for my newsletter to get insider information, and receive a FREE digital download of my Rocky Mountain Romances prequel, *Rocky Mountain Diner.*

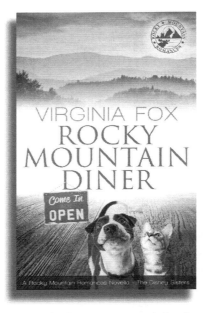

Dive into a little romance, a dab of suspense, and a whole lot of fun!

PREVIEW

Don't miss the next book in the Rocky Mountain Romances series!

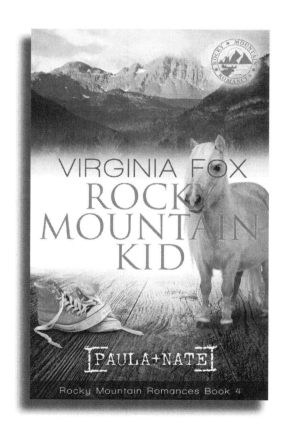

CHAPTER ONE

Paige Nilson stared down the biggest cinnamon bun she'd ever seen. It competed directly against the Rocky Mountain Diner's famous, freshly ground, steaming hot coffee. She looked back and forth between the two, taking stock, and sighed. *What came first? The chicken or the egg?*

Slightly overwhelmed, she stared at the dessert. *There's no chicken here. Or eggs. Just a luscious cinnamon bun. So, I'm safe!* She shook her head. *No. No. No. I can't do carbs and sugar without anything in my stomach.* She grabbed the coffee and took a big sip. Before she realized it, she promptly burned her tongue. *Great. Just great.* Her streak of bad luck seemed to do splendidly. Tentatively, she nibbled on the thick sugar icing. She closed her eyes and groaned loudly. The sweetness made her taste buds stop hurting. Maybe the gods weren't totally out to get her, after all. A cinnamon bun had *never* tasted so good.

"That's one lucky pastry," an amused, deep voice boomed behind her.

Embarrassed, she turned and stared right into the broad chest and perfectly pressed fabric of a man's uniform. Her mouth watered. At first, and of course, she salivated because she'd taken too long between bites. Why else? A half-dozen other scenarios came to mind on the spot as she slowly lifted her gaze over his broad shoulders and stopped on a handsome, square-jawed face. He possessed the bluest eyes she'd ever seen, military short-cropped dark hair, and a smile that required a gun license. Maybe two.

"So, do you like what you see?" he flirted. He put his hand on his hip and leaned like he was modeling for Michelangelo. His gaze roamed all over her. Paige suddenly felt a kinship with her cinnamon bun...knew he was objectifying her the way she had objectified it! She always figured whenever she'd been eyeballed, it was mainly because of the way her strawberry blonde hair framed her heart-shaped face. She was sitting, so she knew there was no way he could really check out her body.

"I don't know. Maybe it's just that coffee here has mind-altering properties," she said, raising her coffee like she was giving a toast. She caught the name stitched onto his lapel.

Ace O'Neil.

Ace stared at her coffee as if what she'd said wasn't a joke. Had she really been talking about drugs in coffee? Did she imply he only looked good because she was medicated? Had she accidentally insulted him while trying to flirt?

Paige noticed his confusion. Based on his looks, he was probably used to women throwing themselves at him. She pictured him checking himself out in the mirror, thrilled with himself. Then she pictured herself behind him, sliding her hands around his full chest, reaching for his chin to turn his face to hers, their mouths opening in anticipation.

She shook her head like a wet cat shaking water out of its fur to try to shake off the image.

"You all right there?" he asked.

Paige snapped out of it, forced a smile, and blinked several times. "Yeah. Sorry. Just got the chills."

"Miss Minnie's coffee ought to fix that, especially with the trippy sauce," he said with a wink. "But duty calls. So, see you around." He saluted goodbye and turned around.

"Bye," she called. "Nice, uh, meeting you?"

Paige looked unabashedly at his well-sculpted rear end as he left. "Speaking of nice buns," she remarked. "Speaking of buns." She peered down at the cinnamon bun remnants on her plate. She put the coffee mug down and went right for the goodie.

Mid-bite, someone interrupted. "Girl? If you're going to advertise our secret coffee to the fire chief..." a voice said. Paige nearly jumped out of her seat. "You need the real stuff."

Fire...*chief?* She turned and was startled to see the waitress hovering nearby. The woman reached under her apron, pulled out a flask, and poured a generous sip of its mystery contents into her coffee before she could say a peep. Miss Minnie was her name if Paige remembered correctly from last evening's round of introductions, made during her bed-and-breakfast's check-in.

She was about to protest the unsolicited alcohol spike, but thought adding high-proof alcohol was a splendid idea, all things considered. Weren't all the famous journalists drinkers, anyway? A quiet voice in the back of her mind reasoned such sloshed genius consisted mostly of poets and writers, weren't usually journalists, and was mostly male. Paige ignored the voice. *Anything they can do, I can do better.* Determined, she reached for the cup and emptied the spiked coffee in one go.

Miss Minnie raised an eyebrow. Poured another cuppa. "How about you chase that with some coffee?"

Paige nodded and pointed at Miss Minnie's apron, mid-morning hangover be damned.

"Whiskey?" Miss Minnie shook her head and added a shot from the flask to the dark, steaming liquid.

Paige gulped it down almost as fast as the first. Smiled.

"Might need to cut you off."

Paige shook her head no. "I need it to find my writing muse, which walked out the door right before your fireman."

"Chief," Miss Minny said. "Fire chief."

Paige put her head on the table—the booze had kicked in—and sobbed. "Everything runs away from me. My career. The fire *master*! Everything!" She realized she was slurring.

Miss Minnie gently and firmly grabbed Paige by the elbow. "Come on," she said. "No one needs to see this."

She led her into the kitchen, where she hugged Paige, pulling her crying face into her enormous bosom and rocked her back and forth.

"There, there...it won't be so bad."

"Yes, it will!" sniffed Paige. "I'm a journalist. How am I supposed to write when I have no words and nothing to say?"

"Write about things that move you. Then the words will come on their own."

As simple as the advice was, it quickly put Paige at ease. Could it be that simple? Don't try to please some editor? Look for a story yourself—one that was written by life? Why not, actually? As of last night, she didn't have a job because of her unpredictable temper. She was literally stuck until she could figure something out. She had sublet her Denver apartment after assuming she would be a junior reporter for the Daily Mail for the next few months.

She straightened up and gratefully grabbed the paper towel that Miss Daisy, standing by the stove, silently handed her.

"Better?" Miss Minnie asked, pinching her cheek.

She took a deep breath. "Yes. Better. Thank you so much. I'm not usually like this." Embarrassed, she let her face disappear behind her hair again.

"You're welcome. Crying never hurt anyone."

Paige nodded. Fortunately, in her miserable mood, she hadn't put on makeup yet, so she was at least spared from running around looking like a drowned panda.

"And the next time our fire chief flirts with you? I expect a witty response."

Paige rolled her eyes and went back to her place at the bar. She doubted whether her newfound self-confidence was enough for such a task. She could count her male acquaintances on one hand. But that didn't matter. After all, she wasn't looking for a man, but for a story. The story that would change her life.

With the Pulitzer Prize in mind, she ventured back to her seat at the bar and took a hearty bite of her cinnamon bun.

It only took a few seconds for the bite to register. Miss Daisy was right. Life was good. You just had to go about it the right way. And enjoy it along with Miss Daisy's cinnamon bun. Her gaze wandered around the quaint diner, furnished with '50s decor.

Her attention turned to a group of people sitting together at a long table in the middle of the room. An incredible number of dogs sat around the table. A German Shepherd watched the entire room, his ears pricked up. He seemed to keep an eye on the comings and goings of the customers like a security guard.

Two huge auburn bulldogs lay close by. Hadn't there once been a movie with a very similar drool monster? And at the end? Was that a giant poodle? Paige shook her head in disbelief. She felt as if she had landed in a parallel universe where dogs had taken over. *Like Planet of the Apes, only with dogs!* She spotted an incredibly ugly, medium-sized, dark brown dog. His physique was stocky, almost squat. She shuddered involuntarily and turned away. She hadn't been much of a dog lover since an unfortunate dog encounter in her childhood.

Uneasily, she eyed the group again. Who on earth brought so many dogs into a restaurant? Wasn't there some law against that? Although she had to admit, the animals all seemed very well-behaved. None of them barked or whined. None tugged at their leashes. *How could they?* She noticed none were leashed, either. Really amazing. At such moments, her aversion to dogs seemed ridiculous. Whenever she saw them in real life, her feelings changed and she sometimes hated to admit she might like them.

Meanwhile, she inhaled the last bite of her dessert. *Nom. Nom. Nom.*

Paige watched the group from her safe place and from the corner of her eye. *Don't make it look obvious. Great reporters blend in and gather all the details while remaining anonymous, right?* She recalled Miss Minnie's words: *Write about life,* she had advised. Paige guessed that meant she had to go where life was actually happening instead of always staying at home and behind her laptop. *Get closer. Get some quotes.* Prompted by her sudden inspiration, she mustered all her courage—with coffee in hand—and changed seats. Her courage was not enough to introduce herself to the group, but she sat at a right angle to them in the next window niche. From there she could observe them inconspicuously and listen in. Maybe she'd overhear a bright idea for her next story.

Jaz was getting excited. Paula, Leslie, Tyler and Pat, Jake, Sam and his girlfriend Kat were all present. The Carter siblings' parents, Brenda and Stan, were about to arrive. Even Cole, Paula's youngest brother, had taken the day off and joined them. After all, there was something to celebrate.

"Do you think there's enough cake for everyone?" Paula asked, who had helped Jaz bake the night before.

"I'm sure they will," Jaz reassured her. "And if they don't? I'm sure the Disney Sisters have a backup plan. They always do."

The two sisters, who ran the restaurant, had agreed to make a one-time exception and allow outside cakes to be brought in. Originally, Paula and Leslie had invited everyone to the ranch. But when one of Jake's deputies had suddenly fallen ill, Jake had to cover the shift. He could still attend so long as he stayed in close proximity to the police station and, of course, on call. They improvised and moved the party to the diner downtown.

The Disney Sisters' concession was not entirely altruistic. The diner was not just any restaurant. No, it was still the only place in Independence that served hot meals, coffee, and alcohol. This made it the primary meeting place for social gatherings and the corresponding daily exchange of gossip.

To make things a little more interesting, the diner also ran a sort of betting shop. They bet on everything and everyone. No one was immune from becoming the subject of a bet.

Independence followed the mystery of what would happen to Leslie. Everyone familiar with the situation agreed the best thing that could happen to the girl was a permanent place with Paula. Recent betting centered solely on when that might officially be the case. In her infinite wisdom, Miss Minnie suspected just they would announce such an arrangement during their lunch. Why else would they be bringing in cakes? She knew it wasn't any of their birthdays, after all. She even checked her Birthday notebook, a place where she kept track of such things. Even though she appeared to be filling coffee and bringing and taking plates, Miss Minnie hung on every word.

Brenda and Stan arrived, causing some chair-waving among the humans and tail-wagging among the dogs. After going down the line greeting folks, Brenda could make her way to Leslie, who looked nervous.

Brenda was not empathetic to the child if she even noticed her discomfort. "Come here, little one. Let me hold you." She hugged Leslie in a vice grip. Leslie squirmed, so Brenda let up just enough so she could see the kid's face. "What's wrong?"

Leslie looked to the side, embarrassed. "You're not mad at me for intruding on the family?" she asked. Her palms were sweaty, and she wiped them on her jeans.

"No. Of course not, sugar. Do you think I'd be shy about saying something if I thought you were?"

Silently, Leslie shook her head.

"There you go. If that were the case, I would have said something long ago and not waited until now. Just think: I'm ahead of all my friends by having my first granddaughter. And one this big already, at that." She smirked. "No, my dear. You're not getting rid of us that easily. You've got the whole Carter family on your back now, like it or not."

Relieved, Leslie hugged Brenda back. "You bet I do. It's my greatest wish."

"Then everything is fine."

"What's that I hear?" Stan's voice sounded behind them. "My favorite granddaughter wants to get rid of us again already?"

Leslie blushed. "No way, Mr. Carter. Uh, Stan." She'd only recently gotten up the nerve to call him by his first name. Stan himself did not know where she had gotten the idea that he would attach importance to the formal form of address. But since his mind was usually on his inventions and calculations, it had only occurred to him when his wife had pointed it out. By that time, however, Leslie had become so accustomed to it that she found the change to Stan difficult.

Paige, sitting right next to them, followed the conversations of the various people at the table with growing interest. It seemed to be a family gathering of sorts. Family stories were good. They moved the reader and evoked emotions. She leaned forward a little, just so as not to miss anything.

When everyone finally sat around the table and grabbed a piece of cake, Paula stood up and clapped her hands.

"Everyone, listen up. Leslie and I have some good news."

The entire party—and the entire diner—watched Paula intensely.

"As you know," she said, "I was approved as a foster parent a few months ago and can now officially take in a foster child." She beamed as though the sun itself shined through her face.

"And you just happened to run across one? Are you sure you want to keep the first puppy you find?" Cole winked at Leslie, who promptly stuck her tongue out at him. He liked the little one and made a point of raising her like a real big brother whenever he had the chance, even though he was really more her foster uncle when you got right down to it.

Leslie pretended to be upset about it on the surface, but secretly she was excited about her new "big brother." The others were all very nice, too, but somehow took on different roles. With Cole, she could fool around and just be herself. Paula was more like a mother. At least that's what she imagined. While they both had fun together too, the dynamic was quite different.

"You know that strays who make it to my farm stay there forever," Paula countered glibly.

Leslie grinned. She didn't mind Paula calling her a stray. She knew how hard Paula had fought to make the celebration possible. Leslie felt overwhelmed that Paula wanted her in her life permanently. She was even believing it.

"What does that mean exactly?" Jake asked. He was familiar with the problems with her previous foster family.

Leslie had not run away from there for nothing. She was afraid to go back there, and so, had long kept quiet about her origins.

"We have completed the investigation against the previous foster family," Paula said, trying not to lose her breath from talking so fast. "In a few weeks, the trial will begin. Hopefully, they'll never be allowed to take in children again."

Tyler snorted. "I hope so. Collecting money for months on a kid who isn't even there anymore? A child they did not know was even alive? It's unbelievable how greedy and unsympathetic they were."

Paula nodded. "That's what the juvenile authorities thought, too. It was clear Leslie needed to be re-homed. That cleared the way for her to come to me officially." She shrugged. "Basically, they don't have enough foster homes, these days. It would have been silly and awful to rip Leslie away from what's become a familiar environment for her. Especially since she's also acclimated very well at school." She gave Leslie a sidelong glance. "School seemed to have been a...ahem...not-so-unproblematic issue in the past."

Leslie hunched her shoulders and tried to hide her grin behind her long brown hair. Paula pulled her close and tickled her.

"But she promised I wouldn't have to worry, right?"

"Yes. Yes. Scout's honor. If you'll just stop tickling me already." Leslie felt she'd grown from a shy little girl and was finally embracing being a happy teenager.

"Now didn't you end up getting in trouble for not reporting Leslie right away?" asked Brenda.

"Let's just say it helped that Jake could prove, thanks to his logs, that he had been asking around at the various offices and combing through missing person reports. Having a police officer for a brother certainly didn't hurt either. And that I had already attempted to be recognized as a foster parent was also viewed positively. I got off with a warning and a minor fine. The Judge will probably still keep an eye on me a bit, but not too harshly, especially after the huge scandal they've just been through. After that, there's nothing standing in the way of adoption."

Leslie looked up at Paula, surprised. She knew nothing about that. Adoption? She didn't know whether to cry or hug Paula.

Paula grinned at her. "You should have guessed as much. You know by now that I don't do things halfway."

Leslie swallowed. She had an enormous lump in her throat. To hide her mixed feelings, she threw herself against Paula and hugged her. Firmly.

"There, there," said Paula, stroking her back in soothing, circular motions. "You're not going to start crying today of all days, are you? After all, there's cake."

With her head still buried in Paula's shirt, Leslie giggled, even though she had been on the verge of tears only a moment ago. That was the best thing about Paula. She always knew the right thing to say.

"Now that's something to celebrate, sis!" Cole stood and raised his glass to toast. The others followed his lead.

Leslie also dared to join in with her glass of apple juice. She never thought her life would be so beautiful. She finally had a family. And a huge one at that! She patted Ranger's head, who had stood up in all the commotion and came to stand at her side. "Well, what do you think? Will I keep getting lucky?"

The German shepherd licked her hand. Satisfied she was okay, he settled down at her feet.

"I guess that means yes, handsome," she concluded, turning back to the others.

Paige could hardly believe what she heard. An orphan, a deceitful and abusive foster family, and a person who had apparently just taken the little girl in. The story had the makings of a hit. Emotions guaranteed. Every local newspaper would fight to run it, she was sure. Or would she rather run the story as a blog? Admittedly, she was still missing a few details. But she was confident she'd find them out. Not for nothing, but Paige knew she was a damn good reporter. In Independence, everyone seemed to know everything about everyone else. It was ideal for her research. She would uncover the missing information in no time. Once her name was on everyone's lips, her former boss would surely realize he missed out and gotten rid of her too soon.

She was in a much better mood than half an hour earlier, so she let Miss Minnie refill her coffee. After all, she needed all the energy she could get to listen to the rest of the conversation and take notes.

THE UTE INDIAN PEOPLE

THE UTE PEOPLE EXTEND a warm welcome to all visitors interested in the Southern Ute Indian Reservation in beautiful Southwest Colorado, home of the Southern Ute Indian Tribe. The second weekend in every September is an Annual Southern Ute Tribal Fair and Powwow. The general public is welcome to attend the dance, drum and fair contests. *Máykh* means hello in Ute Indian language.

HISTORIC UTE

The Ute people are the oldest residents of Colorado, living in the mountains as well as the plains of Colorado, Utah, Wyoming, Eastern Nevada, Northern New Mexico, and Arizona. The word "Ute" comes from the word *eutaw* or *yuta*, which means "dwellers on the top of mountains." The number of Ute people left in the United States is few—they number in the thousands. The old ways and wisdom are precious, and we now realize it needs to be preserved. Cooking, hunting, medicinal plants, and a nomadic hunter-gatherer lifestyle were and still are samples of the expertise of Ute Indians.

FOOD

As expert hunters and gatherers, the Ute found food already growing in their environment to add to the meat of animals native to the region: buffalo, deer, elk, rabbits, and meat birds are just a few. Food was plentiful and nutritious. The Ute devised ways of drying and storing foods for the leaner winter months.

Chokecherry, wild raspberry, gooseberry, and buffalo berry were gathered and eaten raw. Occasionally, juice was extracted to drink, and the pulp made into cakes. Seeds from flowers and grasses were added to soups and stews. Earth ovens were made by digging four-foot deep holes and lining them with stones. A fire was started on top of the stones and food was tucked between layers of damp grass and heated rocks. Covered with dirt to hold in the heat, everything cooked overnight.

WAY OF LIFE

Historically, Ute families lived in *wickiups* and *ramadas* in the western and southern areas. A wickiup was a frame hut covered with a matting of bark or brush. Ramadas were shelters with a roof but no walls or only partially enclosed. Hide tepees were found in eastern territory.

Men and women kept their hair long or braided. Clothing clanged depending on weather temperature and seasonal conditions. They wore woven fiber skirts and sandals, rabbit skin robes, and leather shirts, skirts, and leggings. Baskets were woven to carry food and objects. Animal-skin bags were also useful for carrying goods. Tools were handmade from bone, stone, and wood.

TODAY

Very few Ute people are left and now primarily live in Utah and Colorado, within three Ute tribal reservations: Uintah-Ouray in northeastern Utah (3,500 members);

Southern Ute in Colorado (1,500 members); and Ute Mountain which primarily lies in Colorado, but extends to Utah and New Mexico (2,000 members). The majority of Ute people live on these reservations although some reside off-reservation. Tribal leaders and associations are developing businesses and securing outside opportunities for Utes now and in the future. These are a magnificent people who hold a meaningful and respected place in the rich tapestry of American life.

MISS DAISY'S
RECIPES

THE DINER IS KNOWN FOR ITS DELICIOUS HOME COOKING!
THE RECIPES ARE EACH FOR FOUR PEOPLE,
UNLESS OTHERWISE NOTED.

———————

Miss Daisy's
Buttermilk Pancakes

(MAKES 6 PANCAKES)

INGREDIENTS

2 egg whites

1 egg yolk

2 tbsp. sugar

1 pinch salt

²/₃ cup flour

½ cup buttermilk

1 pad butter, for pan

INSTRUCTIONS

Bowl 1: Beat the egg whites until semi-stiff. Add 1 tbsp. sugar and beat until stiff.

Bowl 2: Mix the egg yolk, salt, flour, and buttermilk.

Fold beaten egg whites into Bowl 2.

For variations, such as adding blueberries or chocolate chips, mix them into the batter now.

Melt butter in a frying pan. Fry the batter in 6 equal portions (two generous tablespoons of batter make 1 pancake), flipping so both sides are golden brown. The pancakes should be small, about 4 inches in diameter:

To keep pancakes warm, place in the oven at 200°F on plate covered with aluminum foil.

Traditionally, pancakes are eaten with butter and warm maple syrup. Other possible toppings are powdered sugar, bacon, stewed fruit, honey…really, anything you feel like.

Miss Daisy's
Baked Potatoes

INGREDIENTS

1–2 potatoes and/or sweet potatoes per person
Olive oil
Sea salt
Thyme

INSTRUCTIONS

Preheat oven to 425°F.

Wash potatoes under cold running water.

Peel potatoes and cut into wedges. (If potatoes have a nice skin, you can leave them on.)

Put wedges in a bowl and mix in olive oil until thinly coated.

Add sea salt and thyme, to taste. (You can also use other seasonings, like pepper.)

Spread the wedges on a baking pan lined with aluminum foil.

Bake the potatoes at 425°F 25–30 minutes, flipping them halfway through. Sweet potatoes take less time—only about 15 minutes—so add them later.

Miss Daisy's
Honey Lemon Chicken Wings

INGREDIENTS

2¼ lb. organic chicken wings

2 tbsp. olive oil

Salt

Cayenne pepper

1 onion, chopped

1 clove garlic, pressed

1 tbsp. olive oil

2 tbsp. lemon juice

2 tbsp. honey

2 tbsp. soy sauce

2 tbsp. water

INSTRUCTIONS

Preheat oven to 400°F.

Rub chicken wings with olive oil, and season with salt and cayenne pepper.

Line a baking pan with aluminum foil and brush with olive oil.

Spread chicken wings on baking pan and bake at 400°F for 30 minutes.

While chicken is baking, sauté the olive oil, onions, and garlic.

Add lemon juice, honey, soy sauce, and water to sauté pan and simmer.

When the 30 minutes are up, take the chicken out of the oven and brush with the sauté mixture.

Return chicken to oven and bake for 5 more minutes.

Take the chicken out of the oven and turn the chicken wings over. Then brush with the sauté mixture.

Return chicken to oven and bake 5–10 minutes until golden brown.

Serve hot with baked potatoes, or rice and vegetables of your choice.

Miss Daisy's
Chocolate Chip Cookies

(makes approx. 16 cookies)

INGREDIENTS

1½ cups of flour (wheat also works, of course)

½ tsp. baking soda

1 cup salted butter

½ cup sugar

½ cup brown sugar

1 tsp. salt

1 tsp. vanilla extract

1 egg

1 egg yolk

1¼ cup dark chocolate chips (or 1½ cups chocolate chunks)

INSTRUCTIONS

Preheat oven to 375°F.

Bowl 1: Mix flour and baking soda.

Bowl 2: Melt butter in a water bath.

Bowl 2: Mix in sugars (white and brown), salt, and vanilla extract until sugar is dissolved.

Bowl 2: Add egg yolks and whites; beat until foamy (you can use a mixer up through this point).

Bowl 2: Fold in contents of Bowl 1 with a wooden spoon or dough scraper until combined (do not mix too much!).

Fold in chocolate chips with a wooden spoon. Mix until there are no more pockets of flour.

Chill the dough for at least 2 hours, or overnight.

NOTE: This is the most important step in the whole recipe, because the butter needs time to solidify again. If this step is skipped, the cookies will be quite uneven and will not have a smooth surface.

When the dough is cold:

Create balls using 1 tbsp. of dough each, placing two inches apart on greased cookie sheet (you can also use baking paper).

Bake in center of oven at 375°F for 10 minutes.

Let cool (or not ...) and enjoy.

NOTES

This recipe can be varied by adding white or milk chocolate, nuts, dried fruit, or even cocoa powder (for the latter, adjust the amount of flour slightly).

BOOK CLUB QUESTIONS

1. Is Kat's dog salon an attractive business to you? Would you own one? If not, are you a dog-grooming or pet-care customer?

2. How do you feel about Kat rescuing her mother and bringing her to America? Did she do the right thing? Or did she actively interfere in her parents' marriage?

3. If you were a store owner presented with a flyer to help an injured pit bull, would you put it up? Or would you be fearful about "the wrong people" blaming you for unwanted attention?

4. Is Mr. Wilkinson similar to any old-timers in your community? Does he make good points? Or is he just stuck in his ways?

5. Was Kat right to go "undercover" to the farm, or did she take an unnecessary risk that should have been left to the sheriff to resolve?

6. Jaz, Tyler, and now Kat, are leaving work and businesses for love relationships. How do you feel about this? Are all three doing what's best everyone involved?

7. How do you feel about Leslie giving Paula a fake name before telling the truth? Should she have been punished? Or was it okay because she was protecting herself until she knew she could trust Paula and the Carter family?

ROCKY MOUNTAIN ROMANCES

Rocky Mountain Yoga

Rocky Mountain Star

Rocky Mountain Dogs

Rocky Mountain Kid

Rocky Mountain Secrets

COLLECT THE ENTIRE SERIES!

ABOUT THE AUTHOR

AUTHOR, MOTHER, HORSE WHISPERER, and part-time healthy food cook, Virginia Fox is a woman who cares deeply about family, animals, the environment, and friendships.

Creative from a young age, she turned her love of books into a prolific career as a writer. Her German-language Rocky Mountain series saw every volume enter the Top 50 of the Kindle charts on day one of launch. Now the bestselling Rocky Mountain Romances series breaks onto the US scene.

Virginia Fox lives on a small ranch near Zurich with her family, her Australian cattle dog, and two moody tomcats. When she isn't writing, she delights in caring for her horses and cooking for her family. Discover more on her website:

WWW.VIRGINIAFOX.COM

Printed in Great Britain
by Amazon

17262098R00172